DEFILED

Do not plant two kinds of seed in your vineyard;
If you do, not only the crops you plant
But also the fruit of the vineyard will be defiled.

Deuteronomy 22:9 (NIV)

MARGARET BUFFANO

DEFILED

DEFILED by Margaret Buffano
Copyright © 2020 by Margaret Buffano
All Rights Reserved.
ISBN: 978-1-59755-600-2

Published by: ADVANTAGE BOOKS™
                   Longwood, Florida, USA
                   www.advbookstore.com

Library of Congress Catalog Number: 2020951167
1. Fiction: Mystery & Detective -Woman Sleuths
2. Fiction: Mystery & Detective - General
3. Fiction: Detective Books

Cover Design: Alexander von Ness

First Printing: January 2021
20 21 22 23 24 25   10 9 8 7 6 5 4 3 2 1
Printed in the United States of America

One

My Guy

She walks for what feels like miles in darkness. She came in late to work, which forced her to park at the far back in the newly paved area. Working late, leaving late, as she's done many times before. Lights and security cameras are not installed yet. Finally, she comes on her parked car. She reaches for the door handle. Before she can open it, a dark figure comes up from behind, grabs her, and throws her to the ground on her back. He crashes down on top of her and pins her down with his full weight. She frantically struggles, but it is useless.

She strains her eyes to see through the darkness. His form, his shape is that of a man, but a flash of light shows he is not what she expected. His face is deformed – no, distorted – hideous, that of a demon. His eyes glow yellow like a mad dog. His hands, callous leathery claws, tear at her clothes. He pounds her with his fists, in the face and side of her head. The first few hits hurt like being struck by a cannonball and then numbness takes over. The sound of his fist hitting her is like a faraway pillow fight. Blow after blow till all the strength to fight back leaves her. She tastes blood in her mouth; it's wet and salty.

He begins to howl and curse in a strange, unknown language – like someone speaking backwards, like a wild animal possessed.

She flops about like a rag doll under him. His body stiffens and shakes for a moment. It is over. There is no warmth, just ice-cold inhumanity. He punches her once more into darkness.

****

She comes to, having no idea how many hours passed. Not knowing where she is, fear takes hold of her. She raises her hands and feels bandages on her face and begins to cry. It's not a dream – not a nightmare – it is real. Remembering what happened, she calls out for a nurse.

"I need a pregnancy test," she pleads.

The nurses in the room, standing at her bedside look at her like she's crazy.

"Ain't gonna do you no good, honey; it's just too soon," says one of the nursing staff, trying to calm her down. But when her demands became louder, her arms waving frantically, they decide to sedate her again.

The steel-metal point of the syringe feels like a red-hot poker plunging into Helen's arm. The drug works fast. Her entire body drifts away. The two heavyset nurses holding her down gently float off her. Voices fade away, echo, and then are soon gone.

"It was the only way," says the head nurse.

"A pregnancy test . . ." whispers Helen with what feels like the last breath of air in her lungs. She can't say anymore. Even her lips feel heavy and numb.

This drug is stronger than the first. There's a buzzing in her ears. She closes her eyes, and waves of dancing electrical pulsations appear behind her eyelids. The buzzing grows louder – the waves brighter and brighter. Then, as if unseen hands pull out some cosmic plug, the waves disappear, and the buzzing stops. Unconscious and drugged, still she can find no peace. Visions of horror play over in her head.

****

When Helen opens her eyes again, it is morning. Daylight floods the hospital room. It's a single room. The shades are down, and still the daylight pours into the room. The brightness hurts her eyes – she becomes aware of pain in different parts of her body. Sensing the presence of someone else in the room, she turns her head slightly. Sitting next to her is a thin, white-haired, middle-aged woman, smiling calmly.

"How are you feeling?" asks the woman.

Helen doesn't reply; somehow, she can't.

"Would you like some water?" the woman asks.

Helen blinks and shakes her head.

"My name is Dr. Angela Mitchell . . . but you can just call me Angela. I'm a psychiatrist with Rape Recovery here at the hospital. You do remember what happened to you last night?"

Helen nods and bursts into tears.

"Here, drink this," Angela says, holding a glass of water to Helen's lips. She takes a few sips. Angela places the glass on the nightstand.

"If you don't feel up to this . . ."

"How am I?" Helen asks.

Angela's smile melts away, and she places her hand on Helen's. A somber look comes over her face.

"There are no broken bones, but you have three cracked ribs, a fractured collar bone . . . of course, burses, cuts and scratches."

"I don't mean that; I mean . . . how am I? Am I pregnant?"

"There is no such thing as an accurate, immediate pregnancy test. It takes a few days."

"But I thought nowadays…?"

"There are tests, but they are questionable at such an early stage. To be honest, you're understandably upset right now. A false positive would be an unnecessary stress for you. I'll have a blood and urine sample taken and have tests run as soon as I believe it's possible to get a true reading." Dr. Mitchell looks curiously at Helen. "They told me you were persistent about asking for a pregnancy test last night. I agree, it is a concern, but tell me why it is your first concern?"

Helen sighs ever so gently. "Because…bones mend, bruises heal, and in time, we forget even the harshest of memories. It's all temporary. If I've contracted a deadly disease, it only means I become ill and die. And I couldn't care less. But if I were to become pregnant because of what happened last night, it will haunt me every minute of every day for the rest of my life."

"And do you believe yourself to be pregnant?"

"My husband and I tried for a baby for years. It would just be my luck to become pregnant by that animal…to carry the child of that monster!"

Angela assures her the likelihood she is pregnant is slim and unlikely, but the worried look on Helen's face remains.

"The hospital contacted your husband. Word is he's in en route from Montreal and will arrive soon."

"Does he know? I mean, does he know everything?"

"Helen, your husband loves you. There's nothing to fear or be upset about."

That means Richard knows. Helen feels shame. Why does she feel shame for something beyond her control? She doesn't understand, but she feels it nonetheless. If love conquers all, what does she have to fear? Yet still fear fills her.

"You know, Helen, at some point, you have to speak to the police."

"Oh, no, not now – it's too soon. Please!"

No matter how she dreads speaking about what happened, she knows in her heart each moment she doesn't talk to the police is perhaps another mile *he* is farther from justice.

Helen changes her mind, "No, wait, I'm sorry; I'll talk to the police. But if I do, I want you with me. I couldn't take the police right now, alone."

"And you won't have to. I'll be here," Angela says reassuringly.

Angela sits forward in her chair and places her hand once more on Helen's.

"Your parents are here."

"My parents…?"

A chill runs up Helen's spine. She knows it will be a scene. She can just picture it: her excessively dramatic mother crying and carrying on, shifting everyone's attention to her – it happened many times before. She holds no reason why this time things would be any different. Her father always tries to be a tower of strength by not showing any real emotion or expressing himself – the exact opposite of her mother. It will be a scene, and she does not feel up to it. But for whatever reason, she cannot decline. She agrees to see her parents.

"My poor baby!" cries Mrs. Russell, her arms flying about and tears running down her face. Running to the edge of the bed, she tosses herself onto her daughter, kissing her.

Mrs. Russell is a middle-aged woman, short, big boned, and big breasted. Her heavily hair-sprayed hair is firm as rock and is the same color as her daughter's, only no longer natural. It comes in a bottle. But her jewelry is real.

Mr. Russell stands firmly at the foot of the bed. He is a middle-aged man with salt-and-pepper hair – more salt than pepper. Unlike his wife, he walks every day and plays eight holes of golf three times a week to keep his weight down.

"Mrs. Russell," smiles Angela, "we mustn't get her too excited…she's been through a lot."

"Yes, of course…I'm sorry," says Mrs. Russell. She sits up and wipes tears from her eyes – her gestures large, grand, and overdone, like some forgotten silent film star. "Oh, darling, tell mother how you feel!"

"I'm okay, Mom…really."

Just one look at her – the bandages, the bruises – it is impossible to believe it true. Helen is beautiful and has always been beautiful, though she learned early not to rely on looks only. Looks can be deceiving. She was a lovely child. In high school, she was a cheerleader and voted class queen at the prom. In college, she was top in her class and sought out by every available young male. Now, Helen is a successful woman – tall, slender, blond, and sexy – yet not looking or feeling so at the moment.

There is a long and uncomfortable moment of silence before her father speaks up.

"Richard called us last night from Canada when he was waiting in the airport. …He told us what happened. We got here as soon as we heard. He just called us again; he should be here any minute." A look of true sorrow comes over her father. "I'm so sorry, Princess, I feel…so helpless." His voice begins to crack.

Helen thinks, *Richard told them what happened? How much information does Richard know, and how much did he tell my parents?* Again, the sharp pain of guilt washes over her.

Not wanting to be outdone by her own husband, her mother lets out a bursting howl, her arms fly toward the ceiling, and again she comes crashing down on her daughter.

Angela places her hands gently on Mrs. Russell's shoulders, trying to lift her up. "We need to let Helen rest now," says Angela. "You can come back later."

"Yes, of course," says Mrs. Russell, lifting herself off the bed, wiping her eyes once more. Then she reaches out and places her hand on her husband's shoulder for support for the long, unbearable journey to the door.

"If there's anything we can do, if there's anything you need, Princess…all you need to do is ask," says Mr. Russell.

"Would you drop by the house and feed Chelsea?" Helen asks. "The poor cat's probably half starved."

"Consider it done."

"Don't worry, sweetheart. We'll take care of everything. You just get well," says Mrs. Russell, gearing up for her grand exit. "And remember…your parents love you!" Her arms go up again as she boo-hoos herself out of the room, seemingly leaving stage right – Garbo style.

Angela turns to Helen before leaving also. "Try to get some rest. Don't worry; I'll wake you when your husband gets here."

****

Richard jumps out of the taxi, nearly forgetting to pay the cabby. Physically, he is the perfect match for Helen. He's tall, slender, with dark hair and chiseled good-looks. He's kept his tight, firm body that he had in college on the wrestling team, but now plays tennis and handball.

Once inside the hospital lobby, his first impulse is to head for the elevators. There he spies his in-laws.

"Tom! Delores!"

"Oh, Richard!" cries Mrs. Russell, falling into his arms.

Richard holds his mother-in-law and looks to his father-in-law for answers.

"Tom, how is she?"

Mr. Russell stands dumbfounded, unsure of what to say.

"Tom!" Richard speaks louder and more firmly, "How is she? Is she all right?"

There is a choke in Tom's voice. "She's bad, Richard. She got beat-up bad. They expect a full recovery, but you'll need to brace yourself. She's all bandaged up, and the parts that aren't, are black and blue."

Delores sobs harder into Richard's shoulder.

"But the doctors say there's nothing too serious. I mean, she's going to be okay, thank God. We've been here hours since we got word. We promised her we'd see to some things at the house, but if you need us to stay…"

"Besides being beaten, did he…?" Richard asks with a worried look on his face.

Tom doesn't answer. He looks away from Richard. The gesture tells Richard the full story.

Feeling awkward, Tom repeats, "Do you need us to stay?"

"No, it's all right. What room is she in?"

"Seventh floor…room 716." Tom places his hands on his wife's shoulders, gently guiding her from Richard. "Come, Delores. We promised Helen we'd feed the cat."

****

On the seventh floor, Richard flies out of the elevator as if shot out of a cannon – there is a frantic and bewildered look in his eyes. He walks past the information desk and down the hall. One of the nurses gets hold of him and escorts him back to the front desk. "Please, sir, we can't let people just wander about, you do understand? Now, how can I help you?"

He speaks in short puffs of breath, "Helen Haywood…I'm her husband!"

"It'll be just a minute. You can wait over there if you like." She smiles and points to a small row of chairs off to one side of the elevators.

Richard remains in front of the desk and paces. Hospitals always make him feel uneasy. The antiseptic smell turns his stomach. He keeps looking at the overhead clock.

"Please, sir, if you could step to one side? It'll be just a minute," repeats the nurse.

"'Just a minute'," Richard thinks out loud. "That's what you said twenty minutes ago!" It hasn't been twenty minutes; it just feels like it.

He is just about to ignore the warning and go looking for Helen on his own when Angela turns the corner, walks to Richard, and holds out her hand to him.

"You must be Richard."

"Is she all right?"

Angela takes his hand and smiles sympathetically. "Richard, listen to me, this is important. Try to calm down. Helen is fine; she's going to be just fine. She's bruised and swollen, but she'll be just fine. What I'm most concerned with right now is her mental health. She's been through an ordeal When you see her, I'm sure there will be some strong emotion…that's understandable…but I need you to be strong and not carry on, for Helen's sake. You understand?"

Richard fills his lungs with as much air as he can and breathes out slowly through tight lips. "Yes, I understand."

"She's probably sleeping…you need to go in alone. Are you ready?"

Richard breaths out again and then nods.

****

At her bedside, Richard looks down at his wife – she is asleep. Bandages and tape cover most of her face. A feeling of rage comes over him. He remembers Angela's words of warning just moments before. He braces himself and swears not to do or say anything to upset her. He reaches out and gently caresses her forehead. She coos like a dove under his touch. Her eyes open. At first, she smiles, but when reality returns to her, a sorrowful look takes her.

"Helen, sweetheart, it's me…Richard. I'm here, baby. Everything is going to be all right, I promise."

As their eyes met, he realizes there is nothing more to say – no words can express it. He reads in her eyes the love she holds for him, the relief she feels now he has arrived. But also he sees the deep sorrow she is feeling, a sorrow like none he ever knew possible – especially in his Helen.

She, too, is without words; her eyes burn from the salt of so many dried tears. The pain of her body she now forgets, while the unbearable ache in her heart swells. She is proud of him, how he calmly shows his concern for her. She knows inside he must be an explosion of anger. For a moment, she feels sorrier for him than for herself.

He lies down next to her on the bed and holds her close. "I'm here, baby. It's going to be all right; I promise."

****

Lieutenants Goebel and Benson stand in the doorway of Angela's office.

"Knock, knock," says Goebel.

Angela looks up and smiles, "Rick, Jim…what can I do for you boys?"

The two men enter.

"Don't be so heartless, Angela," Goebel says. "You know we've been waiting here for hours."

"Have a heart," Benson adds. "How about giving us thirty minutes with Mrs. Helen Haywood? Till now, I'd say we've been cooperative…perfect gentlemen, but enough is enough, Angela. We need to talk to her, and now."

"Her husband just arrived. Give them some time together, and then you can see her."

"Did she say anything…anything that could be helpful?" Benson asks.

"No." Angela folds her hands on top of the desk. "And I haven't pressed her about it, either."

"Did your people get us a good swab when she came in? We'd like to get some DNA on this scumbag."

"I'm afraid not. He was rough on her…ripped much of her inner tissue, and there was a lot of bleeding. We couldn't get a good sample for a reading…sorry. By the way, I think it best you know she wants me in the room during the questioning."

"That's fine with us," Goebel replies. "Is there anything we need to know before we talk to her?"

"Yes, she has a deep fear she might become pregnant from the rape…so don't mention it."

"Is she?" Benson asks. "Is she pregnant?"

"It's too soon to tell, but there's always that possibility."

****

There's a knock at the door. Richard jumps from the bed and stands at attention. Public displays of affection always embarrass him – Helen knew that about him, even before they married. She accepts it, for he shows his true feelings in so many other ways.

"Come in," Richard announces.

It is Angela. "I'm sorry to bother you, but the police are here."

A look of panic comes over Helen, yet she knows what she needs to do – how important it is. Every minute she puts off the questioning is another minute she might forget some important information that will help the police catch *him*. No woman is safe till he's caught. Helen nods.

"Do you want me to stay?" Richard asks. It's a gesture of affection and concern. He knows she will say no, which is just as well. In truth, he doesn't want to be there to hear all the sordid details. But he feels it is his duty to at least make the gesture.

Helen looks at him. "Sweetheart, you won't feel slighted if I ask you to leave?"

"No, I understand." He kisses her, keeps his head down, and leaves the room. For some strange reason, he feels embarrassed, unable to look into the faces of the two detectives entering the room.

Angela takes her place at the foot of the bed. Goebel and Benson move two chairs bedside and sit down.

"I'm Detective Rick Goebel, and this is my partner, Detective Jim Benson."

Helen just nods in response.

"Mrs. Haywood, we realize how difficult this must be for you, so we'll try to make this quick as we can."

"Do I have to tell every little detail?" Helen asks, nervously.

"You just tell us what you can and in your own words, Mrs. Haywood. If there's anything you feel embarrassed about saying, you can write it down later, or you can tell Dr. Mitchell here."

"Well," Helen says, "I went to work yesterday. I work for Colony Home and Life – you know, insurance. I manage certain projects for the company…pretty much alone, so I can make my own hours.

"I got there late…maybe ten in the morning. Only place to park was in the far end of the lot. It's a new section; they just put down the pavement. They hadn't yet installed the lights and security cameras. I didn't think about it at the time, but I suppose it wasn't a smart place to park.

"Anyway, I worked way past five o'clock. And when I left, it was late and dark, and there weren't many people left in the building."

"What time was it?" Benson asks.

"Around eleven at night, that's right; I remember looking at the clock before I shut the lights out in my office."

"Do you normally work late?"

"Depends…there are times of the year when I work even later."

"Which of your coworkers know this?"

"I suppose, all of them…directly, only ten…indirectly, maybe two hundred … That's not counting security."

While Helen relates the details of her ordeal, Angela keeps a close eye on her. She sees her patient is running on automatic, answering questions in a matter-of-fact manner – with little emotion – but inwardly, flames of anguish rise higher and higher. Angela knows all the telltale signs: biting down hard on the lips, leaving slight teeth marks, clenching the fists till the nails nearly begin to draw blood from the palms. These are bad signs.

"Do you remember what he looked like?"

"I couldn't tell you. He was wearing a ski mask and gloves. But I do remember…he was a black man. Headlights from a passing car in the street – its beams were on him only a second – I saw the skin around his eyes and lips and his wrists between his gloves and coat."

"How old would you think he was?"

"Just guessing…I'd say in his late thirties."

"How was he dressed?"

"The coat was all I saw; it was like a navy peacoat. The ski mask was black with make-believe eyebrows and lips that were bright yellow. The gloves were of the same woven material with a yellow line running along the outside."

"Did he speak to you?"

"Yes, in fact, he never stopped talking. First, he told me if I screamed or made any sound, he was going to kill me. Then he started saying nasty things…filthy words…words I don't feel comfortable repeating."

"What did his voice sound like?"

"It sounded strange. He tried to disguise it by talking unnaturally low, and he spoke with phony accents…always switching them. First, he spoke with a French accent…then German…Spanish…even Chinese. It was so bizarre. It made me think…how insane and dangerous he must be. It was frightening."

"When he was…when he was…you know…" Helen stops for a moment, clearly embarrassed.

"We understand," Angela says, "There's no need to go into those details."

Helen sighs ever so slightly; then she continues.

"He became angry; he began pounding me with his fists. …That's the last I remember. When I came to, he was gone. The end of my skirt was up around my neck, and my…my panties were missing. I hurt all over, but I somehow got up and struggled toward the main building. I collapsed under one of the parking lot lights. Security saw me on one of the cameras and came out to me."

"The missing panties…can you describe them?"

"Just plain, old pink briefs with a small white rose in front, sown into the elastic."

Questioning goes on for another fifteen minutes. It is clear to all that Helen is tiring and needs to stop.

"I wish I could be of more help," Helen says, "but most of it is a blur."

"No, you've been most helpful," Goebel says. "Actually, you've remembered more than most women do."

"Gentlemen, I believe you have enough to start your investigation," Angela says. "We need to let Helen get some rest, and we can continue this at another time."

"Yes, we understand. Thank you again for your help, Mrs. Haywood," Goebel says. "We'll be in touch with you tomorrow. May you recover quickly." The two men leave the room.

Lieutenant Goebel presses the elevator button. He watches the overhead numbers blink on and off.

"So, what do you think?" he asks his partner.

"What do I think? I think it's someone she knows…probably a coworker. I mean, the guy jumps up from behind her car. That tells me he knew it was her car and he knew around what time she would be leaving. A guy can hide behind a car for only so long…you know what I mean?"

The elevator door opens. Inside, Goebel presses the down button. The two men watch the overhead numbers blink off the floors.

"What bothers me are the gloves," Goebel declares. "I understand the ski mask … so she doesn't recognize you, but why gloves?"

"An overly precautious guy…maybe a paranoiac?"

"Could be, but I don't think so. Look at it this way…a black guy decides to do a number on some little, blond, white woman…and he wears gloves! Where's the fun in that? I mean, you can't get prints from torn clothing. What'd he think we were going to do…dust her butt for prints?"

The elevator stops. An unseen electronic voice announces the first floor lobby.

"Maybe he didn't get to finish all his plans?" Benson adds.

"Then why did he leave her?"

They step out of the elevator and cross the lobby.

"Maybe something scared him? Maybe he saw somebody? Maybe somebody saw him?"

"Maybe, maybe, maybe!" Goebel says. "Who knows…maybe he's a cuckoo bird with a woolly glove fetish. I tell you…find those panties and you've found our guy, but that's easier said than done."

"So where do we start?"

"If you ask me, I think our first stop should be to Judge Nelson's office for a court order."

"What'd ya mean?"

"What I mean is…if she does turn up pregnant, we need to be ready. Think about it…you got a scared, married, white woman who gets pregnant from a rape by some black guy; she's only got two choices…have the baby or get an abortion. And when you do the math…white rape victim…black rapist…and throw in one angry white husband…it can only add up to one thing. My money's on abortion; and when she gets it, I want a court order saying we get first dibs on that kid's blood…so we can get some DNA on this scumbag!"

****

Richard nervously enters Angela's office. She motions for him to sit down. He squirms in his chair. The doctor gathers some papers and pushes them to the side of her desk, folding her hands in front of her, looks at Richard and smiles.

"So … tell me, how are you feeling?"

It takes Richard off guard. "I don't know how I feel. You tell me. Besides, shouldn't your concern be more with Helen's well-being?"

"I am, but partners of victims hurt, too…sometimes in silence. So tell me, how do you feel?"

Richard takes a moment to reflect on the question.

"I feel angry…very angry! I've got this urge to run out and find the son of a bitch who did this and tear him apart with my bare hands. No…even better, I'd lock him up and torture him for months till he pleads for death. Then, I'd wait another month and then kill him."

"And…would you feel better then?" Angela asks.

"I don't know…I don't know if anything can make me feel better. I suppose, mostly, I feel shame. My first thoughts should be concern for Helen, not murderous rage. I should put her before everything else, but I don't. I guess I feel ashamed."

"Would it help if I told you what you're feeling is natural, and you needn't be so hard on yourself?"

He looks up with sorrowful eyes, and she knows her words have not made a difference. Perhaps they will take root and he'll find comfort in them at some later time in his life – but not now.

"You need to understand," he says, "when Helen and I first met, we were in love, I mean, head-over-heels in love. But lately…"

"But lately…?" Angela asks.

"But lately…I don't know if there is any love. I mean…we say the words, we go through the motions, but it's not the same. We tried so hard to have a child at the beginning. When it didn't happen, we just somehow lost interest. We haven't been … well, you know…for a long time. We both dove headfirst into our jobs. And now this…I just feel angry and…"

"Guilty?" Angela interjects. "Richard…is there something you're not telling me?"

Richard doesn't speak for a moment, looking lost in thought, and then he changes the subject.

"Doctor, how much longer does Helen need to stay here?"

"How much longer…? If we only consider her physical condition, I would say two or three days more. But I have to consider her mental health as well. I'd like to have some serious sessions with her first. Plus, the police want to talk to her a few more times. It would go easier on her if I were there with her."

"So, how long are we looking at?" he demands.

"Two weeks, at the least."

"Two weeks!"

"Richard, you must understand; Helen has this ungodly fear she's pregnant. If we find out she is, I'm not sure how it will affect her. I don't know what she may do. If she's not, then there's no harm done; she could use the rest. If she is, I would feel better if she were here."

"But, if she's pregnant, it's no big deal. She can just have an abortion…right?"

"Right…but it will be Helen's call, not ours."

****

It is three days later. A nurse pushes Helen's wheelchair into Angela's office, parks her in front of the desk, and leaves.

Angela is on the phone. She holds up one finger to Helen, signaling she will be one minute more.

Helen looks about the office. There are rows of the usual diplomas on the wall one expects in the office of a psychiatrist. Strange – there are no pictures of any people or places, no suggestion of what Angela's life beyond her job might be like.

Angela's outward appearance is one that makes her look older than her fifty-four years. She keeps herself neat and clean, but no frills. She wears no makeup. Her clothes and shoes she chooses for comfort and durability, not style. Her long, frizzy, salt and pepper hair, with much of the pepper fading, held back with a simple rubber band. Save for a wristwatch, she wears no jewelry. Angela is a no-nonsense woman working in a world of nothing but nonsense – the chaos and nonsense of the human mind.

She hangs up and looks at Helen.

"I apologize for not being available for your meeting with the police the day before. I was away on an emergency. I am sorry."

"Don't be, that's all right," Helen says. "It wasn't so bad. The police just asked a bunch of questions about the people I work with, nothing more. It was a relief not to have to talk about *that night*."

Much of the bandages and tape are now gone from Helen's face.

"You're looking much better; the discoloration is almost gone. It won't be long before you look yourself again."

Myself again? Helen thinks. She just smiles, not commenting.

"A penny for your thoughts?" Angela asks.

"I don't know. Lately, I try not to think at all."

"I want to run something by you I think would do you some good," Angela says. "This afternoon, I'm conducting a group session. The group consists of five women…all different ages, all different backgrounds, and all of them…"

"All of them rape victims," Helen interjects, bitterly.

"That's just it, Helen. We never use the word *victim*. Only you hold the power to make yourself a victim or not. It's your decision, not some rapist's. I thought if you sat in today, listened to woman who have gone through what you are going through, you might not feel so alone in this. You might learn to deal with your feelings."

Helen thinks about it for a moment, and then she nods. "Okay, I'll try it…just this once."

****

It is the next day. The small circle of women stands and rearranges their chairs to make room for Helen and her wheelchair.

Helen sits quietly while each woman tells her story.

Angela is right when she said all five women are of different ages and backgrounds – they are diverse – but with one thing in common that binds them.

There is Maria – a small, shy, young Hispanic woman in her late twenties. Her assailant received only five years imprisonment. Three years after the fact, rumor is he may receive an early release for good behavior. Maria agonizes over the notion he will possibly be free soon. The thought fills her with fear.

And Marion – a frail, gray-haired, older woman. It is obvious she must have been a beauty in her day, but that time has come and gone. Her assailant was a twenty-two year old technician who worked at the senior housing development where she lived.

Next is Elsie – a young, good-looking woman whose boyfriend and brothers raped her. She lived with her family then. When her parents heard what happened, they sided with the boys, claiming it was her fault for dressing so provocatively. She left home, heartbroken, and has not seen her parents since. The boys received three years probation.

Then there is Sylvia. She was once a fashion model of stunning beauty who now bears scars of that fateful night. She lives tormented over the memory of when a strange man broke into her home, had his way with her, and left her with two scars from his knife. Scars which burrow deep into her face, from her eyebrows down to her chin.

Lastly, there is Carmen – once an all-American homemaker but whose husband of ten years left her. He was unable to cope with the idea someone else had been with his wife. Even though it was not her fault and beyond her ability to stop or change what happened, he abandoned her. Now she is a radical, angry woman. She cut her hair short, threw away her makeup and all her dresses, and adopted a masculine look – deliberately cloaking any trace of femininity she once held.

Emotions run high. For nearly an hour, the women banter, argue, agree, disagree, laugh, cry – running the gamut of nearly every possible emotion. It frightens Helen, seeming so hopeless. Will there ever be a time when the memory releases its hold on her? These women have been working to break free of such memories – some of them for years – and still the past weighs heavy on them.

Some of them are bitter, like Carmen. Her distrust and hatred for men in general is obvious in the way she mocks them and by the way she dresses.

Others remain confused, like Marion. She can't understand why anyone would do such a thing to her, an old woman whose looks have waned. But, like Angela reminds the group, rape isn't necessarily a sexual act. Often, it is a play for power over another human being, and poor, frail Marion was the perfect candidate for such a twisted personality.

Some are religious, like Maria, who shares her philosophy with the others. "You have to learn to forgive. …It is what God wants," she pleads.

Others are angry, like Sylvia, "I suppose God wants this, too?" she says, pointing to her scared face. Helen is unable from that moment on to look the woman straight in the eye.

Some became philosophical, like Elsie. "You have to go on with your life…put the past behind you."

But how does one do that? Helen seriously thinks.

"Men who do these things are sick…sick in their souls. You must pray for them," says Maria.

"I pray for him every night," Sylvia remarks. "I pray he gets cancer and dies a slow death…the son of a bitch."

This brings an uneasy feeling over the group, except for Carmen who throws back her head and roars with laughter.

"That thinking gets you nowhere," insists Elsie, "What you need to do is adopt a lifestyle where you feel safe."

"Like what?" Sylvia demands, "Get another lock for your door? Get yourself an attack dog? That crap don't work!"

"It's something…you got to do something," says Elsie.

"Maybe, if you carried a gun or learn karate," Marion adds.

"I tell you that crap don't work," insists Sylvia. "If a guy tried anything with me now…I'd kick him in the balls!"

The circle of women starts to giggle at the thought, releasing some of the tension.

"What's with women and kicking guys in the balls?" says Carmen. "I think woman just like doing it. It don't work! I kicked my guy in the balls, and all it did was make him madder.

Carmen speaks directly to Helen, "You see how I call him "my guy"? It's not what they do to your body, as much as your mind. That bastard worked his way into my life…forever. That's why he's 'my guy.'"

Carmen then addresses the entire group, "You see, women got it all wrong. They go for the wrong set of balls. There's only one way to stop a guy. …It takes guts, but it's the only way."

She leans forward in her chair and whispers as if she were sharing some dark, ancient secret. "When he's on top of you, start acting like you're into it…like you're enjoying it. Start going, 'Oh baby, oh baby…you're so good'… They like stuff like that. Then you run your hands through his hair and over his face. When you've got him off guard, ram both your thumbs into the outer side of his eye sockets…real hard…till both his eyeballs pop out!"

A cry of horror and disgust comes from the group of women.

"Oh, I could never do anything like that!" says Marion.

"It's the only way," says Carmen. "Ram his eyeballs right out of his head!"

"I guess he'll see things your way after that!" says Sylvia.

Carmen and Sylvia laugh out loud. The other women sit shocked and silent – as is Helen.

****

Back in her room, lying in bed, Helen thinks about what she heard that day. Angela is wrong; the group session did not help her in any way. She did not learn anything about herself or the way she feels or how she can cope. One saving grace is she knows now what she does not want to become.

****

It is a day later. Helen and Richard sit in front of Angela's desk. Helen is no longer in a wheelchair.

"Thank you for being here for Helen today, Richard," says Angela. "What I'm going to say concerns both of you so I'll come right to the point." She looks directly at Helen, "I'm afraid what you've feared all along has come true. Helen...you are pregnant."

There is a long moment of unbearable silence. Helen stares straight ahead – not blinking.

Richard bursts out aloud, "Well, what we need to do is to set up an abortion as soon as possible."

"That will be Helen's call," Angela insists.

"Hey, what's this?" Richard's voice is angry. "First, you ask me here and tell me it concerns me, and then you tell me I haven't any say in the matter!"

"Helen must be our first concern. She's the one who will have to live with the decision."

"Oh, and I don't!" Richard hollers. "You're supposed to be a doctor. You think anything other than an abortion is the right choice?"

"There are physical and mental repercussions to having an abortion as well. It's not just done flippantly!"

"Stop it...both of you!" Helen cries, grasping her hands on the arms of her chair. "I need time to think."

Richard calms down; he reaches over and places his hand on Helen's. He looks as if he will cry at any moment. "Sweetheart, we can start fresh. We can still keep trying to have a baby. The doctors never said it was impossible, only difficult. There's still a chance."

"I need time to think," Helen whimpers.

"We can be happy again, I swear. If we have to, we can adopt. At least it would be a child of our own choosing. ....But not this child...not this child!"

Part of Helen believes everything Richard says to be true. Why she will not agree to an immediate abortion is something even she does not understand – but she just can't.

"Helen, please!" Richard pleads. "Don't do this to me...to us. ...Another man's baby...and this baby won't even look like mine!"

"I need..."

"You need time!" Richard's voice booms. "To do what – keep us from moving on with our lives?"

"I'm sorry, Richard. I'll have to ask you to leave," Angela forcibly interjects. "I think it would be best if Helen and I talked alone now."

"Please, Richard…no more," Helen begs, rubbing her hand on his. "I can't take this…please, for me?"

Richard looks into her eyes. He sees such pain there – it makes him feel horribly uncomfortable. He tears away from her hold. He feels sorry for her, but it is clear in his mind what steps need taking at this point. He rises without a word and storms out the office, slamming the door behind him.

"I've got to go home. I've been here too long. I can't deicide anything here. I need to clear my head. ...I want to go home," Helen cries.

"What about Richard?"

"Oh, he's just feeling hurt. He'll calm down in time. He's a lot more bark than bite."

"Well, why don't we give him that time…to calm down? We'll schedule your release for the day after tomorrow. But I want to set up weekly office visits for you with me…for a while."

Helen's eyes are misty. She speaks, "Angela, what would you do? If you were in my shoes, what would you do?"

"I've always been a firm believer in a woman's choice, and that includes giving birth as well as abortion. I'll stand behind whatever you decide, but I can't tell you what to do…that's up to you. I know it's incredibly difficult, but it all rests on you."

"Do you?" Helen asks. "You have no idea how difficult this is."

Angela turns in her chair. She stares out the window as she speaks, "Being the head of a hospital's Rape Recovery Program isn't a job you choose…it chooses you."

"You mean…you…?" Helen whispers.

"Yes…years ago."

"And was there a child?"

"Yes…there was a child." Angela's voice cracks slightly.

"And what did you do?"

"I'd rather not say; I don't want to influence your decision. I'm your doctor. I should never have told you this much."

"Then, not as a doctor but as a friend…tell me what you did."

Angel turns to face Helen. "As a friend? I carried the child…full term. Then I gave it up for adoption. I never even asked if it was a boy or a girl…I didn't want to know. He or she must be in their late twenties by now."

"And…was it the right decision?"

Angela pauses, turns her gaze once more out the window, and thinks aloud, "I don't know…I don't think I'll ever know."

Two

Do You Like Flowers?

At home, Helen finds it nearly impossible to relax or sleep, her mind consumed only with thoughts of her problem pregnancy. She tries to fill the long hours, but nothing captures her full attention. She tries to do some work at home. Carol, her assistant from Colony Home and Life, delivers some papers for her to review, but she finds it difficult to concentrate.

Though she feels ashamed to admit it, she is thankful Richard's work on the Montreal deal keeps him away from town most of the time. When he is in town, he often works long hours and comes home late in the night. Helen feels the weight of his body as he slowly gets into bed, gently trying not to wake her. But she is awake. She pretends to be sleeping, afraid of confrontation. When Richard is home, he is cordial, polite, and loving to a point. Intimacy is something Richard does not feel comfortable initiating. He wants to give her space. He believes she'll let him know when and if. As for Helen, for the moment she is not sure if she'll ever feel comfortable being intimate again. Angela tells her this is common and will soon pass. But for the moment, it doesn't seem as if it ever will. Helen is grateful Richard hasn't tried anything.

Neither one of them mention the pregnancy or possible abortion. Helen strongly believes Richard is right – an abortion is the only sensible solution. But a spark somewhere deep inside her prevents her from moving ahead with it.

"I know this child," she thinks silently. "I don't understand how, but it's not a stranger to me. . . .I know this child!"

Whenever Richard is away, Helen's parents visit her, bringing take-out from restaurants so she doesn't have to prepare something. These dinners are exhausting and trying for Helen. Like Richard, her parents became tight lipped, skirting the issue. Save for tidbits of local gossip offered by her mother, they often eat in silence.

Surprisingly, Helen learns during one such dinner that her parents know of the pregnancy – Richard told them. Perhaps he wants to recruit them as allies in his demand for an abortion or thinks if her parents are in the know it puts her under pressure to be of the same mind as his wishes. Helen should be mad with him for doing so, but she never mentions it to Richard. So much of the fight in her has left her recently. She avoids conflict whenever possible.

Sadly, Helen receives no other visitors. She realizes her and Richard's demanding work schedules not only impinged on their intimate personal life, but destroyed their social life as well. The only time her spirit slightly approaches being calm is when she sits, staring out the back window at the garden with Chelsea, her cat, sleeping on her lap. Sweet Chelsea, her unconditional love and affection Helen always valued – especially now going through the most trying time of her life.

Twice a week, she drives to the hospital for a session with Angela. Helen holds mix feelings about these meetings. On one hand, it feels good to let go of some of what is going on inside her, but on the other hand, hashing over the same thoughts and feelings over and over makes them seem larger. Her life feels like it is spiraling downward with no stopping in sight.

She yearns to return to work where she can find solace and fill empty hours. She seriously considers calling her boss and asking to return to work. After all, she is no longer covered in bandages, and what slight discoloration she still has, makeup will easily cover. She believes if she goes back to work, the distraction will give her some release and a little of her sanity back.

"I've been thinking of going back to work, but I'm not sure if it's too soon. Do you think it would be the right move? I'm not sure what I should do."

"What do you feel you should do?" This is Angela's stock answer to most of all Helen's questions – answering a question with a question. This repetition only makes Helen feel more hopeless.

Helen is so close to calling the office and declaring herself fit for duty – just this close – but for some unknown reason, she can't bring herself to make the call. Then the straw that breaks the camel's back unexpectedly arrives at her front doorstep.

****

Helen slowly and cautiously opens the front door where she meets with a face from her past – a man she has not seen in many years, yet still easily recognizable. It's Father Kelly from church. His face is still ruddy and round, even rounder when he smiles. Much of his hair is now gone, and what remains is thin and gray. Lines in his face have deepened and his skin is wrinkled. Even without a clerical collar, which he always wears, Helen easily recognizes him. She will always remember Father Kelly.

She invites him in and escorts him into the living room.

"Please, sit down, Father. Can I offer something? Would you like some…" she hesitates a moment. *What do you offer a priest?* she thinks. "Would you like some tea?"

"Tea sounds fine," he says, his round face glowing. His small eyes and large smile are reminiscent of the Man in the Moon.

Helen excuses herself to the kitchen where she franticly searches for tea bags she believes are still somewhere in the back of the pantry.

All her life, she has known Father Kelly. When she was little attending parochial school, she view him as a large and authoritative figure. She trembled whenever he entered the classroom. As a child, Helen's parents always took her to Sunday services, and there was Father Kelly on the altar, looming over the congregation like some great saint from the Bible. Now, years later, as a full-grown woman, her hands still tremble as she makes the tea, knowing Father Kelly is waiting in the next room. *Good gracious, it's like having Moses over for afternoon tea.*

She knows he came at the request of her parents – most likely, at her mother's asking. She feels angry. How could her mother do such a thing? This is so awkward; she has not been to church in years. She knows why he has come, and she is unquestionably not in the mood for a lecture.

She sits down opposite Father Kelly, places the tea tray in front of her on the coffee table, and pours out two cups. She isn't sure what to say, so she waits to hear what he has to tell her. He takes a sip of tea and then places the cup down.

"How are you feeling, Helen? You have been in my prayers every night since I heard."

"My parents sent you here, didn't they?" Helen wants to come straight to the point. She doesn't want to prolong the uncomfortable feeling she's having. Besides, she is mad – mad with Richard for telling her parents, mad with her parents for telling Father Kelly and whoever else might know.

Ever since the night she was attacked, she'd been losing control of her life. She instantly realizes that if she is ever to get her life back, it will be up to her alone. And that will never happen until she stands up and begins to take it back.

"Yes, they did…because they love you…as does Richard, and so do many other people who care for you."

"And this has less to do with my rape as it does with being pregnant, doesn't it, Father? Well, if I want to have this baby, it will be my decision. If I want an abortion, it will be my decision…not Holy Mother Church!"

Father Kelly is taken aback by Helens straight forwardness. As well, Helen has surprised herself. Yet, inwardly she is pleased with her action. And for the first time in a long time, she feels as if control is returning to her.

"My dear," says Father Kelly, "you misunderstand my purposes. The Holy Mother Church is not without sympathy. Abortion is wrong...but..."

Helen waits for the other shoe to drop.

"But there are certain circumstances where abortion is not a sin. And I believe this is such a circumstance. If you allow me to go before the Bishop for you, I believe I could get you special dispensation...to have an abortion."

Helen is nearly in shock. Her mouth drops open. "You mean to tell me, the Church wants me to get an abortion?"

"No, of course not. ...I'm just saying under the circumstances, I believe, the Church might grant absolution for you to do so."

Helen's mind is swimming. She's had enough. All her life, the Church told her what is right and wrong. Now the same authority that imbedded such notions in her mind wants to retract their once unmovable decision.

"Father, with all due respect, I thank you for coming, but I'm not feeling well, and I'd like you to leave."

"Oh, of course...but think about what I've said," Father Kelly says as Helen shows him to the door. Before leaving, he makes one last plea. "Just think about what I've said. If you need me, just call the church."

She resists the urge to slam the door when he leaves. She closes it gently, turns and leans against the door.

Helen doesn't want to think about it. This is the last straw. She picks up the phone and dials her boss.

"Tracy? This is Helen. ...Oh, just fine. ...Listen...I'm sure I'm ready to come back to work. ...Sure, I'm sure. ...Monday? Monday will be fine. ...In fact, it sounds great. ...See you then."

****

Seated behind her old desk, a sense of normalcy comes over Helen. There are piles of backlogged paperwork needing sorting through. Usually, she cursed the mountains of paper, but now she feels thankful for every sheet.

Carol brings her a cup of coffee.

Carol Hastings, Helen's assistant, is short with a robust figure. She carries herself well and dresses in plain business style. Her dishwater-blond hair is always kept short and neat. She enjoys working for Helen, and it shows by her willingness and enthusiasm to please.

"So, Carol, how have things been while I was gone?"

"Same old, same old…you know." Carol hesitates for a moment to think and then decides to come out with what is on her mind. "Those two detectives…"

"You mean Goebel and Benson?"

"Yeah, those two…Well, they came by a few times and questioned just everybody…especially the men…or I should say the black men who work here?"

"And, what happened?"

"Most of the guys took it all in strides, but it did piss some of them off. They didn't take kindly to being a suspect. I'd be careful with what I say, if I were you. There's a small handful who blame you."

This conversation with Carol is the closest anyone at the office comes to recognizing what happened to her. Of course, all her coworkers stop for a moment at her office door to inquire how she is feeling. But there is no direct questioning from any of them. It is all done with a false air of an illness, as if she had been out with the flu or broken a leg from a skiing accident. This is fine with Helen.

She is not looking pregnant, yet. She is sure no one knows about that. She looks forward to the next few weeks of playing catch-up with her job and pushing all other thoughts to the back burner of her mind. And that is exactly what she does.

But there is still fear one of her coworkers is her assailant. She finds herself staring at all the black men she meets, trying to size them up in her mind.

From indirect contact, the number of possible suspects at Colony Home and Life range from twenty or thirty. But direct contact, she can only think of three.

There is Tito who works in maintenance, but he is from Trinidad, with a distinct accent he surely can never hide successfully.

Next is John Pierce, supervisor over payments. John physically matches the description, but not the profile. He is a kindhearted, churchgoing, temperate man – dedicated to his job, his beautiful wife, Tina, and his two lovely children, Lateasha and Trent, both under five years old. It seems a near impossibility to consider John would do such an act. Still, stranger things happen in the world. Though it is unlikely, Helen does not exclude John from her mental line-up.

Then there is LaDarrell Phillips, head of collections. His office is just a few doors down from Helen's, but she seldom associates with him. He comes across pleasant enough, but he is single and always flirts with whatever woman is in the room at the time. His pencil-stick mustache is as crooked as his smile, which he so freely shows whenever he is in the presence of a female. Whatever the subject of conversation, he finds a way to bring sex into it. He does this lightheartedly, using double entendres, trying to play innocent – and perhaps he is. But Helen is always uncomfortable around him, so she keeps her distance. Could he be the assailant? He fits the profile, as far as she is concerned. But she knows too little about him to make a fair judgment, so she decides to do some investigating on her own.

"LaDarrell…what do you know about him?" Helen asks Carol as they sit eating lunch together in the cafeteria at work.

"LaDarrell?" Carol questions, looking across the room at LaDarrell sitting with some of his friends. "Not much…only that I don't like him. A woman can't walk past him without feeling his eyes undressing her. All you need to do is say 'Hi' to him, and he takes it as an invitation to jump your bones. He thinks he's God's gift to women. He's always bragging about his 'ladies.' I try to stay out of his way and just ignore him."

"Does he do well with the 'ladies'?" Helen asks.

"I'd say he does! Some women have no sense at all. I'll tell you how I know … because it's one of many reasons I can't stand the guy. One day, we were all in a meeting; I excused myself to get some paperwork I forgot on my desk. LaDarrell asks me if I would get some papers he forgot on his desk while I was at it. He told me to look in the bottom drawer on the right side. I guess I wasn't thinking, I looked in the bottom drawer on the left side, and you know what I found? Panties…a drawer full of women's panties…souvenirs from his 'ladies'…his conquests. The man makes me sick; he's such a dog!"

"Panties?" whispers Helen; a shot of red-hot fear rushes through her. Her breathing becomes shallow. Is LaDarrell the one? He has the physical characteristics. She must be careful about false accusations. She isn't sure what she should do.

Alone, back in her office, Helen takes a card from her purse and dials the number.

"Lieutenant Goebel here. How can I help you?"

"Lieutenant, this Helen Haywood. This may be nothing, but I thought it best to tell you. If you remember, my assailant took my panties…perhaps as a souvenir, as you put it. Well…"

"Go ahead, Mrs. Haywood, I'm listening."

"Well, like I said, it's probably nothing. Do you know a Mr. Phillips here at my office, LaDarrell Philips?"

"Yes, I remember him," Goebel replies.

"Well, my assistant was looking for some papers in Mr. Phillips' desk and came across a drawer filled with woman's panties. I haven't said anything to anyone. I didn't know what to do, so I phoned you."

"Mrs. Haywood, you did what was right. Now listen carefully. Don't tell anyone what you just told me – not your assistant, not nobody. And especially, don't try to confront Mr. Phillips. I remember him from the interviews we did. We could be out there in under an hour. What would be best is if you were to excuse yourself for the day and go home and wait to hear from us. Just go home. Don't worry; we'll take care of this. I'll call you as soon as we know anything."

****

Lieutenant Goebel hangs up the phone and turns to his partner.

"That was Mrs. Haywood."

"What did she want?"

"Do you remember that one black guy whose office is near hers?"

"You're talking about the big guy with the wife and two kids?"

"No, the other one. …He was the skinny guy with the thin mustache…LaDarrell Phillips."

"Yeah, I remember him. What about him?"

"Well, it seems Mr. Phillips is not only back on our suspect list, but he's inched his way to the top of it. Come on, I'll clue you in on the rest on the way there."

They arrive at Colony Home and Life within a half hour.

"Knock, knock," says Goebel. He and Benson stand in the doorway of LaDarrell Phillips' office.

"Say, I remember you two," says LaDarrell.

"And we remember you, Mr. Phillips. Do you mind if we come in?"

The two police officers enter, shutting the door behind them.

"I've told you guys all I know," says LaDarrell.

"Just a few more questions, Mr. Phillips…if you don't mind?"

The two sit down. "I'll come right to the point. We have it on good authority you own a sizable collection of woman's panties in the lower left drawer of your desk."

LaDarrell is speechless for a moment. "So…what of it?"

"Nothing…it's just that Mrs. Haywood…you remember the Haywood case…we questioned you on it. Well, it seems her assailant took her panties…probably as a souvenir, of sorts."

"So, what's it got to do with me?"

"Maybe nothing…maybe everything."

"Listen," says LaDarrell, "it's just nothing…just panties from a few hoes I went out with. I get a kick out of it. There ain't no law against it, is there?"

"Probably not, but if you're smart you'll come with us."

"Am I under arrest?"

"No, not really…"

"Then what if I told you guys to buzz off?"

"We'd get a court order to take possession of the contents of your desk. And you still have to go down to the station. Not to mention you'd be on our bad side, which I wouldn't want to be, if I were you."

"Listen, you're making a big mistake! It's all very innocent, believe me."

"Okay," says Benson, "I'll tell you what, come with us now…with the panties…no sirens…no handcuffs – we just calmly walk off the property. We'll run some test on those undies. And if there's no trace of Mrs. Haywood or any other rape victims, we'll not only let you go, but we'll drive you to work and explain to everyone it was all a big mistake. …Fair enough?"

"Do I have a choice?"

"In the long run…no."

LaDarrell Philips follows Lieutenants Goebel and Benson out of the corporate building of Colony Home and Life. True to their word, they don't handcuff him. Benson carries a cardboard box filled with panties.

LaDarrell sits in the back seat, trying not to look nervous, which makes him look all the more uneasy.

"You guys are makin' a big mistake," LaDarrell warns.

"It won't be the first time," Benson replies.

Downtown, they park their car in front of the police station. Benson opens the backdoor and takes hold of Phillips' arm. He is about to guide him toward the entrance when LaDarrell jolts out of his grip. His arms flaring wildly, he doesn't get far. He's not trying to get away; that's not his intent. He purposely runs out into the street and into the route of an oncoming bus. The bus tries to stop in time, but it is too late – LaDarrell Phillips' dead body lies under the weight of the large tires.

The bus driver comes blasting out toward Goebel and Benson, "It's not my fault! You saw him! He came running out of nowhere like he wanted to die!"

"Don't worry about it," says Benson.

"I've been driving this route for twenty-years without a hitch. It wasn't my fault!"

"I said, we know…it's not your fault!"

****

Richard is away on business. Helen spends the night in bed with Chelsea resting close to her. She waits for the phone to ring to hear Lieutenant Goebel tell her they caught Phillips and justice prevails. To have no fear, to put it all behind her and get on with her life. But the phone call never comes. Exhausted, Helen sleeps – bedroom light on and phone by her side.

****

Next morning, Helen isn't sure what to do. Should she call Goebel and Benson? She hasn't heard from them. She decides to dress and go to work as if it were any other day.

At work, Helen begins to organize her day. Carol comes in with her morning coffee.

"This is so weird…don't you think it's weird, especially after we talked about him yesterday," Carol says as she places Helen's coffee cup in front of her.

"What are you talking about?"

"My God…haven't you heard? Yesterday…LaDarrell Phillips…he's dead. He killed himself!"

****

Lieutenants Goebel and Benson sit in their office, gloating over their so-called victory. Surely, Philips is the culprit. He killed himself rather than face the shame of a trial and conviction of the rape of Mrs. Helen Haywood and perhaps others. A phone call from Dodson, their friend and confidant at the police lab, cuts their victory celebration short.

"Benson?" says Dodson. "I'm going to run tests on those panties you gave me, but from experience, I can tell you he's not your man."

"What makes you say that?" Benson asks.

"Because, when they inspected the body of said LaDarrell Phillips they found him clad under his clothes in lacy women's undies."

"You mean he was a fag?' Benson asks.

"No, he probably was a crossdresser. ….He liked to wear women's clothes. I'll run all the tests, but I bet you I'll find nothing."

"So where does that leave us?"

"I suppose…at square one."

****

A quick inspection of LaDarrell Philips' apartment confirms Dodson's suspicions. At first, it looks like any typical bachelor pad – stereo, large-screen TV, open bar, dimming lights. But a locked closet in the bedroom reveals an unexpected secret, LaDarrell Philips' most closely guarded secret.

There are rows of hangers holding costly, flamboyant women's clothing – wigs, shoes, undergarments – all not-so-typically large– LaDarrell Philips' size.

"Say, get a load of this!" says Benson, lifting a stack of mail-order catalogs catering to drag queens. "What do you think makes a guy like Phillips want to do stuff like this?"

"Who the hell knows?" says Goebel. "I stopped trying to figure out why anybody does anything years ago."

Further investigation and interviews with friends and neighbors proves Phillips in fact was a "Lady's Man." His little black book was like a phonebook for a small town – a town of only women – in alphabetical order, starting with "A" for Abby, all the way through "Z" for Zoe. He had a reputation, one he prized. When he realized he would lose it because his dark secret was to come into the light, he freaked. He couldn't live with the stigma, so Phillips bailed out at the first opportunity by diving under a cross-town bus.

****

Helen wears a look of shock after hearing the news of LaDarrell's death from Carol. She immediately phones Goebel and Benson. They tell her of Phillips' innocence and his suicide en route to the Police Station. Both detectives remain tight-lipped about any other information, feeling it bears no direct connection to the case. They see no reason for revealing Phillips' secret.

"Just tell me," Helen pleads, "Did his death have anything to do with what we talked about?"

"No," says Goebel. "I wouldn't worry about it if I were you. His death and your case, they're unrelated. Trust me, it would have happened sooner or later, anyway."

Helen tries hard to believe him. All day long she keeps repeating his words in her mind. But if there is no connection, then why won't they tell her the circumstances? It bothers her. She can't help believing if she hadn't tried to play detective, an innocent man would still be alive.

****

It's dark when Helen finally calls it a day. A security guard walks her out to her car – a new company policy. After hours, security will escort associates to their cars.

Her escort is a young black man in a crisp, starched uniform.

"What's your name?" Helen asks. "I don't think we've ever met. Are you new?"

"The name's Calvin," he says. "Been here five years. We've probably never met because I'm on a rotating schedule. I'm still going to school, and the company has been trying to work with me on the hours."

"What are you studying?"

"Accounting…I hope someday to trade in this uniform for a three-piece suit. Maybe I'll work here. …Who knows?"

Helen listens to his voice, carefully. She watches him walk. She guesses his height at six feet. His body is muscular. She looks at his face and the shape of his head, trying to imagine it covered with a black ski mask.

Then she catches herself – she can't go on with her life being paranoid. She puts all such thoughts out of her mind, thanks the young man, and gets into her car. He waits and watches her pull away.

It isn't late, but there are few cars on the streets. She drives the speed limit cautiously toward her home.

She isn't sure when she first realizes the van is following her. She thinks little of it when it pulls up behind her as she leaves the company parking lot. But now, ten minutes into her drive home, it is still close behind.

She tests her suspicions, making deliberate quick turns down unlikely streets – the van keeps a close tail. It is a familiar vehicle; she has seen it before. Her mind races. She tries to remember who she knows who owns such a van. In an instant, it comes to her. John Pierce, supervisor over payments at work, he owns a van just like this one. As she makes a sharp turn at the corner, the van stays close behind. A flash of light shines through the dark tinted windshield of the van, and she gets a split-second look at the driver – it is John Pierce!

"What does he want? Why is he following me?" Helen cries out loud. She would never suspect John Pierce, but he could be the one. Depraved lusts can harbor in the heart of even a seemingly good man such as John.

She begins to feel threatened and frightened. Her driving becomes erratic; she is all over the road. Up ahead, she sees the lights of a shopping mall – she might have a chance there. She shifts lanes to be ready to turn into the parking lot.

A block from the mall, a traffic light turns red. She guns the engine, hoping to lose the van, but it keeps up with her and runs the light also.

In the mall parking lot, Helen drives to the front of a large, well-lit store. The van stops directly behind her. She looks in the rearview mirror and sees John getting out of the van.

In her confusion, she isn't sure what her next move should be. She can bolt from the car and run into the store, but she is sure he can outrun her. She decides to hold up in the car and call the police on her mobile phone. She grabs her purse and begins to rummage through it, searching for her phone.

A knuckle taps on her window, taking her by surprise. She wants to scream, but can't.

John's face is inches from the window. "Helen, it's me, John. We need to talk."

Her hands are shaking uncontrollably. She turns her purse upside down, letting all contents fall onto the seat next to her. Her phone hits the seat cushion; it bounces and falls to the car floor. She is just about to reach down to get it when she hears the click of the car door – she hasn't locked it. She feels cool night air rushing into the car. In a panic, she takes hold of the steering wheel and begins to press down on the horn, honking it again and again. Then – she feels a hand grab her arm to stop her.

"Helen, are you all right?" Surprisingly, it is a woman's voice. She looks at the hand holding her arm; it is a woman's hand. She turns to see the face of Tina, John's wife, smiling at her sympathetically. "Helen, it's me, Tina Pierce. Are you all right?"

Helen is so relieved to see Tina, she jumps out of the car and into her arms.

"Oh, Tina…" Helen begins to sob, hysterically.

"Oh, you poor dear, God only knows what you've been through," says Tina.

John goes back to the van and returns with their two children, Lateasha and Trent.

"Sorry about all the secrecy," says John. "We didn't mean to scare you. My family and I just want to talk to you."

Helen begins to calm down and looks at him.

"We couldn't think of any other way to tell you what we want to say without causing trouble," says John. "You know the company's policy on religion in the workplace…they don't look sympathetically on it. I just wanted to tell you…that is…I mean, we…our whole family wants you to know Jesus loves you and we have been praying for you every day. In fact, our whole church has been praying for you. Here's a get-well card signed by the entire congregation."

Helen takes the card. Tears begin welling up in her eyes, but now for a much different reason.

"I feel so ashamed," says Helen.

"Our daughter Lateasha made something for you," Tina says. "Give Mrs. Haywood her gift, sweetheart." She guides her daughter toward Helen. Shyly, the little girl hands over a small piece of construction paper.

"Now tell Mrs. Haywood what the picture is of."

"It's a picture of you, Mrs. Haywood," says Lateasha.

"Oh, how sweet of you to do that for me," Helen says, admiring the stick figure of a woman in the middle of the page. "But what are all these white things floating around me?"

A questioning look comes over the child, surprised Helen doesn't know instinctively what they were. A smile comes over the little girl as she softly speaks, "Angels."

****

Helen parks the car in the garage. There is an empty space where Richard's car should be. He is not home yet. The lamp in the living room is on, suggesting Richard was home earlier, but left.

"Chelsea?" she calls out for the cat as she enters the kitchen.

She still can't shake off the feeling of shame. John and his family were so sweet, yet when she first saw him in her rearview mirror, all she thought was the worst. Is this the way it is to be from now on – fear and suspicion?

She takes down a can of cat food, opens it, and places it in a bowl. "Chelsea?" she calls, putting the bowl on the floor.

It is seldom Chelsea doesn't run to the door to greet her whenever she comes home. But the cat is getting older – twelve years now – and is sleeping more and more. Helen knows she will probably find her upstairs asleep on the bed.

She goes upstairs to get out of her work clothes and into something comfortable. In the bedroom, there is no sign of Chelsea. Helen thinks this strange; the only other times she couldn't find Chelsea was when something or someone scared her and she nestled into a remote harbor of the house to hide.

But what could scare her?

A slight twinge of fear starts to come over her.

"Stop being so paranoid," she thinks. "Nothing scared the cat; she's just asleep somewhere in the house."

She places her clothes in the hamper and takes out a light pink sweat suit from a dresser drawer. Before putting it on, she stands in her underclothes, in front of a full-length mirror in the corner of the room. She examines the shape of her stomach – first the front view, then a side view. It is becoming obvious she is pregnant. It won't be long till she'll have to wear larger clothing – then everyone will know.

She runs her hands over her stomach. She admires herself and the way she feels. Part of her still thinks an abortion is the only sensible solution, but she also can't help feeling pleased.

"I know this child," she tells herself again.

Once more, not wanting to face a decision, she puts all such thoughts away and files them somewhere in the back of her mind – at least for another day.

She puts on the sweatshirt and sweatpants and goes downstairs. In the kitchen, the bowl of cat food remains untouched.

"Chelsea?"

Helen is starting to panic. She looks over to the far end of the kitchen where the phone and answering machine are. There is a red blinking signal on the answering machine. She walks over. It isn't a phone call; it is the memo indicator. A message left from Richard, she thinks. Maybe it is about Chelsea. Maybe she became ill and Richard took her to the vet.

She presses down on the memo button.

An icy cold rips through her entire body. Like dry ice, it burns as well as chills. Sheer terror takes hold of her when she hears the low voice of a man – speaking with a phony German accent.

"*Der liebhaber*, where are you? I came by to see my hot little *das Miststück*, but you weren't home! I miss your beautiful *feste Brüste* and your hot, wet *schamlippen*! We get together soon, and make sweet *Sex haben…jah, das is gut, mein Liebchen*.

"I brought you some flowers, but I couldn't find a vase. So I planted them in your garden…I hope you don't mind. I know you're a *der tierfreund*, so I got you some cattails…they're lovely. I will see you again *mein Liebchen*…real soon, *jah*, my dear sweet 'Hell-in'…*Auf Wiedersehen!*"

The message stops. The machine clicks off – all is silent. Helen stands, her head bows down, staring at the machine. Her whole body is shaking. She reaches out for the back of a chair to support herself. She feels she is going to faint. Then she re-exams in her mind what she just heard.

"Chelsea!" she screams.

Quickly, she runs out the backdoor leading to the garden. She grabs the large flashlight they keep hanging by the door as she exits.

Outside, the garden is dark. She switches on the flashlight and holds it with two hands guiding the light beam along the ground from flowerbed to flowerbed.

"Chelsea! Chelsea!" she continues to call, but there is no answer.

The light beam settles on a mound of dirt at the end of a line of flowers, a mound of dirt that should not be there.

Helen slowly walks over to examine. There is a large pile of light-brown soil, and at the top of the mound is the head of the cat protruding up. The body fully buried, only the head is visible. Chelsea is dead, motionless. Her eyes, half-shut and crossed, stare in horror, her tongue sticking out. The familiar black gloves with the yellow stripes wrap around the animal's twisted neck.

"Oh no! Chelsea…no!"

Dropping the flashlight, everything goes dark. She doesn't know where to run. The monster was in her home – nowhere is safe anymore. There is no place to hide, no place to run.

She finds her way back into the house. She runs to the phone and dials 911.

"Police Department…may I help you?" asks a humdrum voice on the other end of the line.

"Please…please…please…I…" is all that comes from Helen's lips. She is so frightened she can't even form a sentence. Breathing deep and sporadic, she starts to hyperventilate. The room begins to spin. Sharp pains shoot through her body. Her knees begin to buckle, and she starts to lose consciousness. She reaches out for something, anything. But instead she goes down, her head striking the edge of the kitchen counter. She hits the floor – hard. Everything goes pitch-black.

****

Helen wakes to find Angela sitting next to her in a hospital room. Helen lies in bed.

All that time, all that suffering and effort, only to realize she has come full circle, back to the beginning of the nightmare. Only now, it has intensified.

Angela reaches over and places her hand on Helen's. She looks sadly and sympathetically into her eyes – knowing there are no words that can help.

Tears begin to stream down Helen's checks; her lower lip is quivering.

"I can't…I can't do this…I can't do this anymore."

Angela stands and wraps her arms around Helen whose entire body shivers.

"I can't do this anymore," she cries, sounding more like a plea than a statement.

"You won't have to. You're safe now, I promise," says Angela, holding Helen tighter.

"The baby…?" Helen whispers.

"Oh…Helen…I'm so sorry. …You've…you've lost the baby."

Helen's quivering stops. Angela gently releases her and tucks her in. "Just try to get some rest…sleep."

Angela leaves the room.

In the waiting room, Angela confronts Richard and Helen's parents. "I know you are all concerned and want to see her, but I think she would do best undisturbed. I've given her a strong sedative; she should sleep the night. Go home…all of you. …I'll call you with a report tomorrow."

With a little more persuading, they reluctantly leave. Angela walks them to the elevator, reassuring them Helen will be fine with rest.

When the elevator closes, Angela turns in relief only to find herself confronted with Goebel and Benson.

"No!" is all she says as she walks away.

The two officers follow her. "'No'? What do you mean, 'no'? You haven't even heard the question," Goebel demands.

Angela stops and turns to them. "It doesn't matter. …Whatever it is, the answer is no. That poor woman is this close to having a breakdown. I don't want you two pushing her over the edge with too many questions."

"Okay…okay!" says Goebel, "Just do us one favor…keep us posted." The two enter the elevator. It closes, and they are gone.

****

Helen keeps slipping in and out of consciousness. Her mind won't let her sleep, though strongly sedated. Instead, the drug gives her a wakened state with a dream-like quality, which frightens her. The white of the hospital room swirls in front of her eyes.

A loud sound, like an alarm, cuts through to her, bringing her to a groggy consciousness. She looks over, next to the bed, on top of the nightstand – the phone is ringing.

It takes all her strength; the drug makes the world heavy and thick. Her body moves in slow motion. Helen reaches over, picks up the receiver, and places it to her ear.

"Hello?" she whispers.

She isn't sure if it is a dream or reality. Either way, it doesn't matter, it frightens her so.

The low voice of a man speaking in a phony French accent comes over the line. "*Bonjour, chérie*…so sorry you are not feeling well. I should send flowers, but I don't think you like flowers…do you? How is our child? All gone, eh? …Oh well, *c'est la vie*.

Voulez-vous coucher avec moi? You know I do. *Tu es une pute*! You know what I'd like to do? *Je vais te juter sur la gueule*! Does that sound good to you? I'm sure it does. *Au revoir…pétasse…à bientôt*!"

****

The instant the elevator door closes on Goebel and Benson, a terrifying scream echoes through the entire seventh floor of the hospital. It's coming from Helen's room. Angela takes off running. Hearing the scream coming from the floors above, the two detectives get off at the lower floor and run up the stairs to the next floor.

They find Helen with her face on the floor, but most of her body is still on the bed – she slid down the side.

Two of the nurses help pick her up and place her back on the bed. Angela sees the phone on the floor; she bends down and picks it up.

"I gave strict orders…no phone calls! You were to hold all phone calls. I want her to rest."

Goebel and Benson come running into the room. They're out of breath from the run, so they stand and wait.

Helen pushes her hands into the mattress and sits up straight. "It was him. …He called."

Angela looks at Helen.

Goebel and Benson move in closer.

"It's okay," Helen announces. "I'm all right. I'm not going to break over this. I'm not going to let him hurt me…ever again."

There is a renewed freshness and conviction on Helen's face. This leads Angela to wonder if Helen somehow tapped into some unknown strength within or pushed all the way to madness. It is too soon for Angela to tell which of the two happened.

The two detectives look on, feeling helpless.

Angela shoots them a look. They understand there will be no questioning tonight. The best they can do is go to the front desk and see if anyone there knows where the call came from.

"Who forwarded that phone call to Mrs. Haywood's room?" Goebel asks the two nurses behind the front desk.

Angela comes up and stands silently next to the two detectives. She wants to hear the answer as much as they do.

One of the nurses, the head nurse, is an older woman with hair as white as her scrubs. She doesn't answer, but looks to the younger nurse.

The younger nurse steps forward. She bows her head in shame. "I put the call through," she confesses. She looks up at the trio with her sad eyes. It's clear to see how upset she is. Any angry words Angela planned to shout at her get pushed aside.

"I don't suppose there is any way of tracing that call from here?" Benson asks.

"No, sir, I'm afraid not," the young nurse says shyly.

Angela steps forward and address the young woman as calmly as she can.

"I gave orders for Mrs. Haywood to not be disturbed. That includes phone calls. Why did you put the call through?"

"I'm sorry. I thought it was important. He said he was a family member."

"What name did he give?" Benson asks.

"He said he was her Uncle Jerry."

Three

Surprises

Dodson casually strolls down the hallway toward Goebel and Benson's office. He is a burley little man in his mid-fifties. As a young man, he studied medicine; his goal was to be a doctor. But as his distrust and distain for his fellowman grew over the years, he set his sights on police work where he would have little dealings with other human beings – living human beings, that is. He works with fingerprints and samples of skin, hair, blood, and body fluids. His only dealings are with the dead – entire cadavers or parts of people recently or long gone, which is just fine with Dodson. Though, for some reason, he does seem partial to Goebel and Benson, and they to him.

"Got some interesting stuff this time for you two on the Haywood case," says Dodson. With a folder in his hand, he enters the office and sits down like he owns the place.

"Like what?" Goebel asks. "You want some coffee?"

"No thanks…just had some. Like this…the gloves you found around the neck of the cat. They're rather expensive…made by a Swiss-Italian company that folded in the late sixties. Where your guy got them is a mystery in itself."

"What about the memo on the answering machine?" Benson asks.

"What about it? There's not much I can do with it. We can always compare it to someone else's voice, if you have a suspect. But by itself, it's not much help. I'll tell you one thing, though…from his pronunciation, I can tell you the guy ain't German. You know, I looked up the meaning of those words…what a mouth on that guy!"

"Yeah…and he called Mrs. Haywood in her hospital room and played the same number on her, only this time in half-assed French."

"Trace the call?" Dodson asks.

"Yeah…and here's the kicker…we traced it to a payphone downstairs in the hospital lobby."

"So, what do you two geniuses have on this case?" Dodson asks.

Normally, Goebel and Benson never discuss a case they are working on, but they don't mind answering Dodson's questions. Sometimes it is good to bounce ideas off a third party. Besides, Dodson has a good head for such matters.

"Well…" Benson says, "what we've got is some cuckoo who won't let go of his victim. We're sure it's someone she knows because he knows too much about her. Besides, the ski mask and the gloves were a sure give away he wanted to hide his identity."

"He must know her real good to get into her house and leave her a message," says Dodson.

"Hell, there ain't much to getting into a person's house," Goebel says. "The Haywoods had gotten out of the habit of always setting their alarm. Anyone with a little know-how, and I mean anyone, could sneak in. Besides, the husband said he was there earlier to change clothes. He admitted he left the garage door up. …That's as good as having a key."

"What about the international dirty-talk?" Dodson asks.

"Who knows? …Like I said…he's probably some cuckoo. I guess we'll find out when we catch him. That's if we can get some DNA evidence from Mrs. Haywood's miscarriage…if you know what I mean?"

"Oh yeah…the DNA results. Luckily, we got enough skin and hair from inside the gloves to run a test." Dodson opens the folder. "You guys are all alike. You think DNA is going to solve all your problems. You think we put this stuff under a microscope and up pops the guy's name, phone number, and address. DNA can only tell you so much."

"So what does it tell you?" Benson asks.

"You're not going to like it," Dodson smiles. "It's going to throw a monkey wrench into your investigation."

"So…what is it?"

"Your guy ain't black. …He's as Caucasian as you or me."

"Are you sure?"

"Yeah, sure I'm sure."

The room goes silent for a moment, and then Goebel hammers his fist down onto the desk.

"The gloves…now, I get it! He wore the gloves because he put dark makeup around his eyes and lips…and with gloves on, all he needed to do was color his wrists. I knew there was something about those gloves."

Benson quietly stands and starts for the door.

"Where the hell are you going?" Goebel asks.

"I'll see you in the morning."

"But it's only three o'clock in the afternoon!"

"I got a hunch I want to check out. If I'm right, we'll have our suspect. I'll see you in the morning."

"He's a nutcase," Goebel remarks.

"*He's* a nutcase?" Dodson laughs. "I don't know if you realize it or not, but if you two didn't have different names, I'd have no way of telling you two apart."

****

Angela has never seen Helen looking so well. Her energy is up, and her spirits are high. She wonders if it's real or a put on.

"I'm almost afraid to ask," Angela says. "Why the sudden change?"

Helen sits up and smiles. "After the miscarriage, I felt like I couldn't go on. Then something dawned on me...something you once said to me. You said it was up to me to decide if I were to be a victim, not some rapist. Right there and then, I decided to not be a victim. I have a good life...a good job...and a marriage needing a little work, but it's fixable. I won't be a victim and let some monster take it all away from me. From now on, I call the shots! I'm going to reclaim my life. This caused a wedge between me and Richard. I won't let that happen. He's not going to win...I am."

Angela doesn't know what to make of Helen's quick about-face. She wonders if it is only the calm before the storm.

"The police called me," Angela says. "They're concerned for your safety. They suggested on nights when Richard is away, you shouldn't be alone. Maybe on those nights you could stay with your parents?"

Helen laughs incredulously.

"My parents...? I don't think so!"

"How bad could it be?" Angela laughs as well. "It'll only be until they catch this guy."

Helen shakes her head. "You don't know my mother."

****

The following day, Helen packs an overnight bag and puts it in the trunk of her car. After work, she reluctantly drives out to her parents' to spend the night. It's a large one-story house in an old part of town, a well-off area walking distance to the country club.

It is exactly as Helen feared. Her mother takes up the dual role of martyr and ringmaster. She was always a suffocating woman, but now it is more than Helen is able to tolerate. She spends most of her time in her room.

Her bedroom has not changed since she left home. High school memorabilia and little girly frills her mother preserves like a shrine.

Though the thought crosses her mind, Helen knows she must at least spend some time with her parents, especially at dinnertime. Outside of a few questions as to how her day went and how she is feeling, her father speaks little at the dinner table. He seems to sense Helen's need to not talk. But not her mother – the woman is a bottomless well of questions and an eternal fountain of opinions.

Helen does her best to answer the questions and to block out the opinions. She rushes through her dinner and then excuses herself to her room.

One night as she lies in bed reading, a gentle tap comes at her door. The door opens slightly and her father's smiling face comes in.

"I saw your light was still on…hope you don't mind. …Can I come in, Princess?"

"Sure, Daddy."

He closes the door behind him and sits down on the edge of the bed. He is holding a small, oblong, wooden box.

"We haven't had a chance to talk. Are you all right?"

"I'm fine, Pop."

"And you and Richard?"

"Well…it's been better. He gets back home tomorrow. I'm sure it's nothing we can't handle."

"I'm sure it isn't." He smiles and then he offers the oblong box to her. "Here…don't let your mother know I gave you this. …She'd have a fit. I bought it for her years ago, but she wouldn't take it. She doesn't even know it's still in the house."

Helen opens it. There inside, resting in velvet, is a revolver.

"It's a .38…small enough to carry in a purse, but it can stop a train."

"Pop…I don't…I mean…"

"Don't worry, Princess. I'll take you out to the range and show you how to use it. Just remember…hold it in both hands and aim for his chest and don't stop shooting till all six bullets are gone…and the son of a bitch is dead."

With tears in his eyes, he leans over and kisses her forehead.

"You use it and kill the son of a bitch if you have to."

He rises from the bed, overcome with emotion, and starts out the door. "Goodnight, Princess."

"Goodnight, Daddy."

Alone, Helen takes the gun in her hand – it is heavy. She puts it back into the box and places it on the nightstand. She turns off the light and closes her eyes.

****

Helen spends hours in the kitchen preparing some of Richard's favorite dishes. It will be their first night together in weeks. She plans a quiet dinner and romantic evening, determined to get their love-life back on track.

Richard is downstairs in their home office, working at the computer. She doesn't want to disturb him, but dinner is almost ready. She sneaks quietly into the office and places a glass of wine near him.

"Dinner will be ready soon."

"Mmmm…" is all he says, lost in deep concentration. He doesn't look at her and continues to tap-tap on his computer's keyboard.

"The other night," says Helen, "when I was at my parents, strangest thing happened. My father gave me a revolver. I just thought you should know…I've got a gun now."

Richard stops typing and takes a sip of his wine. He then continues what he's doing without looking at her.

"I know. Your father told me about it on the phone today. Seriously…Helen…I don't think running around with a gun in your purse is a good idea…do you? I mean, you've never shot a gun in your life, and in the state of mind you're in…if you don't shoot someone else, you may shoot yourself."

"There's nothing wrong with my state of mind! Besides, my father will teach me how to use it."

Richard finally turns to look at her.

"I still think it's a bad idea," says Richard. "That's why I took the gun out of your purse and put it someplace safe."

"You what? My father gave it to me! Where did you put it?"

"I put it someplace safe."

"But you've no right to take it. He gave it to me!"

Richard doesn't answer. He turns to the computer and continues his typing.

"Dinner will be ready in ten minutes," Helen says, trying to sound calm, doing her best to keep her composure.

"Thanks…but I've got to get this stuff done."

"But, I've made all you favorites." Helen is still sounding calm.

He turns and stares her down.

"Are you going to disagree with everything I say and do? I said, Thank you, but not right now!"

Helen feels a strong urge to slam the door when she leaves the room, but she doesn't.

****

During her session at the hospital the next day, Helen tells Angela about the gun and how distant Richard has been.

"He had no right to take the gun from me. And to hide it from me, as if I were a child, is…is…degrading."

Angela comes to the defense of Richard, "For the longest time now, he hasn't felt like the man of the house. He's just throwing his weight around. It's his way of taking control of his life, which he feels has been taken from him. Give him some time; he'll settle back down."

Helen thinks about it. Perhaps, Angela is right. But what truly matters to Helen is getting her gun back.

****

Benson comes into the office early the next morning. He places a bag on the edge of Goebel's desk. Goebel pulls out a container of coffee. His hand feels around inside the bag.

"What the hell is this? Where's my Danish?"

"No Danish…bagels," Benson says.

"Bagels…? My wife put you up to this, didn't she? Eat healthy, my foot! Did you at least bring some jelly?" Goebel rummages again through the paper bag.

Benson ignores his partner's tantrum and sits back with coffee and bagel in hand.

"So what was this big secret investigation you needed to do?" Goebel asks.

"You've been doing this as long as I have," Benson says. "You have the same suspicions I do. I just wanted to get some stuff confirmed before we go any further.

"When Dodson told us the assailant was in fact a white guy, the wheels started to turn in my head. I checked with the airlines. On the night of Mrs. Haywood attack, her husband was not in Montreal like he claims. I checked the phone records. All his calls during that forty-eight hour period were local. He was nowhere near the airport."

Goebel puts down his bagel and coffee. "So he wanted to kill his wife…that I get…but why the rape?"

"Who knows? Maybe the guy's kinky…beating on his wife gives him the hots. Maybe he wanted to give her one last turn? Maybe he did it to throw us off course? How do I know?"

"And, the reason he didn't finish her off is…?"

"Because…something spooked him. …That's why he wore the disguise and the dark makeup in the first place – in case he got spotted. Something spooked him, and he couldn't finish the job.

"Now he thinks he's got her on the run. And if he doesn't kill her, she'll probably go mad. Either way, he gets his wife out of the picture.

"It would have been easy for him to kill the cat and leave the memo – and to make the phone call from the hospital lobby to her room. He's our prime suspect."

"Yeah, it all fits," Goebel agrees.

"So you want to pick this guy up?" Benson asks.

"No…let's wait. If we arrest him now, we'll just get a song and dance routine from him. Without some real evidence, a conviction is a long shot.

"First off, I want to know why he wants her dead. There is such a thing as divorce in this state…there's more here than meets the eye.

"I say, let's not mention to anyone concerned we know the assailant's a white guy, even to Mrs. Haywood. …Let him think we're not on to him. Let's keep a close eye on Mr. Richard Haywood. We dog him day and night till we get some evidence or he screws up…whichever comes first."

Goebel tosses his bagel into the wastebasket.

****

Helen is spending the night at her parents'. She looks at the clock on the nightstand – it is nine o'clock. There is a gentle rapping on her bedroom door, followed by her mother's voice.

"Helen, there's a Carol Hastings on the phone."

"Be right there, Mom."

Helen is staying with her parents for three days while Richard is out of town on business. Her assistant, Carol, is working late, and some of the numbers just aren't adding up. There is no way out of it. Helen needs to go to the office, or there will be hell to pay in the morning.

"It's late, dear. Why don't you let your father drive you?" her mother suggests.

"It wouldn't be any trouble, Princess," says her father.

"No, it's okay. I may be awhile. . . . Depends on how bad the damage is. Don't worry; I'll be all right."

Her father smiles and gives her a knowing look. She has not told him Richard took the gun from her.

****

"That's it, Carol. You've been at it all day. You need to get home to your husband," Helen announces, storming into the office.

"But there's still some numbers that don't line up!" Carol moans.

"That's why I'm here; I'll take it from here."

"But…"

"No buts!"

Carol looks at her with sad puppy-dog eyes. "Are you sure?"

"I'm sure, I'm sure. Besides, I work best alone. I'll have it wrapped up in half an hour."

Carol reluctantly leaves. "Call me if you need me," she calls over her shoulder as she makes her way down the hallway.

"I won't!" Helen hollers back. "Be sure security walks you out!"

Helen removes her jacket and sits down in front of the computer. She looks at the sheets with rows of numbers on them and then the rows of numbers on the computer screen. They don't match. It's going to be a long night.

****

It's just passed midnight when she finally finishes and shuts down the computer.

Her security escort to her car again is Calvin.

"So, how are your studies going?" she asks.

"Not bad. Working the late shift gives me time to study."

She tries not to show it, but she is still nervous. She has not stopped sizing up every black man she meets as a possible suspect. Of yet, Goebel and Benson have not let her in on their findings.

In true gentlemanly fashion, Calvin holds the car door open for her. He waits till the engine turns over and she is on her way before waving goodbye. Helen smiles and waves back as she pulls out of the parking lot.

The streets are empty. Halfway home, Helen stops at a red light; a pair of bright headlights comes from behind. She lets out a sigh of relief when she realizes it's a police car. It pulls alongside. There are two officers sitting in the front. The officer on the passenger side motions for her to pull over to the side of the road. She can't imagine what they want – she hasn't been speeding.

She does as they direct. The officer gets out and walks alongside and signals for her to roll down her window.

"Good evening, Officer. Is there something the matter?"

"Please turn the car off," he says firmly. She does. "Did you know your right rear light is out?"

"I had no idea. I'll get it fixed first thing in the morning."

She is half-hoping he lets her go with just a warning. She places her hand on the steering wheel and prepares to turn the car key and shift into drive.

"May I see your license and proof of insurance, please?"

This is going to take longer than she thinks. She nervously digs for a minute inside her purse till she comes up with her driver's license. She hands it over; he eyes it for a moment, then hands it back.

"Your insurance card, please?"

Helen leans over to the glove compartment and reaches in. She feels something strange – something smooth and silky. She grabs it and brings it out into the light. To her surprise, it is a pair of woman's panties – a pink pair with a small white rose sown to the front waistband. The same pair she wore the night of her attack – the same pair her assailant took from her. The front of them stained and crusted. In disgust, she tosses them down onto the car floor. She cannot imagine how he was able to put them in her car. She begins to feel excessively vulnerable. She begins to tremble; tears are rolling down her cheeks.

"Are you all right, miss?" asks the officer.

She doesn't answer as she borders on the edge of hysteria.

The next few hours are a blur to Helen. She finds herself at the police station with Goebel and Benson questioning her. She tells them again and again that there is no way he could have put anything in her car. When she is at work, she keeps her car locked, and it is always under surveillance of company security. On nights she stays with her parents, she parks her car on the street – again, always locked. Only when she is home and the car is safe in the garage does she leave it unlocked.

"Then you're saying only you and your husband had access to the car in the past few days?" Benson inquires.

"Exactly! That's why I can't understand how this happened."

Benson looks at Goebel. They smile knowingly at each other.

****

Angela listens intensely while Helen relates all that occurred in the past week they have not seen each other.

"But you…" Angela asks. "Tell me, how are you holding up?"

"Honestly, rather well; better than you can imagine. The night I found the panties through me off center for a while, but I know I've recovered from that. I feel…strong and determined. I told you I refuse to be a victim! He may continue to try to turn that around, but I'll never let him." There is a look of resolve in Helen's eyes.

"And Richard – how are you and he getting along?"

"We're not…we're not even ships passing in the night. We live on completely different shores. But then again, Richard loves me – I know he does. I thought about what you said the last time. He needs to heal as much as I do. In time he'll come around…I just know it."

"That's just the point," Angela says. "No one heals until the hurting is over. This fiend's determined about going after you. You must take protective measures. I know you're staying with parents when Richard is away, but is it enough? The police would like you to move to a safe place, somewhere where he can't find you and the police can protect you better."

"You mean, hide under a rock? I'm not going to let him have control. I told you that. If the police can't do their job, then I will."

"Now, Helen, you don't mean to do anything foolish?"

"Don't worry; I won't. But, I'm not going to live in a hotel with armed guards at my door…I refuse!"

"Well, if it all becomes too much for you at your folks or you need some time away, call me. I've got a big old place in the Madison District; it's too big for even two people. Heck, I'm hardly home anyway. …You could have the place to yourself. If it gets crazy, you'd be welcome."

"Okay," Helen smiles, "but only if it gets too crazy."

"You promise?" Angela says.

Helen nods. "I promise."

****

"Knock, knock," says Goebel. He and Benson stand in the doorway of Dodson's office. Dodson looks up from his desk, looking puzzled.

"The panties…?" Benson reminds him. The two officers enter the office.

"Oh yeah…the panties…the Haywood case," Dodson says in true absentminded-professor style. "It's too soon. I'm only half done with all my tests."

"The stains in the front of the panties," Benson asks, "is it what we think it is?"

"Sure is," says Dodson, "About 10ccs of male spermatozoa…no more than four days old. I did run some tests on it and came up with some interesting information."

"Like what?" Goebel asks.

Dodson continues, "Well…I don't know if your guy is trying to be funny or he still believes he has you bamboozled into thinking Mrs. Haywood's attacker was a black man. The DNA from Mrs. Haywood's baby proved without a doubt it was a white guy, but the stain on the panties could only come from a black man."

Goebel and Benson remain silent, not knowing what to say – their mouths fall open.

"That's about how it affected me," Dodson goes on. "It didn't make any sense. So…on a hunch…I ran a few more tests and I came up with the guy's name and address."

"Quit screwing with us," Goebel says.

"I'm serious! I told you it was only a hunch, but it paid off. I can take you to the guy who stained those panties, right now. Follow me."

Dodson walks out of the office. Goebel and Benson look at each other, shrug their shoulders in confusion, and tag along behind Dodson.

As they walk down to the far end of the hallway, it doesn't take Goebel and Benson long before they realize where he is taking them – the morgue.

Dodson pulls one of the long drawers out. A white sheet covers the cold dead body before them, save for the corpse's right foot, which has a tag dangling from the big toe. It is the foot of a black man.

Dodson turns down the sheet disclosing the body of a black man – young, maybe thirty, extraordinarily muscular, and looking to a certain extent rather healthy, if not for a deep bullet hole in his right temple.

"Gentlemen, may I introduce you to the late Mr. Donald Johnson. His body was found three days ago in his car hidden in a back alley."

Goebel and Benson take their time examining the body.

"And you say this is the same guy whose juice is on the panties. …How do you know for sure?" Benson questions.

"Well, allow me to digress," says Dodson. "I did some detective work on my own. It seems Mr. Johnson, here, was of the homosexual persuasion, last seen Saturday night at the Velvet Hammer, a gay bar in the Industrial District. Most likely, he met someone to his liking, and they left the club together. . . .Other patrons and workers at the club say they never saw him leave or whom he was with.

"It seems they left in his car together and made their way down a dark street for a romantic rendezvous that turned bad. They found Mr. Johnson Sunday morning in the driver's seat of his car. His pants were down around his ankles, and the front of his shirt and underwear stained with his. . .you know. . .I ran some tests on his stain alongside the stain on Mrs. Haywood's panties. . . .It's the same guy, all right. On further investigation of the body, I would say just when he was experiencing a sexual climax that his partner shot him in the head and cleaned most of the mess with the panties. And, well. . .you both know the rest of the story. Whoever did this is the same man who is after Mrs. Haywood. . .I'd bet on it."

"Any fingerprints?" Goebel asks.

"None. . .we dusted everything – the car, the body, everything. . . .No prints. Your guy is extraordinarily careful."

Benson bends down, taking a closer look at the bullet hole in Donald Johnson's temple.

"What caliber gun would you say killed him?"

"At such close range, no question about it," says Dodson. "It's from a .38. . . .I'd bet on it."

****

The Velvet Hammer is much larger inside than its façade leads one to believe. Goebel and Benson stand in the doorway until their eyes adjust to the darkness. The club has no windows.

For a weekday afternoon, it is surprising how much business they are doing. The dance floor is empty, but there are several customers at the jukebox and even more gathered around the pool tables. For all intents and purposes, it looks like any other dance club in town, only there are no signs of even one female.

Goebel and Benson step up to the bar. There is a lone bartender on duty – a handsome, young black man wearing a muscle shirt, with the muscles to go with it.

"May I help you two officers?" asks the bartender.

Goebel spreads his arms out at his sides and looks himself up and down.

"Is it that noticeable?"

"Noticeable. . ." laughs the bartender, "Does Jack Webb know you're wearing his clothes? You two guys look like the poster for Dragnet. If you're here to ask me about what happened last week to Donald, you're too late. I already told that other cop everything I know."

"Well, we'd like to hear it again, if you don't mind." Benson says. "First off, what's your name?"

"Josh…Josh Rogers…but all my friends call me Tink…short for *Tinkerbell.*" He starts to laugh.

"Well…Tink…" Goebel says. "Without sounding too much like Jack Webb, could you please give us just the facts?"

"Well, it's like I told that other cop, Don was a regular customer. He was here last Saturday night. I remember serving him…a scotch and soda man…"

"Was he with anybody? I mean, did you see him leave with anybody?"

Tink laughs again, "Man, you don't know what it's like here on a Saturday night? Wall to wall…butts and balls! I didn't notice anything…nobody did, man."

"Did you know the deceased?" Goebel asks.

"Kind of. …All the brothers know one another…like a minority within a minority. You dig?"

"Yeah…I dig," Goebel says. "Did you and he ever…get together?"

"You mean…were Don and I ever lovers?" The smile leaves Tink's face. "Oh, I get it…you think, I'm gay…he's gay…I'm black…he's black…so we must have gotten it on. Jeez…talk about your stereotyping. You guys are something else, you know that?"

"Don't give us a hard time," Goebel says, "I'm uncomfortable enough just being here. Just answer the question."

"No, man. …I ain't ever been with him. Like I said, we were just acquaintances. Besides, I'm not his type, anyway."

"Oh, and what was his type?" Benson asks.

"White guys," Tink says, his laughing smile returns to his face. "Don was the original Little Eva. He was into white guys – tall, short, old, young, fat, skinny – Don liked them all…as long as they was white."

"I see," Benson says, taking a snapshot of Richard Haywood from his coat pocket, "Ever seen this guy?"

Tink takes the picture and examines it closely. "Yeah, man. I've seen this dude here before. …No, wait…" He takes another look. "Maybe not…I'm not sure. Hell…I don't know. Cute-looking white boys…turn them upside down, and they all look alike. Ya know what I mean?"

"No, I don't know what you mean," Benson says. "We thank you for your time. If we have any other questions, you'll be hearing from us."

Goebel and Benson start for the door.

"Drop in anytime," laughs Tink. "I'll be here…I'm always here. I live here, man. Say, why don't you two do yourselves a favor and send those suits out to be dry cleaned and burned?"

They still hear his laughter as they stand outside the Velvet Hammer.

"So now what?" Benson asks.

"I'm more convinced than before," Goebel says. "We need to start tailing Mr. Richard Haywood.

"Come on, let's get the hell out of here. I don't want anybody to see me standing in front of this place…especially with you."

Four

You Remember Uncle Jerry

Chez Michelle is by far the most respected and expensive five-star French restaurant in town, and her parents' favorite. Helen made all the arrangements, despite her mother's constant onslaught of suggestions. She reserved one of the smaller, private dining rooms, selected the menu, and sent invitations to all her parents' closest and dearest friends. It is her parents' fortieth wedding anniversary, and she wants everything perfect for them, so Helen labors over every single detail.

Night of the party, Richard is running late. Helen looks at her watch; it is seven thirty. She can't hold the festivities up any longer so she gives the maître d' the go-ahead to begin serving. Helen excuses herself and heads for the parking lot to look for Richard.

When she reaches the front door, Richard comes storming in. Under his arm is a large package giftwrapped in silver and gold, with a large bow on top.

"Sorry I'm late." Richard is huffing and puffing.

"Here, give me the present," says Helen. "I'll take care of it. Go in and say hi to everyone before they start eating."

"Need to go to the john first!" He runs off into another direction.

Back at the party, they are just beginning to serve the main course. At the entrance of the room, there is a long table set up for gifts. Helen places the package on it. She turns to see her father standing next to her.

"I just wanted to let you know how happy you've made us, tonight, Princess."

"It's the least I can do. You and Mom have done so much for me all my life." She kisses his cheek. "Why don't you go sit down, Dad, before your food gets cold?"

He is just about to turn around, when an idea strikes him. "Say, Helen, why don't you and I go to the pistol range this weekend and get you used to firing that .38 pistol I gave you?"

"Gee, Dad…I don't know…" Helen's voice is hesitant.

"What do you mean you don't know? Why, what's the matter?"

"Well, Richard thinks a gun is a bad idea and…"

"He does, does he? Well, we'll just see about that!"

He looks around the room for Richard.

"Please, Dad…not now…not here…not tonight…for me, please."

There is such pleading in her voice he finds it hard to say no to her.

"All right…for you, but I'm going to have to talk to that boy." He turns and makes his way to the head table and sits down next to his wife.

There is another table next to the gift table. On it is a framed picture of her parents dancing at their wedding. It is an old black and white photo, her mother in a long white gown and her father in black tie and tails. So young and beautiful – they look so happy.

Also on the table, her mother laid out all the old family photo albums for all to see.

Newer-looking albums are mostly pictures of Helen – first day at school, birthdays, Christmases, high school graduation – every major event of her youth. Older books are of her parents wedding and honeymoon. As well, there are photos of their first house, parties, and vacation trips with old friends – most of them now sitting in the same room, looking much older than their now fading images in the photo albums.

Helen flips through one of the older books. Her heart leaps from her body and she holds her breath when she comes to an old black and white photo of her parents on a skiing trip. There are high mountains of ice and snow in the far distance behind them. Her father and mother are on skis, smiling at the camera. But, there, standing between her parents is a man – he is on skis also, and he is wearing a ski mask over his face – a black ski mask with light-colored, make-believe eyebrows and lips.

Helen turns to see her parents standing at their table. They are giving a speech to all the other guests. Her mind can't hear what they are saying. She hears her name mentioned and everyone in the room begins to applaud. It all sounds faraway and muffled, as if being underwater. She can't take it any longer. She rushes out of the room and into the lady's room, runs cold water, and splashes her face.

When she comes back out, Richard is waiting for her.

"Are you all right?" he asks.

"Oh, yeah, I guess it's all the excitement."

"Well, don't scare everyone like that, especially me."

She starts back to the party.

"I love you," says Richard.

She turns and smiles, "I love you, too."

Later, after everyone has eaten, most of the guests walk about the room, cocktails in hand, talking and laughing and looking at the old photos.

Helen motions to her mother to come to the photo table. She points to the ski trip photo and the man in the ski mask.

"Who's that?"

Her mother takes her time and eyes it carefully.

"Oh, that…it was years ago…way before you were born…a skiing holiday in the Swiss Alps. That's your father, there…and that's me…and the guy in the middle with that ridiculous mask on is your Uncle Jerry…your father's brother."

Helen's parents have not heard all the gruesome details of the night of her attack, so the sight of the now-familiar mask doesn't send terror into her mother's heart as it does in hers.

"I believe his wife took this picture…your Aunt Eleanor. You probably don't remember much about either one of them. Your Uncle Jerry died when you were about thirteen years old. Aunt Eleanor still lives in Tannersville, fifty miles north of here. We haven't kept in touch over the last few years. …Christmas cards…that's about it. The poor woman's lost most of her marbles over the years.

"They used to come and visit every summer when you were little. Do you remember? They had two sons. …Now let me think…what were their names? Oh, yes…Nicholas and Victor. They were a couple of years older than you. Oh, how you hated those boys," she laughs.

"But what did Uncle Jerry look like? Are there any other pictures of him?" Helen asks.

Her mother thumbs through all the photo albums.

"That's strange. I could swear we had some pictures of Jerry somewhere, but I don't see any. There are a few empty spaces; maybe they fell out. Whatever, he wasn't much, not a memorable character, anyway."

Her mother puts down the book and turns. "Margaret! So glad you made it!" She is off to another part of the room.

Helen's first thought is to call Goebel and Benson and tell them about her findings. But what could she say? Her attacker is in fact a ghost.

She decides to not say anything to anyone. She would research it further on her own. She is becoming more and more reliant on her own judgment and abilities, and less and less on others – especially the police.

She quickly turns when she hears loud talking from the other end of the room – Richard and her father are arguing. Helen runs to them.

"With all due respect, Tom, but I think it's none of your business," says Richard.

"None of my business…? Your daughter's your daughter for the rest of your life! Haven't you ever heard that?" Tom bellows.

"I'm sorry, Tom, but I think a gun is just too dangerous for Helen to be carrying around. She's my wife and my responsibility."

Helen's father is fuming. "You can't be with her all the time, but a gun can. Next time could be worse; she may wind up dead! With a gun, she at least has a fighting chance!"

"She's my wife, there will be no gun, and that's my final word!" Richard turns and looks Helen in the eye. "I'm going home. . . . Are you coming?"

Helen looks at her father. "Dad, I'm so sorry. . ."

Richard starts to walk away.

Helen's father grabs her, pulls her in close, and whispers to her, "Don't be upset. We're family. . . we can disagree without it being the end of the world. I like the boy, even though I know he's wrong. . . and you tell him so for me. But he's your husband. . . so go."

"Thanks, Dad. I love you." She kisses his cheek and runs after Richard.

She catches up with him just outside the front door of the restaurant. He turns in surprise, "You're coming? Aren't you going to stay with your folks?"

"Richard. . . my father thinks you're wrong about the gun. I think you're wrong about it too, and I wish you'd reconsider. But you're my husband and I love you, Richard."

Richard's eyes have a look of relief in them, as if some intense weight just lifted from him. Maybe Angela is right; he just needs some time to heal. He takes her in his arms. They kiss.

"Where are you parked?" he whispers. "I'll walk you."

"Over there," she smiles. "Come on. . . I'll race you home."

****

Tailing Richard Haywood slowly becomes routine, fruitless, boring, and seemingly a waste of time. He spends most of his days – and much of the nights – at the office, on the phone or computer. His lunch meetings are just that – long, drawn-out get-togethers with other professionals like himself. His business trips are all legit. In the short time of Goebel and Benson's surveillance, he went to Montreal twice and once to Atlanta.

"I think we're wasting our time," says Benson, sitting behind the steering wheel of their unmarked car. "All this guy does is work, work, and more work. . . what a dope!"

"Yeah, not smart, like us," Goebel laughs. "I tell you, Jimmy, this guy is dirty. . . . I just know it. . . . I can taste it."

"Better step on it, or we'll lose him," Benson says.

It is Friday afternoon. Richard is driving toward the airport for what appears as another weekend business trip. As they pass downtown, Richard suddenly takes the next turn off the highway.

"Well, what do we have here? It looks like we're not going to the airport after all. I think I smell a rat!"

They follow as close and as safely possible down winding streets, till they come to a row of new two-story townhomes. Richard parks in the middle of the block. Goebel and Benson pull to the curb some spaces behind. Richard gets out, takes his overnight bag out of the trunk, dashes up the stairs of one of the townhomes, and rings the doorbell. A moment later, a tall, slender redhead opens the door. She flies into his arms, and the two kiss long and hard before going inside.

"Bingo!" yells Goebel. "I told you the guy was dirty! Now we've got our motive!"

At first, Benson doesn't say anything. He is browsing through a folder resting on his lap. He runs his finger over a long list of names and addresses before finding what he is looking for.

"Francis Crawly...works for the same company....Her office is right next to his. She does much the same job he does...been with the company for three years..."

"Who cares?" says Goebel. "We've got our motive. In this state, divorce means splitting everything fifty-fifty. But if your wife dies...you keep one hundred percent; it all fits into place. Let's stick around for a while...maybe we can get some photos."

"That leaves us with a big decision to make," says Benson. "Cheating on your wife is a motive, but it's not evidence. We got nothing that'll stick."

"So, what's your point?" Goebel asks.

"I'm saying...if we run him in for questioning at this point, he'll know we're on to him, and we may never get anything on him. On the other hand, it may throw him into a tailspin, and he may confess. If we wait any longer, he may still get to his wife. This way, even if he doesn't confess...we've got him off guard and on the run. ...He's bound to screw up."

"You think we can pressure him into talking?"

"If anyone can...we can."

Goebel thinks about it for a moment, "Okay...let's call him in." He looks out at the townhouse. "Hell, they'll be in there for hours doing the horizontal mambo. Let's go get something to eat and then come back."

"I know a place on Montgomery with a great salad bar," says Benson.

"Salad bar...what's with you lately? You've been talking to my wife again?"

It has been a long busy workday for Helen and Carol. There is a conflict between payment slips and claim amounts in the computer. They need to pull each payment slip, compare them to ones in the computer, make changes, and refile them. By five o'clock, the problem is only half resolved.

"I hate to ask you this," says Helen," but I'm afraid we need to stay late tonight, till we get this fixed."

"Gee…Don's not going to like this," says Carol. "My car is in the shop so I told him he needed to pick me up. I'll call him. What time do you think we'll finish?"

"That's no problem," says Helen. "Call him and tell him I'll take you home."

Carol phones her husband, and after a long explanation of how to warm up leftovers from the previous night, she hangs up and returns to her filing.

Carol is a hard worker and has moved up fast within the company. She is young, bright – eight years Helen's junior – somewhat round and voluptuous, with dishwater blond hair that is close to being brown.

At ten to seven, Helen backs her chair from her computer.

"I'm hungry. …Are you hungry?"

"I thought you'd never ask. …I'm starving!"

Helen looks at the clock on the wall. "Cafeteria's closed…been closed for more than an hour…anything in the snack room?"

"Just cookies and chips," moans Carol. "We can order a pizza?"

"Pizza…? No, I've got a better idea. We just held my parents' fortieth anniversary party at Chez Michelle…phenomenal French food! They've got a lobster bisque and a crème brulee that's to die for. I'll call in the order, if you go pick it up. It's on me."

Helen calls in the order, while Carol puts on her coat.

"Here's the money," says Helen, handing Carol a fifty-dollar bill, "and here's the keys to my car."

"Gee, I've never eaten lobster bisque before. I'm excited!" Carol says, making for the door.

"Don't forget to get someone from security to walk you out," Helen yells down the hall to Carol.

Carol leaves at seven twenty. Helen returns to her work. Twenty minutes later, she looks up at the wall clock – she is only slightly concerned. But when another twenty minutes passes, she becomes worried.

She calls Chez Michelle, and they tell her Carol has come and gone nearly half an hour ago. She calls down to security; there is no sign of Carol.

"Maybe she's having car trouble?" thinks Helen. She looks up Carol's mobile phone number and dials.

"*Hola*, Senora Haywood! It's me...*el huele todo!*"

She knows the voice immediately.

"How are you, my little *conchuda*? I'm so sorry you're not my guest, instead of this fat cow, but any port in a storm. Besides, this will teach you who's in charge – not you, my dear."

"Let her go, you bastard!"

"Sticks and stones, my love. ...Sticks and stones...don't bother me."

"I'm not afraid of you. ...I'll kill you...you son of a bitch!"

"That's good...I like my women sassy. But you sound so tense...maybe a little *beso negro*, might do you good? We need to get together soon. I have such wonderful visions. You...*chupa mi pinga*. ...*me*...*te voy a hacer la sopa*. ...Sound good?"

"Let her go you animal! I swear I'll kill you. ...By God...I'll kill you!"

"Eh...*esta vida es un asco. Hasta luego*...my love."

There is a click in her ear and the frightening hum of disconnection.

After phoning the police, Helen again finds herself confronted with questions from Goebel and Benson – most of it routine.

The police find her car in the parking lot of Chez Michelle. Carol is missing. The driver's side door is wide open, the keys still in the ignition. The overhead light is on, the car-door alarm is chiming, and the take-out dinner for two is on the passenger's seat. They find Carol's mobile phone blocks away, clearly intentionally crushed under a car wheel.

They dust the car – nothing. They question the restaurant workers and valet, but no one saw or heard anything out of the ordinary.

****

Following day, Helen finds herself once again in Angela's office – sobbing. There is nothing Angela can say. No words of comfort will stop her from blaming herself for what happened to Carol.

She can't stop picturing the scene in her mind, over and over – two police officers standing in the doorway telling Don, Carol's husband, she is missing, most likely kidnapped, and possibly dead.

She weeps uncontrollably.

"Oh…I do hope she's dead," cries Helen. "I know it sounds like a horrible thing to say, but I would hate to think she is still alive and with that madman. She'd be better off dead!" She starts to tremble. "Maybe, I'd be better off dead?"

Angela writes her a prescription for her anxiety. Helen knows well enough not to argue with Angela about it. In her mind, she knows she will not take any pills; she wants to remain sharp for whatever is to come next.

****

Helen wakes to the smell of breakfast coming upstairs. She looks over to the other side of the bed. Richard's place is mussed, but there is no Richard. He must have come in late, got up early and is trying to surprise her with breakfast. Her robe lies at the foot of the bed. She puts it on and goes downstairs.

Richard is in the kitchen doing his best not to burn three pans of eggs, bacon, and pancakes – there is a pot of hot coffee.

"Smells good. …What's the occasion?" Helen asks.

"No occasion. …Do I need an occasion to make breakfast for my wife?" Richard puts down the utensils, takes her in his arms, and kisses her. "Well, maybe it is an occasion…more like a peace offering."

Helen looks confused. He sits her down and serves her. Then he sits down next to her and holds her hand.

"I want to ask your forgiveness. I was wrong. After I heard what happened to Carol, I thought…that could have been you. I was wrong. I've put the gun your father gave you back in your purse…right where I found it…like nothing ever happened. Do you forgive me?"

"Of course I do, darling."

Helen remembers Angela saying Richard only needed to heal and in time will come around again. She was right.

"I've been such an ass lately, and I don't know why." he says.

"It's all right, honey." She runs her hand along his arm. "We've all been through lots lately. It takes time to return to normal."

"But I don't want to return to normal; I want everything better than it was. I want you happy. When you were pregnant, all I did was pressure you for an abortion. When you had the miscarriage, I showed more relief than caring. And all this time, when there was danger, I wasn't there for you. That's all going to change. I want to be the husband you expect me to be. I swear I'm going to try."

"Oh, Richard!" Tears fall from Helen's eyes. To the sound of clattering plates, she somehow makes her way onto Richard's lap. "Oh, Richard, I love you so much." She begins to shower him with kisses.

"I love you, too, baby," whispers Richard. "You remember the first time we were in Angela's office? I meant what I said…there's still a chance we could have a baby together."

Richard tries to be macho and carry Helen upstairs to the bedroom, but for all his efforts, he can't even get up from his chair with her in his arms. His effort is comical, and the two of them burst into laughter. It feels good to laugh together again. They laugh all the way upstairs.

****

Richard walks out into the hall and looks into Francis' office, half expecting to see her sitting at her desk. She is nowhere to be found. It isn't like her to be so late – he thinks it odd.

He receives a call from Detective Goebel asking him to come down to the station for further questioning. He assumes it is nothing more than more routine questioning.

After following directions down a long corridor, Richard finds the Detective's office door and knocks on it.

"Come in," he hears a voice announce from within. He enters.

Detectives Goebel and Benson stand next to a desk, and there, sitting in front of the desk is Francis – his Francis. She turns to look at him. Her expression tells the entire story. Her eyes say, "I'm sorry, but I didn't know what else to do."

"Sit down, Mr. Haywood. ….I'm sure you know Miss Crawly," Goebel says.

"Don't try to be funny, detective. You know very well about Francis and I, or you wouldn't have asked her here." Richard sits down in a chair next to her. She reaches over to him, and the two hold hands. "So…what now? You're going to tell my wife? I don't see the point."

"That's not our job," Benson says, "We're not private dicks working on a divorce case. We're city detectives working on an assault and rape case…and…maybe a kidnapping and murder case."

"Murder…? What the hell are you talking about?" Richard demands.

"We were hoping you could tell us," Goebel smiles.

"Listen, if you think I did anything like that, you're crazy. I wouldn't do anything to hurt Helen."

"How about having an affair behind her back?"

"That's different! You can't blame a person for whom they fall in love with. Besides, I was planning to tell her a long time ago, but all this stuff started to happen. I've done my best so Helen would never suspect. We're doing the best we can, under the circumstances."

"Oh yeah...you two deserve a medal," Goebel says.

"We've been talking with Miss Crawly here, and I'm afraid, she can't vouch for your whereabouts on the night of Mrs. Haywood's attack," Benson says.

"That's not what I said!" Francis is nearly in tears as she speaks to Richard. "They asked me if we were together that night. I said I don't keep track of the time we spend together. I just couldn't remember."

"Of course you remember, darling," pleads Richard. "Don't you remember? It was the night we were drinking wine in front of the fireplace, and I received a phone call from the office, there was an emergency, and I was to call my in-laws. I waited at your place till enough time passed, and I then called and told them I was at the airport?"

"I...yes...yes...now I remember!" says Francis, turning to the two detectives.

"How convenient. ...You remember after being reminded."

"It's our word against yours," smirks Richard.

"There is a way to clear this up," Goebel says. "We still have the DNA from the stillborn. If we were to get a blood sample...you could clear your name."

"No!" shouts Richard.

"And why not? What are you afraid of? Just a swab of your saliva, and you could clear your name."

"Because, I have no need to clear my name. ...That's why! I'm innocent, and there's no reason I need be on the defensive. I've done nothing wrong, and I'm offended from all these accusations. You idiots have nothing, and you can't make me do what I don't want to do."

"We can get a court order."

"Then get one! But, I'm not your dog to jump whenever you command. Now, if you two gentlemen have nothing further to tell me, I've wasted enough time." He stands up and looks at Francis. "Come, sweetheart. Let's go."

"Oh, you can go, but we have a few more questions for Miss Crawly."

"Remember...you don't have to say anything. I love you," Richard's last words to Francis before he lets go of her hand and heads for the door.

"Oh, Mr. Haywood," Benson calls to him, "one last question."

"What's that?"

"Ever read Shakespeare?"

"What's that got to do with anything?"

"Methinks thou doth protest too much."

"Go to hell!" He leaves, slamming the door.

They wait a moment for Richard to be well on his way.

"So, tell us, Miss Crawly, how did this love affair with Richard come about?"

"Our offices are right next to each other. ...It just happened. ...We didn't mean for it to happen. ...It just did," she speaks softly and sadly.

"And what plans have the two of you made? I mean, did he mention anything about leaving his wife?"

"Yes, many times, but he's afraid something like that, right now, might even kill her! I mean...in the condition she's in, after all she's been through."

"I see. Tell us, Ms. Crawley, how much do you love each other?"

"That's a silly question. Why...with all our hearts, of course."

"You love him enough to do anything for him...even lie?"

"But that's just it! I don't need to lie. I'm telling you the truth!"

"And he loves you very much...enough to commit murder?"

"That's not true! Richard would never do anything to hurt Helen or anyone else for that matter. He's not that way. He hates violence. He even took Helen's gun from her, afraid she might hurt herself."

Goebel and Benson pause to look at each other.

"Gun...?" Benson asks, "What gun is this?"

"I don't know...some gun her father gave her. He took it from her, afraid that in her state of mind she might hurt someone or herself. He showed it to me one night. Then when all that horrible business happened to that other woman...he thought it over and gave her back the gun. Now I tell you, if he didn't care about her safety, if he didn't want her able to protect herself...why would he give her back the gun? Why?"

"That's a good question, Miss Crawly. Why?"

****

After Francis Crawly leaves the office, Goebel opens the top side drawer to his desk. He lifts a small recorder from the drawer. There's a long cord connected to the recorder that runs along the side of the desk to a small microphone taped to the corner of the desk. Goebel presses a button to shut off the recording. He rewinds it and then plays it back. They hear Richard's voice from a moment ago. Goebel stops the recorder again.

"Well, we got it," Goebel announces.

"Yeah, and if his voice pattern matches the one on the message machine, we've got our man."

Five

International Nancy

At the end of the day, it seems like it will be another late night of work for Helen. It feels strange and sad alone in the office without Carol. Helen can't help thinking about her. She keeps expecting to hear her voice or see her come walking in at any minute.

It has been a week since Carol's disappearance. The police have not come up with even one clue. She calls Goebel and Benson daily, in hopes they learned something, but every day is the same. No one has any idea what happened to Carol.

As sad as it may seem, Helen still secretly hopes she is dead. The thought her assistant, her friend, being alive and in the clutches of him is torturous.

Helen is sure most, if not all, her coworkers think it strange she would come back to work so soon without missing so much as a heartbeat. She realizes it must seem she is heartless and cold – without feelings. But it is her feelings she is trying to get away from. So, as always, she hides herself from the world in her work. At work, she doesn't have to think of anything but her job. Thoughts of what happened need pushing aside, or she is sure she'll go mad. And as for guilt, there is more than she can carry. And fear – no matter how brave a front she puts up, her fear eats at her. She hates to admit it. On the phone, the night he took Carol, she told him she was not afraid of him – that is just a lie. She fears him more than death itself. But for Carol's sake, she swears she'll continue until his capture.

She is getting hungry. She looks at the clock – it is seven. In the snack room, nothing in the vending machines appeals to her. She decides to be content with just a cup of black coffee.

Walking back to her office, she realizes she has gone the entire day without once checking her office mail box. She looks inside. There are stacks of the usual memos, a few pieces of mail of no immediate concern, but what she does not expect is a small oblong package wrapped in brown paper, the kind that grocery bags are made of. Tied around it is brown twine. She looks at the address on the box – it is to her, all right. The writing is in pencil, and the handwriting is barely legible, as if a small child wrote it.

She sits at her desk, staring at the package, afraid to open it. There is something not right about it. She is sure of it. Eventually, her curiosity gets the best of her; she knows she must open it and see what is inside. She takes her letter opener and cuts the cord. She carefully tears away the brown paper. It is an old cardboard box, soiled and torn. She opens it and finds herself confronted with something that brings up memories of long ago – memories not thought about since she was a child.

It is a doll. Not just any doll – it is her doll. A doll she loved and cared for when she was a little girl. A doll she lost and has not seen since she was nine or ten.

She takes it out of the box and examines it. It is a ragdoll. On its back is a pull string that no longer works. Its clothes – dress and stockings – are made of small, stitched-together flags of different nations.

"International Nancy!" Helen says aloud. The name comes back to her in a flash the second she holds it. "But I lost you years ago…when I was little. Who could have had you all this time; and why would they return you to me now?"

Helen isn't sure what to do. She picks up the phone and dials.

"Mom, it's me. …You got a minute?"

"Your father and I are watching something on the TV. …There's a commercial on. …Why, is something wrong?"

"No…nothing's wrong, Mom. I just want to ask you something. Do you remember when I was little I had a doll…International Nancy?"

"Why are you bringing that up now? The show is about to come back on."

"Please, Mom, think. …Do you remember the doll?"

"Of course, I remember it. It was an ugly little ragdoll made of different flags or something. It had a string in its back, and when you pulled it, it spoke something in different languages. You loved that stupid doll…wouldn't go anywhere without it. If you only knew the time I had trying to get you not to take it in the tub with you."

"Mom, do you remember what happened to it?"

"Sure, I remember. You lost it. …You were about nine, I think."

"How did I lose it? Do you remember how and where I lost it?"

"How could I forget? It was the last summer that your Uncle Jerry and his family came to visit. You know…Aunt Eleanor and their two boys. Oh, what were their names, again? Anyway, we went to Hourglass Lake, to Sandy Beach, for swimming and a cookout. You stayed much to yourself. Their boys were a couple of years older than you. And how you hated those boys…you hardly talked to them. So you stayed to yourself, walking up and down the beach and carrying that stupid doll… International… whatever her name was.

"Just a few minutes before your father and I were getting ready to leave, you came out of the woods, crying. You didn't have your doll; you obviously lost it in the woods. And you cried...you cried all the way home, and didn't stop till you fell asleep in your bed."

"Oh, dear, the show is starting again! I need to get back, if that's all you called about."

"That was all, Mom."

"Call me tomorrow, sweetheart. ...Love you."

There is a click when her mother hangs up. Helen continues to stare at the doll. Bits and pieces of that day long ago at Sandy Beach come into her mind, but the images appear blurred and not in any particular order.

"I did lose you that day, didn't I?" she says to the doll in her hands, "But that wasn't why I was crying. I was crying because...because..."

She can't answer the question. She knows the answer is somewhere in her mind, but something stops her from recollecting it. She knows something happened to her that day, something horrible, something that made her cry for hours on end – and it wasn't the loss of her doll. There is a dark veil between her and the hideous truth, locked away somewhere in her mind. She needs the key to get to it, to the truth. But where will she find the key – if it even exists anymore – if it ever existed.

Then, it dawns on her in a flash. She knows where to find the key. She takes her purse and makes sure the gun is there. She knows where she can find the key to the memory of that day – at Sandy Beach.

****

Helen feels both fearful and foolish as she drives along dark country roads toward Hourglass Lake, but she knows it is something she must do.

In the dark of night, she is unable to see any familiar landmarks that might trigger any old memories. A signpost up ahead reads, "Sandy Beach, 8 miles." She will be there soon.

Thankfully, the chain-link fence surrounding the property is unlocked. The overhead sign at the opening spells out "Sandy Beach" – all the letters made of old horseshoes on an old, gray, wooden sign.

She continues down a long dirt road. To her left, she sees the lake through the trees. The moonlight flickers on the water.

At the end of the dirt road, it opens to a large empty parking lot. She shuts off the engine and turns on the overhead light. Taking the gun from her handbag, she slips it into her coat pocket. Under her seat is a flashlight; she takes it and turns it on.

When she slams the car door shut, the thump sounds off the lake and echoes back. The moon isn't full, but it is bright. And the sky is clear, making it easy to see. The flashlight proves useful for finding good footing as she walks.

Looking around the empty lot, she senses old memories stirring within her. Walking onward, toward the lake, the sand is white and reflects the moonlight – giving a glowing halo appearance to everything. There is a trail of whitewashed wooden planks, now cracked and broken – walking on the sand is easier and safer.

Standing in the picnic area near the shoreline, the memories flood back to her like old ghosts that have haunted the beach for years. She can almost hear people talking and laughing, having a fun day at the lake.

She remembers the vision of her father standing over a hot coal grill, cooking hot dogs and hamburgers while her mother and Aunt Eleanor prepare salads. It is all coming back to her, but it is all in pieces. Sights and sounds are but a blur, especially faces of people.

She suddenly begins to feel vulnerable, as if she is a little girl again – a little girl of nine years.

She remembers the two brothers, her cousins Victor and Nicholas, how they taunted and teased her.

The image of her Uncle Jerry is coming back, too. He sits on the edge of the picnic bench, talking to her father while he cooks. At his feet, there is an ice chest full of beer. He continuously drinks a bottle and drinks another, then another, till the chest is empty.

She pictures his shape, but no matter how hard she concentrates, his face is a blur in her mind.

Again, she begins to feel vulnerable and frightened. A strong impulse to leave the picnic area comes over her – to get away from her two bullying cousins – and from her drunken uncle.

She heads for the shoreline. She recalls what it's like to be nine years old, smaller than most people around her.

She remembers walking along the beach, holding her doll, International Nancy. She constantly pulls the string in her back over and over – the doll says phrases in different languages from all over the world.

Helen looks out on the lake. There are two roped off areas – the kiddy section, and the adult swimming area. Far off in the center of the lake is a large, wooden swimming platform painted white. She has always dreamed of someday learning how to swim and being able to go out to the platform. But it never comes true; she never learned to swim.

Further down, along the shoreline, is a diving board. There is something about it that calls to her. She approaches it. There she sees a walking trail just behind it – going into the woods.

"That's where I went. ...I remember now...I went into the woods," Helen says to herself. "I was carrying my doll...pulling its string. ...I went into the woods. I felt scared, but I kept on walking."

Helen starts down the trail, flashing the light on the ground before her feet. Far into the woods, the trail ends and then opens to a large clearing surrounded by thick bushes and high trees. The moonlight cannot penetrate – darkness is all around.

A sense of terror comes over her. "It happened here," she whispers. "But what happened here? In this clearing, a million years ago, when I was only nine...what happened?"

She strains to remember. But whatever it is, it is so terrible her mind won't let her touch it.

Helen hears the snap of a twig from behind her. She spins around and shines the flashlight down the trail she has just come. Her hands are trembling, her breathing is loud and labored, and her heart is pounding so hard she hears every beat throbbing in her ears. The sound of another twig cracking echoes round her.

"Who's there?" cries Helen, shining the light down the path. "Is there anybody there?" Her voice echoes back from the dark, "Is there anybody there?"

"Just the devil," a voice says behind her. She spins around in horror, and the flashlight flies out of her hand. There, standing just a few feet in front of her is the silhouette of her attacker.

"Welcome, my dear Helen. You finally came back...back where it all began. We've missed you...me and the boys. ...They send their regards."

He isn't speaking in his usual foreign accent jibber-jabber. He comes in closer; she clearly sees the black ski mask.

"We used to have so much fun together...you, me, and the boys...you remember? You were so tiny then...so innocent and tender. I'm sorry the others couldn't make it, but that's no reason we can't..."

"You're not who I think you are! You're dead!" Helen shrieks.

"Dead...I can never die! I'll always be alive...in your mind...forever."

Helen searches in her coat pocket; she pulls out the gun and points it at him.

"What's this? A toy…how exciting!" He laughs. It sends a cold shiver all through her. "Well, here's a toy for you," he says, grabbing hold of his crotch. "Do you remember how we taught you?"

He steps toward her, and she pulls the trigger. The first shot sends him back three or four feet, the sound echoing across the lake and back. He is still standing. Her next shot pushes him back another foot. The echo returns. She shoots two more times in succession. This sends him to the ground. After the echoes stop, he is motionless. His body lies there, twisted, his legs tucked far back under him. All is quiet again.

Helen slowly walks over, never once taking her aim off him. She examines him closely. He isn't breathing. Slowly, she bends down and reaches for the ski mask. She has to know who he is – she has to.

She hesitates for a moment, and then grabs the mask at his neckline. She is just about to pull it over his head when his hand comes up and seizes her wrist. She screams. He begins to laugh. His grip is strong. She can't pull herself free. The louder she screams, the more he laughs. Finally, she remembers the gun; she places it down on his chest and blasts the last two shots into him. His hand releases her and falls to the ground. He is motionless again – she hopes, at last, dead.

Helen is frantic. She drops the gun and runs back down the trail toward the lake. She runs as fast as she can, tearing her clothes and skin against trees and bushes.

She makes it back to the diving board. She runs along the shoreline, past the picnic area, and back to the parking lot. Back in her car, she locks the doors, reaches into her handbag for her mobile phone, and dials the police.

****

"He's dead. …I shot him six times. …He's got to be dead. …There's nothing to fear anymore," Helen tells herself as she sits trembling in her car, waiting for the police.

A half hour passes – it feels like an eternity. Then in the rearview mirror, she sees bright headlights coming down the dirt road to the parking lot. It is two black and whites, and two unmarked cars. They come screeching to a halt alongside her. She feels relieved, especially to see one of the cars contains Goebel and Benson.

The two detectives walk over to Helen's car as the others gather equipment. Helen jumps out of her car, runs to them, and starts to relay her story, but she is nervous and out of breath – she is rambling.

"Hold on, Mrs. Haywood," Goebel says. "Try to relax. …Now, take a deep breath." She does. "Now, calm down. Just let me ask questions. First…are you all right?"

Helen nods.

"Good. ...Now...on the phone you said you shot and killed your assailant. ...Are you sure it's him?"

"It's him, all right...ski mask and everything."

"Well, Mrs. Haywood, could you take us to the body, please?"

They follow at her side, asking questions as they walk. She tells them about receiving the doll, how it triggered memories leading her back to Hourglass Lake – back to Sandy Beach.

Other police officers are carrying equipment and excessively large flashlights, which nearly light up the entire beach.

They walk passed the picnic area, along the shoreline, and up to the diving board. She stops, turns, and points down the dark path into the woods.

"Down that way," she says. "There's a clearing. ...The body's there."

Benson guides Helen to walk behind him. The path is easier to walk with all the lights on, but this causes hundreds of shadows that move as they do. Once again, she is beginning to feel frightened and vulnerable.

The body is motionless, lying at the far end of the clearing –legs awkwardly tucked-back under the torso, just the way she left it nearly an hour ago. With all the lights, now it is easy to make out more details.

"So how many times did you shot him?" Benson asks.

"All six..." Helen replies.

"And where is the gun now?"

"I shot him four times. ...He went down. I bent over him to take off the mask. He was still alive! So I shot him again. I got scared...dropped the gun and ran."

"Give me your flashlight," Goebel says to one of the officers. "Wait here, Mrs. Haywood." He looks to his partner, "Well, let's see who he is."

Goebel and Benson walk over and bend down over the body. Goebel holds the flashlight as Benson eases the ski mask over the face and off the head.

"Who is it?" Helen cries. She can't see around the two detectives. "For God's sake...tell me who it is!"

Goebel and Benson do not respond. They remain hunched over the body, whispering to each other.

"Why won't you tell me?" Helen screams, walking forward to get a better look.

Goebel jumps to his feet and gently guides Helen back.

"It's not him." says Goebel.

"Not him? What do you mean...not him! I shot him six times. ...He fell. ...He died. ...There's the body!"

"It's not him." repeats Goebel, "It's Carol...Carol Hastings."

Helen collapses in his arms. Goebel has two of the officers take her back to the cars.

She sits in the back of the squad car. Goebel and Benson return and get in the front seat.

"Mrs. Haywood, I think it would be best if we took you home. Don't worry; we'll make sure your car gets back to you safe.

"About the gun...you said you dropped it near the body."

Helen just nods.

"Well, we can't find it anywhere. This gun...it wouldn't be the same gun your husband withheld from you?"

"Yes, but how did you know?"

"We have our ways," Goebel says. He motions for his partner to step out of the car with him.

"Well, if you ask me, I'd say someone loaded the gun with blanks...and the last person with it was her husband. I think we have enough on him now. Put out a call for the arrest of Mr. Richard Haywood."

****

Angela is no stranger to late night emergency calls, so she doesn't question why her phone is ringing.

"Yes?"

"Angela, this is Helen Haywood."

"Helen! Are you all right?"

There is a pause before she speaks.

"Angela, remember when you said if it got...too crazy...I could stay at your place? Well, I'm afraid it's gotten that bad."

"Of course, you can stay here. Why...what happened?"

"It's a long story. I'll tell you when I get there."

The patrol car drives Helen home. Officers wait as she packs an overnight bag, and then they drive her to Angela's.

Angela lives in the Madison District of town – large, older homes with finely manicured lawns, mostly colonial-style houses that have been in the same families for generations.

The officers escort Helen to the front door where Angela is waiting.

As soon as she locks the front door, Helen nearly collapses. Angela guides her to the living room sofa and pours them both a tall brandy.

"Here, this is one prescription I insist you take," Angela says.

Helen takes a few sips, sighs heavily, and begins to relax. Angela pulls up a chair beside her.

"So, tell me," Angela says.

Helen tells her story, sipping now and then at her brandy – about the doll, the lake, the shooting, finding Carol's body.

"And now they tell me they've put out a warrant for Richard. They say there's evidence pointing to him. How could that be? He's my husband! I don't understand."

Angela pours another small amount of brandy into Helen's glass.

"What you need to do is get a good night's sleep and not think about it till the morning."

"That's just it, I can't stop thinking about any of it. Sometimes, I think I'll go mad. The images racing through my mind as I walked along that shoreline of the lake. ...I couldn't grasp one thought long enough for any of it to make any sense. And in the clearing...I had the strangest feelings.

"He said certain things to me that don't make sense – 'I've missed you.' ...'The boys missed you.' ...'The way we taught you.' What does it all mean? It's torture not knowing.

"Something happened to me in that clearing that day when I was nine. If I could only remember...maybe then I'd know what to do."

Helen takes a long drink, sighs, and calmly looks at Angela.

"Those diplomas on the wall of your office," Helen says, "I remember one of them was for hypnosis. Couldn't you hypnotize me to remember?"

Angela sips her drink as she speaks, "Yes, I suppose, it's possible. But I'm not sure if it would be a good idea. You see, the beauty of the mind is its ability to forget...forget things we can't live with...and in your case, it thoroughly buried it...perhaps, for your own safety. If we dig this thing up again, it might be something you can't handle."

"I can't handle this," Helen says. "If I don't find out what happened, I think I'll go insane!"

Angela puts down her drink.

"Very well...we'll try it...but not tonight. You need sleep. When you're rested and strong would be a better time."

Angela walks off to prepare a bedroom for Helen. When she returns, she finds Helen fast asleep. She covers her with a blanket and turns out the light.

****

"Knock, knock," Dodson says, entering Goebel and Benson's office. He doesn't wait for an invitation before he pours himself a coffee and sits down. A folder is tucked under his arm.

"So you two geniuses have solved the Haywood case?"

"We picked the husband up last night. We've got him locked up now."

"What makes you think it's the husband?" Dodson asks.

"It all adds up," Goebel says. "The guy's having an affair with some woman from work. . . . He decides he's in love and wants to bump off his wife. So he comes up with this plan – a bizarre plan, I must admit – but he thinks it will work.

"We checked him out. He hasn't any alibis for any of the times his wife was assaulted or contacted. He hasn't an alibi for the night someone milked and shot Donald Johnson. Bartender at the gay bar even said he looked familiar. The night of Carol Hastings' kidnapping, he was nowhere to be found. The night of his wife being attack at Sandy Beach, he couldn't account for himself. She tried to shoot her attacker, but the gun didn't do a thing to him because it was full of blanks – the same gun he's had in his possession for nearly two weeks. . . . Plenty of time to switch the bullets for blanks. I tell you, Richard Haywood is our man."

Dodson puts down his coffee, puts his hands together and applauds.

"Bravo! Bravo! That's one hell of a story. . . . Only, it's a fairytale."

"What do you mean?" Benson asks.

"Your case has more holes in it than a piece of Swiss cheese. It's all circumstantial evidence.

"Take for instance the night of Mrs. Haywood's attack. So he's bopping another broad . . . So what? You've got no witness, no fingerprints or original ski mask.

"The night the gay guy's killed, bartender says 'He looks familiar.' . . . Give me a break! Again, you've got no witness, no fingerprints, and no murder weapon. This gun, with or without blanks . . . where the hell is it? All the dirty phone calls . . . nothing but bull! Richard Haywood's voice patterns don't line up with the voice on message machine. They're two different voices. And at Sandy Beach, it's the same. . . . You got squat.

"Swiss cheese is what you two have . . . Swiss cheese with holes! And here's the biggest hole of them all." He tosses a folder on top of the desk.

"What the hell is this?" Goebel asks.

"That's the test results from a blood sample I got from one Richard Haywood."

"I thought he was refusing to give a blood sample?"

"He changed his mind. Prison bars have that effect on some people."

"So what did you find?" Goebel asks, opening the folder.

"I checked him against the stillborn samples. No way is he the father. ...I guarantee he's not. Richard Haywood may be a cheat, a liar, and an adulterer, but he's not your man."

"So? He still could have switched the bullets for blanks. He knows someone is after his wife, so he makes sure she's defenseless. Who knows...maybe he hired this guy to do a number on his wife? I still say, this guy is dirty," Goebel demands.

"Yeah, but without the gun to prove it, you've got squat!" Dodson insists.

"Back to square one...dammit." Benson falls back in his chair.

Dodson continues, "I suggest you guys stop feeling sorry for yourselves and hit the pavement running. Whoever this guy is, he's one sick puppy. And this ain't the end of it, by no means. This guy kills because he loves it. It's like mother's milk to him...he's gotta have it.

"I ran an autopsy on Carol Hastings. I've seen some sick bastards in my time, but this guy takes the cake. What he did to her down below must have taken two...three hours. And, it's not just knife cuts. ...It's pins...nails...thumb tacks...and God knows what else.

"She's got teeth missing, and there's the missing left ear unaccounted for. I'm sure you two saw what he did to her throat? He cuts her throat nearly from ear to ear ... reaches into the opening and pulls her tongue out and has it sticking out of the slit. I thought I'd seen it all, but this guy..."

Goebel and Benson look at each other. They know they have to continue the investigation – but where to start?

"You guys going to release the husband?" Dodson asks.

"After what you just showed us, we have to," Goebel says. "But do us a favor; tell him you couldn't run the test on the blood sample right away. Let the bastard sit for a day or two."

Six

Remembering

Angela draws the curtains across the windows. The living room goes dark with just enough light to make out shapes – no colors, just faded grays. Two overstuffed chairs are arranged in the middle of the room with a small floor lamp next to them. She directs Helen to sit in one as she takes the other. She turns on the lamp, dimly illuminating only the space where they are – all around is blackness, as if they are in a bubble of light, a bubble suspended in a sea of shadows.

"Now, just relax," Angela says. "Close your eyes and take a few slow, deep breaths."

Helen closes her eyes and breathes deeply, her hands resting on the arms of the chair. Angela holds her hand up two feet from Helen's face.

"Good…Now, I want you to open your eyes and follow my hand. Don't move your head; just follow my hand with your eyes."

Angela moves her hand slowly back and forth in front of Helen's face. She begins to move her hand close and then faraway as well.

"That's good. …Just follow my hand…keeping it in focus always. …Good…just keep it in focus. It's so difficult for you to keep focused on my hand. It's so tiring. Your eyes are beginning to feel heavy. You can hardly keep them open. They're getting heavier. …You can't keep them open any longer. Close your eyes and relax. The sound of my voice is all you hear. Relax."

Once Helen's eyes close, Angela puts her hand down. She taps a small tape recorder at her feet to turn it on.

Angela begins asking questions of Helen, trivial things, to allow her to relax and go deeper into the trance.

Finally, when Helen is well under, Angela slowly begins regressing Helen through the years of her life, back to being a little girl.

"You're nine years old, Helen. I want you to go back to a summer's day when you and your family took a trip to Sandy Beach."

"I'm wearing my new swimsuit today," Helen says, in the tone and manner of a small child. "See? It's lime green with a big yellow flower and made of elastic and all stretchy."

"Who's going to Sandy Beach with you?" Angela asks.

"There's me...Mommy and Daddy...Uncle Jerry and Aunt Eleanor...my two cousins, Nicholas and Victor, and International Nancy."

"Nancy's your doll...isn't she?"

"My favorite. ...When you pull her string, she says stuff from all over the world. 'Wherever you go...you always know...just how to say hello.'"

"Is it a long ride to Sandy Beach?"

"A real long time...we're in Uncle Jerry's station wagon. I'm riding in the back with Victor and Nicholas."

"Tell me about your cousins, Victor and Nicholas."

"I hate them. They're stupid boys. They think because they're older and bigger they can be mean...always pinching me and pulling my hair. Hey, stop that!"

"What just happened, Helen?"

"Nicholas pulled the elastic on my swimsuit and snapped it back on me. Hey, stop that!"

"Helen, you're no longer in the car. You're at the lake...at the picnic area with your family. Tell me about your aunt and uncle. What's your Aunt Eleanor like?"

"Daddy says she looks like a scarecrow...she's really skinny. Mommy calls her 'The woman who wasn't there,' and not very smart. But I like her. ...She's nice."

"And what's your Uncle Jerry like?"

Helen is silent for a moment.

"He's got so much hair on his arms, but hardly any on his head. And he's got a big, fat belly that sticks way out. I don't like him much; he's always teasing me. He don't shave real good. And when he kisses me, it scratches my face."

"Does your uncle kiss you often?"

"All the time. ...I wish he wouldn't. ...It scratches."

"Now, Helen...it's later in the day. ...What are you doing?"

"Walking up and down the beach. ...I've got Nancy in my arms. ...I'm pulling her string ...I'm going to learn how to speak every language there is."

"Why aren't you playing with the other children?"

"I don't know anybody. Nicholas and Victor are no fun. Besides, everyone is swimming. I don't like the water. I'm afraid of it. I can't swim. One day, I'll learn how to swim, and I'm going to go all the way out to the platform in the middle of the lake."

"Where are your two cousins?"

"I see them over by the diving board. They just went into the woods. Mommy says we're not supposed to go into the woods. I'm running to the trail behind the diving board. …I can't see them. Now I'm following them. I'm afraid, but I keep walking and pulling the string on my doll. It's getting darker, but I keep walking. Oh…my…!'"

"What is it, Helen? What do you see?"

"I'm in a clearing…with trees all around. …It's dark!"

"Who's in the clearing with you?"

"I'm not sure. …I'm scared."

"Don't be afraid, Helen. Tell me who's there."

"I'm not sure. …I see…Nicholas…and Victor…and Uncle Jerry."

Helen flinches in her chair.

"Helen, what just happened?"

"Somebody just took my picture…flashbulb went off in my eye. …I can't see too good. Nicholas and Victor are picking on me, but Uncle Jerry is stopping them. He says I can stay if I join the club. What am I supposed to do? Hey, give that back! They just took my doll. They say I'll get it back later, but first I've got to join the club. I'm supposed to do whatever Nicholas and Victor do."

Helen begins to laugh and giggle.

"What are you laughing at, Helen?"

"Nicholas and Victor…they just took off their swimsuits…they've got nothing on. Their…things…are so tiny and funny looking. They're doing silly things."

"What silly things, Helen?"

"To each other…you know…silly things."

Helen flinches again.

"Did someone take another picture?" Angela asks.

"Yeah…of Nicholas and Victor…Uncle Jerry is taking off his swim trunks, now. He's doing silly things with the boys. They want me to take off my swimsuit. No…no…I won't…I won't! Uncle Jerry told the boys to grab me. …They're holding me down on the ground! No…no…no!"

"It's all right, Helen. You don't have to stay there. Let's jump ahead in time. It's an hour later. You're safe now."

"I can't find my doll. Where's my doll? They said they'd give her back."

"Where are you, Helen?"

"I'm lost in the woods. I'm trying to get back to the beach. I hear voices. I'm just following the voices. I'm crying. I can hardly see. I hurt…it hurts to walk…I hurt so much."

"Where do you hurt, Helen?"

"Down below…in my private place. I see my parents. My father is packing the car. My mother wants to know where I've been, but I just keep on crying. She sees I don't have my doll. …She thinks that's why I'm crying.

"During the drive home, I make-believe I'm asleep. …I don't want to look at anybody.

"At home, my mother puts me to bed. My father comes in to kiss me goodnight. He says I shouldn't cry over my lost doll. He's going to take me to the toy store to buy whatever doll I want. But…I want Nancy!"

Tears begin flowing from Helen's eyes. Angela slowly brings her back through the years.

"Now, Helen, when I count to three, you're going to wake refreshed, as if after a long night's sleep. All the images you've seen are nothing but shadows. …They can't hurt or touch you any longer. …There's nothing to be afraid of. …They're just shadows. One…two…three…"

Helen opens her eyes and stares expressionlessly. She finally speaks, "That was only the first time."

"What do mean? What are you saying?" Angela asks.

Helen shakes her head, trying to clear her thinking. "None of it is completely clear still, but I remember more than ever. That day at the beach when I was nine was only the first time. It happened other times over the years till I became a teenager. Then it stopped – that is, until recently."

"How many times did this happen?"

"I'm not sure. I just know it was a few times."

"Was it by your uncle or your cousins?"

"I only remember that there was always more than one, perhaps all three, for all I know. Or maybe I'm mixing it up with the first time, and there was only one of them. Maybe after the first time it was only one of them. I'm not sure. I only know…I'm sure…it happened many times."

Helen is shaking, half from fear, but also from anger.

"How do you feel?" Angela asks.

"I feel…defiled. …I feel…dirty. What they did to me that day …I wouldn't let anyone do to me now…and I'm a grown woman! But to do that with a child is…is…I can't express how it makes me feel."

"Didn't your mother say your uncle died years ago?" Angela asks.

"So she says…so she believes…but that doesn't make it true. Perhaps, he's not dead! Stranger things have happened. It doesn't matter, though…dead or alive…I know two boys who were there who are now grown men.

"It might be a good time to renew some old family ties. I swear…I'm going to get to the bottom of this!"

****

There is a knock at Angela's office door. It is open, and she looks up to see Richard Haywood.

"Richard?"

He walks in and stands in front of her desk.

"Helen tells me she's been staying with you. I've tried to get her to come home, but she won't. I called her at work, but all she says is she's not ready to talk. What the hell is going on?"

"You must understand Helen's position," Angela calmly says, "She's frightened and confused. She's learned from the police about your…affair. She feels betrayed by you. She doesn't know where to turn. It'll be a long time before she feels she can trust you again."

"Oh, and she trusts you, huh? Why doesn't she stay with her parents? Why did she run to you? Something's not right here."

"What are you implying, Richard?"

"Oh, get off it, doctor. I see through your game. Helen's vulnerable right now. I've heard about psychiatrists taking advantage of the doctor-patient relationship, but this is a new one on me."

Angela stands up, indignant.

"If you've got something to say, Richard, say it and then get out of my office."

"Do I need to spell it out for you? A good-looking young blonde…running scared… A has-been, old, hippie dike…takes her under her wing…"

"Get out of here, right now. Get out of my office!" Angela points to the door.

"This isn't the end of it…*doctor*…" Richard says, walking to the doorway, pointing back at Angela.

"Are you threatening me?" Angela says through gritted teeth.

"No, I'm warning you. I can make things pretty hot for you around here. I wonder what the superintendent would say if he knew what was going on right under his nose."

Angela rushes forward, pushes Richard out, and slams the door.

"Get out of here with your filth!"

Helen sits at a corner table of the café. Her mother Delores walks in and makes a beeline toward her.

"This is so nice," she says to Helen as she sits down, "having lunch together. Why don't we do this more often? Oh, iced tea, please, and a Cobb salad," she coos, smiling at the waiter.

"I'll have the same," Helen adds.

The first minute of their lunch conversation centers on her mother's concern for her daughter. Then, Delores rambles on through the entire meal about trivial matters, which Helen always finds boring and trite, but is always willing to tolerate.

When the waiter removes the empty plates, Helen abruptly changes the subject.

"So…the other day, you told me Aunt Eleanor is still living in Tannersville, and I was wondering…"

"What's with all these questions lately about your Uncle Jerry and his family?" her mother interrupts.

"Oh, it's just that I have to go to Tannersville on company business, and I thought it would be nice to take in a visit with her."

"What for?" laughs her mother. "We haven't seen each other since your Uncle died."

"That's just it," Helen says, "She's still family, and I'll be in Tannersville."

"I suppose I could call her and tell her you'll be coming," her mother says thoughtfully.

"And Nicholas and Victor, my cousins, do they still live in Tannersville?"

"My goodness, don't you remember? Nicholas died in a car accident when he was still in high school. Victor married…has a couple of kids…two boys, I think. Last I heard, he's still lives in town not far from his mother's.

"When your uncle died, he left a good amount of life insurance money to your aunt. Which was a good thing…poor dear. …Fifteen years ago, your Aunt Eleanor had a stroke. She's been in a wheelchair since. Has a live-in nurse to cook, clean, and take care of her. Good thing she has that money."

"How did Uncle Jerry die?" Helen asks.

"Heart attack…fell facedown dead in Barcelona, Spain…on the steps of that big church they have out there. He and your aunt were there on vacation. He was walking up the stairs to the church and feel facedown dead…heart attack."

"And you went to the funeral?"

"Why, of course; we went to the funeral."

"And you saw the body?

"What a strange question to ask. But, now that you mention it, there wasn't a body...not really. Your poor aunt was there in Spain alone...the poor dear. ...She didn't know what to do. Found out it costs a fortune to ship a body back to the states. So she had him cremated there and came back with his ashes in an urn.

"I don't like the idea of cremation. ...But then again, being in the ground with all those worms – it makes me shiver. What do you think, darling?"

"So if you call Aunt Eleanor, you think I could visit her?" Helen asks, ignoring her mother's question.

"Oh, I suppose so. I'll give her a call tonight."

Her mother picks up the tab the waiter left on the table.

"And lunch is on me. This was fun! We should do this more often."

Seven

Don't Go in the Basement

Tannersville is no different from any other small rural town. In the center of town stands its hundred-year-old, two-story city hall, surrounded on all sides by small, family-owned businesses: the feed store, shoe repair, hardware, clothing, furniture and food. No frills, just the basics.

In front of city hall, on both sides of the walkway to the entrance, are rows of empty park benches – empty save for one. On it sit four old codgers, each dressed in blue overalls and straw fedoras. Each with a mouth full of chewing tobacco, taking turns spitting brown spittle on the grass. It is late in the day. They talk about the weather, the price of feed, the local gossip, and when being all talked out, they sit silently together watching the world. They watch Helen as she gets out of her car and approaches.

"Howdy," Helen says, thinking a country style greeting would be more fitting, and then feeling foolish for saying it.

"Howdy," says one of the men. "Can we hap ya?"

"Yes, please. I just got into town. I'm here to see my aunt, Eleanor Russell. Would any of you gentlemen know where she lives?"

The oldest-looking fellow, sitting at the far end of the bench, speaks up.

"Old Jerry Russell's widow…sure do…Just follow this road here, 'bout a mile and a half, till you see an old gray house with a white porch and trim. You can't miss it. …It's the biggest dang house in the county."

"You mentioned my late Uncle Jerry – did you know him?"

He turns his head and spits into the grass, takes a handkerchief from his chest pocket, and wipes his lips before speaking.

"Sure, I knew him; everyone knew him. He was a good ole boy, always smiling and willin' to hap a friend. He coulda run for mayor, if he wanted. He would have won, too. …Everybody liked Jerry." The others nod. "Always helping out at church and the school…ran the Boy's Club down at the gym till the day he died."

"The Boy's Club, you say?" Helen's eyebrows go up. "Well, gentlemen, thank you very much."

She makes her way back to her car, feeling their eyes on her. They watch in silence till the car is out of sight.

****

The old fellow told it true. A little more than a mile down the road is a large gray house with a white porch and trim. It is huge, even bigger than it seems in the flashes of memory she has of the place

Helen stands on the porch, looking through a screen door into the dark house. She can't see anything except for the shapes of windows.

"May I help you?" The voice startles Helen. It is an older, white-haired woman dressed in a nurse's smock.

"Yes, I'm here to see my Aunt Eleanor."

"You must be Helen," says the woman, opening the screen door. "She's been expecting you. My name is Joyce McDonald. I'm Eleanor's caretaker and companion."

Inside, Helen's eyes adjust to the dark. It is a large home, plainly decorated, neat, clean, and comfortable.

"She's asleep in the living room. Let me tell you something before we go in. And, please, don't take offense at what I'm about to say. I tell this to all of Eleanor's visitors. She's a very ill woman; that's why I'm here. Her speech is slurred from the stroke, but if you listen carefully, she's not hard to understand. Her memory is poor. ...She often gets the past and present mixed up...so don't let that throw you. All in all though, she's a very smart and sensitive person. Don't talk down to her. She's not stupid, and she's not crazy. Those are the ground rules."

"I understand," Helen says.

Joyce walks ahead; Helen follows.

"Eleanor, there's someone here to see you. Wake up. ...It's your niece, Helen, all the way from the city to see you. Remember your niece, Helen?"

Sitting in a wheelchair in front of a large window and warmed by the sunlight pouring down on her is Aunt Eleanor, looking as one would expect – a worn, old, sickly version of what Helen remembers.

Her eyes open slowly. Then her face shows bright with delight as she focuses in on Helen.

"Helen!" she calls, "Your mother said you were coming. How wonderful! Let me look at you. My...I haven't seen you since you were little. Just look at you! What a lovely woman you've become."

"Thank you, Aunt Eleanor," Helen says, sounding slightly embarrassed.

"I'll just leave you two alone," says Joyce. "I'll be in the kitchen, if you need me."

Helen spends the next hour answering one question after another. It clearly gives the old woman pleasure, so Helen does her best. She realizes none of her own questions are going to be addressed for now.

"I'm here on business; I'll be staying in town at the hotel. I was hoping I could come and visit again tomorrow?"

"A hotel? Don't be silly. …You're staying here with me. Joyce! Joyce!" her aunt hollers.

The woman comes running in from the kitchen.

"My niece is staying with us. Help fetch her belongings and set her up in the upstairs guestroom."

"Aunt Eleanor, that's very kind but…"

"No buts," says the old woman, "You're family…I won't hear another word about it."

"Thanks, Aunt Eleanor," Helen leans over and kisses the old woman's cheek.

****

The guestroom is no different from the rest of the house – clean, comfortable, and decorated in a simple country style. The ceiling slants with the angle of the roof. Two small windows overlook the back of the house. The one-car garage by the large backyard is open. There is the memorable station wagon – idle and rusting.

Dinner is simple fare, meat and potatoes. Helen has no trouble getting Aunt Eleanor to answer questions about her uncle; only, the answers shed little light. As far as Aunt Eleanor is concerned, Uncle Jerry hung the moon. He could do no wrong – he was a wonderful husband and father. Still, there is a single piece of information which might hold promise. When speaking about how great a father he was, Aunt Eleanor mentions the many hours he and the boys spent making pieces of small furniture in their makeshift woodshop in the basement. Helen knows somehow she will have to go down and investigate, and the thought of it stirs up some deeply buried fears.

When speaking about her two sons, the subject of the now-deceased Nicholas is never mentioned. She focuses her praise on Victor, the oldest, how he has done so well for himself with two strong, handsome boys and a newborn daughter, a lovely wife, and a beautiful home. It is not until later Helen learns this is all to be only wishful thinking. While helping with the dishes in the kitchen, Joyce gives her the true story.

"I'm not sure if your aunt doesn't remember or refuses to admit the truth. Victor and his wife separated nearly a year ago. We have no idea where he is or what he's been doing.

His wife and kids live in some rundown old shack on the poor side of town. I'll give you her address. …Maybe she knows where he is."

After they put up the dishes, Joyce writes the address for Helen on a slip of paper. As Helen leaves the kitchen, she notices the dark wooden door in the corner of the room – the door to the basement.

The next two hours they spend sitting in the living room, Aunt Eleanor asking questions about Helen – her parents, her marriage, her life. Helen shares only as much as she thinks will be enough to leave her aunt content.

"Time for bed, Miss Eleanor," Joyce says, standing in the doorway.

"I'm so happy you're here, my dear. It's been such a treat to see you again," Aunt Eleanor says to Helen. "Make yourself at home. I'll see you in the morning. Goodnight, dear."

"Goodnight, Aunt Eleanor, and thank you," Helen says as Joyce wheels her off.

Twenty minutes later, Joyce reappears in the living room.

"Well, don't forget to turn off the lights before you go to bed. This is a small country town. There's no need to lock up at night, but if it makes you feel better, then go right ahead. Don't worry; I've got a key."

"But I thought you stayed here?" Helen asks.

"Oh, I only lived here for the first year of your aunt's condition; there's no need anymore. Don't worry; she'll sleep through the night. A cannon blast couldn't wake that woman. TV is in the back sitting room over there. There are books in there if you feel like reading. I'll be back early morning. Breakfast is at seven. Have a goodnight."

"Goodnight, Joyce."

Helen is relieved; it makes investigating the basement possible and trouble free. Still, she waits more than an hour, reading magazines until she feels it safe to assume her aunt is most likely asleep.

She doesn't turn on the kitchen light. She feels what she is doing isn't right, and the cloak of darkness comforts her.

She tries the door to the basement – locked. There must be a key somewhere. She rummages through every drawer in the kitchen – nothing. Finally, in despair, she turns on the light. She takes a knife, figuring she can jimmy the lock.

When she turns to the door again, she notices something not seen when the light was off, but now visible with the kitchen fully lit up. Over the door is a wooden shelf. On it is a dark piece of metal – the key. She moves one of the kitchen chairs in place. Standing on it, she takes down the key. She slowly places it in the lock and turns it. It opens with a click.

She searches for a light switch and finds it on the wall to one side. The light coming from the cellar below is brown and weak, just barely enough to see by. Each of the wooden steps creaks under her feet as she slowly descends.

At the bottom of the stairs, Helen looks around the dimly lit basement. Sprawled about the room are pieces of incomplete furniture. A dirty old mattress is on the floor in the corner. The main wall has a workbench in front of it. Above it is a large pegboard with various tools attached. To the right of the workbench is an electric saw with cobwebs now decorating the rusting blade. To the left of the bench is a tall metal cabinet. Helen tries the dual handles – locked.

She runs back upstairs to the kitchen, selects the longest and thinnest knife from a wooden block, and returns to the basement.

The thin blade slips easily into the front chink of the cabinet – just under the lock. She slowly raises the blade up. And with little force, the lock clicks, and the two cabinet doors swing open.

Inside are rows of old work clothes dangling from rusting metal hangers. There are glass jars filled with nuts and bolts, screws and nails – all in all, nothing of any great interest. But at the bottom of the cabinet is a metal box, the kind used to store important documents.

Helen takes it out and places it on the workbench. It is large, perhaps two feet by two feet and one foot deep. There is a small, inexpensive lock on the front – poor security, but a lock, nonetheless.

Helen looks over to the pegboard and spots a hammer. So as not to make too much noise, she wraps a dirty old rag around the lock. She hammers until it gives way, breaking into pieces.

At a glance, the contents of the box tell volumes to Helen. Inside are hundreds of photos of naked boys in compromising positions – mostly of Nicholas and Victor, but there are one or two of other boys. Most of the photos were taken there in that basement, many on top of the same mattress now lying discarded in the corner, filthy and molding.

Though it sickens her, Helen searches through the photos, looking for evidence of her past – and she finds it.

She holds in her hand a faded picture of a little girl in a lime green swimsuit with a ragdoll in her arms. It is a picture of her at Sandy Beach in a clearing in the woods. She is sure she'll find more photos of herself on that fateful day, but at the moment she does not feel strong enough to look further through the box. She tosses the photo back in and closes the lid.

That instant, she hears a click come from the top of the stairs. The light goes out; the basement is pitch-black. The sound of heavy feet rushing down the stairs sends terror all through Helen. She can't move.

When the intruder lands at the bottom, Helen feels strong hands grab her and toss her aside. She tumbles over the disarrayed pieces of furniture and lands face down on the discarded mattress.

There is the sound of metal clanking. The stranger fumbles about and then runs back up the stairs. Helen hears him run across the house above her and rush off the front porch. Next is the screeching of car tires and the roar of an engine fading off into the distance.

Helen slowly shuffles her way through the dark to the top of the stairs. She turns on the light and looks back down at the workbench. The metal box is gone.

Upstairs, Helen looks around – nothing else is missing. Whoever it was knew she was there and suspected she would be looking for something, anything. Also, they knew their way around the house and basement like the back of their hand.

For a moment, Helen considers calling the police. But that would only hinder her plans. She must be brave and continue on her own.

Small town or not, Helen locks every door in the house, goes upstairs to her room and locks the door. Not until well into morning does Helen get any sleep. Most of the night she spends seated on the edge of the bed, holding the long slender knife in her hand.

****

Next morning, Helen descends the stairs following the pleasant scent of morning coffee and bacon coming from the kitchen. Joyce is standing at the stove cooking. Her Aunt Eleanor sips coffee at the kitchen table.

"Good morning," Helen says.

"Good morning," Aunt Eleanor smiles. "Sit…sit…Joyce can whip up anything you'd like."

"Oh, just coffee, please."

"Did you sleep well, my dear?"

"Okay, I guess. I always have a hard time sleeping in a new place."

Helen decides not to say a word about what happened last night. What could she say? *Last night, while I was burglarizing your house, someone snuck in, knocked me down, and ran off with your late husband's collection of child pornography.* That, surely, will not go over well.

"So, Helen, what would you like to do today?" Aunt Eleanor asks.

"Well, I am here on business. I'm afraid I won't be back till late this evening."

"Oh, what a pity," pouts Aunt Eleanor. "Oh, well…business is business…my husband used to say…and it must come first."

"I'm afraid so," Helen says, feeling a twinge of guilt for lying to the old woman.

"Will you be back in time for dinner?" Joyce asks.

"I'm not sure," Helen responds. "I'll call and let you know as soon as I do."

"I'm making my pot roast," Joyce beams with pride.

"Joyce makes the most heavenly pot roast," coos her aunt.

****

It is still early morning when Helen drives back toward City Hall. She has the address and instructions to get to the home of Victor's estranged wife and kids.

Theresa Russell
421 Mockingbird Lane.

Just before the town square, while she is passing the high school, she sees a small group of young boys holding basketballs and waiting for the gym to open.

"The gym…the Boy's Club," she whispers, remembering what the old men on the bench told her about her uncle.

Her curiosity stirred, she parks the car and walks over to investigate. As she approaches, a man comes from the opposite direction, dangling a set of keys. He opens the door, and the boys all dash inside.

The man is tall, well-built, and handsome with a country-boy charm in his eyes and smile. His hair is sandy and full, and his skin tan from outdoor sports. He looks to be around Helen's age. He is just about to enter also when Helen calls out to him.

"Sir…excuse me…sir, may I have a minute?"

"A minute…sure…how can I help you?" He smiles. His tone says even if she asked for an hour, he would gladly give it.

"Is this the Boy's Club?" she asks.

His smile gets even bigger.

"You must be Helen Russell…Eleanor Russell's niece?"

"It's not Russell anymore; I'm married now," Helen says, tangling her fingers to draw attention to her wedding ring. "But how did you know?"

"Heck…small town like this, everybody knows everyone else's business. It's hard to keep a secret around here. You spoke with Toby and the old boys in front of city hall, yesterday. …That's as good as takin' out an ad in the local paper. My name's Kyle Adams. …It's a pleasure to meet you." He holds out his hand for Helen to shake.

"I hope you don't mind me intruding, but they tell me my uncle used to donate his time to this gym. Did you know my Uncle Jerry?"

"Sort of…not really…I mean, I saw him around when I used to come here as a kid. I went to the same school as his sons. …Didn't hang out with them much; they were a little too wild for me." He tilts his head to one side. The thoughtful look leaves his face and his smile returns. "So how do you like our little town?"

"It's charming, at least what little I've seen. I've mostly been with my aunt at her home."

He tilts his head in the opposite direction, never losing his smile. "Listen, maybe later, I could show you around?"

"I don't think that's such a good idea. Besides, I'll be leaving first thing in the morning, and I've a few things I need to do before I leave."

"Well, how about having lunch with me? You do eat lunch, don't you? It's just lunch…all very innocent and respectable. Besides, I'll let you in on all the local gossip."

Helen smiles and thinks for a while. It is obvious he is coming on to her. Normally, she would never even entertain the notion, but normalcy changed drastically in her life lately.

"Okay," she says to her own surprise, "What time and where?"

"Just follow this road, two blocks north…Kathleen's Copper Kettle. You can't miss it. They've got great hamburgers. I've got a late lunch, today…how's two o'clock sound?"

"Sounds just fine. See you then." Helen turns and walks toward her car. Kyle stands at the door and watches her every move, then waves as she drives away.

****

Helen follows Joyce's direction to a Tee. She parks in front of an old, wooden-frame house whose powder-blue paint job is in desperate need of refreshing and much repair.

After no response to her knocking at the front door, Helen presses her face up against one of the windows. The house is dark, save for a light coming from the kitchen in the back of the house.

Helen walks around to the back of the house. In the backyard, she finds herself confronted by a very unfriendly dog, thankfully, tied to a tree. The dog strains against the rope, choking itself. The yelping is loud and sharp.

The backdoor opens and a woman holding a small baby on her hip stands behind the screen door. Two small boys play at her side.

"Can I help you?" the woman asks.

"I'm looking for Mrs. Victor Russell...Teresa Russell?"

"You found her."

Helen steps forward so each of the two women can get a better look at each other. The dog is still barking loudly.

"My name is...my name is..." Helen can't make herself heard over the dog's barking.

The woman pushes open the screen door and steps out. "Poncho...Poncho...shut up, boy. It's all right. ...Shut up, Poncho!"

The dog whines for a moment and then lies down under a tree.

"I'm sorry; he's just thinks he's a big dog with big responsibilities. Like I said, I'm Teresa Russell."

Helen starts again, "My name is Helen Haywood. I use to be Helen Russell before I married. I'm Victor's cousin."

"Well, I'm sorry, but Victor doesn't live here anymore."

"I know that. I was hoping you could tell me where he is."

"Why don't you ask his mother? I could tell you where she lives."

"I've already been there. She doesn't even know about your separation."

"I suppose not," says Teresa. "Poor woman...doesn't know much about anything lately. I guess I could write down his address for you."

"I was hoping you and I could talk," Helen moves in closer to Teresa.

"What about?"

"About Victor?"

"Well, I don't know," says Teresa.

"Please, I've come such a long way to get some answers. It's so important to me. Please?"

Teresa senses the urgency in Helen's voice.

"Okay, come on in." She holds the door open for Helen and then looks toward her two sons. "You two boys go outside and play. I'm going to have a talk with this nice lady."

Inside, Teresa pours two cups of coffee and places them on the kitchen table. As she sits down, she motions for Helen to do the same. This is all done one-handed and with great finesse while never taking the baby from off her hip.

Up close, Helen is able to get a better view of Teresa. She is perhaps a couple of years older than she – slender and pale. It is clear to see she is attractive, despite her mussed hair, her old torn housecoat, and an unmade-up face. Understandably, being a single mother to three young children is slowly taking its toll and aging her.

"So what is it about Victor you want to know? I haven't seen him in three months, but he phones now and then. He's working at the cement plant. Most of the time he's good about sending child support. He's got himself an apartment on Cloister Avenue. I'll give you the address."

"To be honest," Helen says, "I have some questions about my Uncle Jerry…Victor's dad."

"What can I tell you? The man's been dead since I was a little girl."

There is a noticeable strain in Teresa's voice.

"Anything you can think of," Helen asks. "Did Victor ever mention what his relationship with his father was like?"

A look of deep sorrow sweeps across Teresa's face. She stands up and places the baby down gently into a playpen. She walks over to the sink. She stares out the window – her back to Helen. She knows she can't look into her eyes and say what needs saying.

"Victor always feared someday you'd come looking for an answer. He told me what they done to you that day in the woods. He told me how his father molested him and his brother, as well as one or two of the local boys around town.

"Those memories haunt and torture Victor every day of his life. It tormented his brother, Nicholas. …The boy was always drunk or high on something. He died in a car crash in his senior year. Victor was wild, too, in those days. But when his brother died, he straightened up. …That's when we started dating.

"Like I said, those memories are Victor's cross to bear. I tried to help him. …I tried to understand. Till one day…" Teresa's voice trails off. There is a knot in her throat, but she continues. "Till one day…I caught him with Travis…our oldest boy. I kicked him out. I told him not to come back or I'd press charges."

"Why didn't you press charges, or at least try to get him some help?" Helen interrupts. "I mean…the man is out there…free to do whatever he wants!"

"I know you're not going to understand this," says Teresa. "But my children must come first. He sends money every week…not much…but lots more than I would be getting if they locked him away."

"You're right," says Helen, "I don't understand."

Teresa takes up a pen and pad; she begins writing.

"This is Victor's address. Be careful. …I'm pretty sure he's started drinking again."

Helen stands to meet Teresa and takes the slip of paper.

"Thank you," says Helen.

As she looks into Teresa's troubled and sorrowful eyes, she feels pity for the woman. She reaches out and puts her arms around her.

"Thank you very much," whispers Helen.

Teresa begins to cry. "I do love him, you know. …I still do."

****

Kathleen's Copper Kettle is everything Helen imagined – simple country décor with a no-frills menu of stick-to-your-ribs breakfasts and hearty down-home lunches and dinners. Helen looks about the restaurant. Kyle stands and waves from a table in the back of the room.

Kyle holds her chair for her.

"I hope I haven't made you wait too long."

"If you did, the sight of you made it all worthwhile," he says, taking his seat across from her.

"You know, Kyle, there is a fine line between being friendly and flirting. I am married, you know."

"Well, let's just say it's friendly flirting. …Don't take it wrong. …I find you attractive, but I know my place. I just thought it would be great if we had lunch and got to know each other. I don't want you to feel uncomfortable."

"I don't." Helen smiles now that she has lain down the ground rules. "So…I think I'll try one of those world-famous Kathleen burgers you told me about."

Their lunchtime passes with the usual polite chitchat. Helen answers questions about her job, her home, her family, her likes and dislikes – all very sedate – without a mention of her true motive for coming to Tannersville.

Kyle turns out to be an interesting character. After high school, he signed up with the Army on their college benefits program. In those short four years, he finds himself stationed in the Far East, the Mediterranean, as well as six months' duty in South America. For a small-town boy, he is well traveled, and it shows. He has an air of sophistication not obvious in any of his fellow townspeople. After the military, he came back home to attend the state university, taking a variety of courses before selecting his major. The degree he earned qualifies him to be a sports coach at any reputable college, but with a sick father at home, he applied for a simple gym teacher/coaching job at the local Tannersville High School.

"You know the old saying: 'those who can't do, teach. And those who can't teach, teach gym,'" he laughs.

"And your sick father…?" Helen asks.

"He died over a year ago. …Left me the house…nice little place…I'm comfortable there."

"And, there's no woman in your life…handsome guy like yourself?" Helen kids.

"Like I said, it's a small town. All the good ones are taken. I guess I'm going to have to import one. You wouldn't consider the position, would you?"

"I thought all flirting was going to be kept friendly."

"Sorry, I guess I forgot myself."

Over coffee, Helen questions Kyle about her family members in Tannersville.

"Earlier, you said you remembered my Uncle Jerry?"

"Mr. Russell…I remember seeing him at the gym. …Seemed like a nice enough guy. It was all such a long time ago; I hardly remember what the man looked like."

"And you knew my cousins, Nicholas and Victor?"

"I used to see them at school, if that's what you mean. When we were little, we never spoke at all, but then again, Nicholas and Victor never spoke to anyone. They were always quiet and kept to themselves. But when their father died…about the time we were all becoming teenagers…all hell broke loose. Boy, did they break out of their shells with a vengeance. I guess, without their strong-handed father to keep them in line, they just ran wild.

"All through high school, they had a bad reputation. If you wanted drugs, and who knows what else…just ask the Russell brothers. They drove their cars like they didn't care if they lived or died. The sheriff warned your aunt more than once about her boys. But what's a sweet, country-town woman supposed to do with two wild animals?

"Finally, one Saturday night your cousin Nicholas took it too far. He was high as a kite…in no shape to walk, let alone drive a car. He ran into a pole on Main Street, just a few blocks from here. Paper said he must have been doing ninety.

"I guess Nicholas' death scared Victor straight. He settled down, got a job, and married. I thought they were going to live 'happily ever after,' but I hear now they've been separated for a long time. I see Victor around town now and then, but we never talk. He's usually drunk, from what I can tell."

Kyle looks at his watch. "Gee, where does the time go? I better get back to the gym before those kids burn it down or kill one another." He stands and picks up the check. "Say, am I going to see you again before you leave?"

"I'm afraid not," Helen says. "I've got an appointment this afternoon, and I promised my aunt I would spend the evening with her. I'll be leaving early in the morning if I'm to get back to the city in time for work on Monday."

"Well, it was sure nice meeting you. If you ever come back to town, look me up. You know where to find me."

"Same here," Helen says.

"Well, *arrivederci, Signora* Haywood."

The sound of the foreign language takes Helen off guard; it is too reminiscent of what she heard from her attacker. It scares her. Then she catches herself. Why is she torturing herself with such thoughts? Many people say things like that everyday just for the fun of it. She remembers Kyle told her he spent time in the Mediterranean. He is just showing off, trying to be cute. She realizes she is being foolish and resolves to ignore it.

Kyle turns away, takes two steps toward the cash register, and then turns around again.

"If I keep it friendly, do you think you could handle one more small piece of flirting?"

"I suppose so," smiles Helen.

"If I ever find myself up your way, would it be all right if I call on you?"

The question takes Helen aback, but something inside her tells her to answer him quickly and truthfully.

"Of course. In fact…I'd feel disappointed if you didn't."

A boyish smile appears on Kyle's face.

****

Helen knocks on Victor's apartment door as hard as she can. The sound of a blaring TV blots out her efforts. She tries to look in the window, but the blinds are closed tightly. She can see a light is on, and there is movement. She decides to try one more time. Clenching her fist, she slams it as hard as she can. Inside, the volume on the TV lowers. She hammers again on the door. It opens. A vague likeness of the young Victor she once knew a long time ago stands in the doorway.

His hair is mussed. His face is unshaven, his clothes wrinkled and soiled, and his hands dirty and rough. He has a pungent body odor, and his breath has the distinct stench of alcohol.

"Well, well, well…who says God doesn't answer prayers? Hey beautiful, come on in. Let's take a flying shot at a rolling doughnut together."

"Victor, it's me, Helen – your cousin, Helen. Listen to me!"

He stands there for a moment. Recognition shows in his eyes, and the drunken smile leaves his face.

"Go away. …Isn't there enough misery in the world? Don't you have enough turmoil in your life?"

He tries to shut the door, but Helen forces herself inside. He staggers about the room, trying not to look at her. An overhead light bulb dangles from the ceiling, the only light in the one-room apartment. There is a small black and white TV resting on a wood box, a torn up old couch with missing legs, newspapers and magazines covering the floor, and scores of empty wine and whiskey bottles strewn about the room.

"Victor, I need to talk to you."

He staggers to the couch.

"Go away! What did you do…forget to pay your back dues into the club? Ah…yes…the club."

"Victor, I need to speak with you. I remember what happened that day at the beach. I remember everything!"

Victor sits up straight and throws his arms out wide.

"Ladies and gentlemen of the jury, I throw myself on the mercy of the court! I plead the fifth! I was young and foolish! Forgive me Father, for I know not what I do." Victor begins to laugh loudly. "You remember one day in your life…one horrifying moment. Well…Cuz…I remember a thousand days and a thousand nights! I'd be glad to change places with you any day."

"Victor, I know what you've been through. There's help for you. It's not your fault, what your father did to you. Victor, tell me, what did you do with the box of photos you took from the basement last night?"

Victor just smiles.

"Victor, I need your help. I don't think your father is really dead. I think he faked his death for the insurance money. And for some reason, he's resurfaced, and he's been attacking me."

"Oh, he's dead all right. Momma showed Nicholas and me the ashes."

"They could have been anyone's ashes," Helen pleads.

"No, he's dead all right. His ghost comes to me at night."

"You don't believe in ghosts…you can't…it's not a ghost, Victor. Your father never died."

Victor speaks out loud, as if talking to no one in particular, as if Helen isn't there.

"His ghost comes to me at night; it tells me what to do. He told me to be with Travis! He comes into my bed at night and…"

"Stop it…Victor…stop it!"

It is useless. He slowly falls into a stupor and into unconsciousness. Helen searches the apartment, but there is no sign of the photo box or anything else that might appear of any use to her investigation.

She finds an old blanket behind the couch, covers Victor with it, and walks out of the apartment.

****

Following morning, Helen is up early. Carrying her packed bags, she goes downstairs. Joyce is in the kitchen cooking breakfast.

"Good morning," says Helen, placing her bags down.

"Good morning," Joyce turns around from the stove, "What can I get you…coffee?"

"No, thank you. I need to get going. I've a long drive and I have to be in the office today early."

"Well, at least say goodbye to your aunt before you go. She's still in bed. She's not feeling well this morning, so I was going to serve her breakfast in bed. Go ahead, she's awake. …It would disappoint her if you didn't see her before you left."

Helen slowly makes her way into Aunt Eleanor's bedroom. The old woman is sitting up in bed. Her eyes open, and a smile comes on her face when she sees Helen.

"Helen, sweet girl, you're not leaving, are you?"

"I have to, Aunt Eleanor. I have to be back at work this morning."

"Business is business, my husband used to say." Her aunt points to a portrait on the wall. It is a photo of Uncle Jerry. Helen has since forgotten exactly what he looked like, but now, looking at the portrait, even more harsh memories flood her mind. She is beginning to feel queasy.

"You'll come back and visit us soon?" the old woman asks.

"Of course, I will, Aunt Eleanor. …You stay well until I do."

Helen bends down and kisses the old woman's cheek before leaving the bedroom.

"You sure I couldn't make you a thermos of coffee to go, at least?" Joyce asks.

"No, thank you. You've been more than kind, but I must be going." Helen picks up her bags and heads out the front door. "It was nice meeting you. Thank you again for everything."

"Nice meeting you, too," Joyce calls out from the kitchen. "Don't be such a stranger. Come back real soon!"

Helen tosses her bags in the backseat and drives off. She drives past Kathleen's Copper Kettle, past city hall in the town square, and past the high school gym, all the while hoping she sees Kyle one more time. But it is early, and the streets are empty.

Once she is on the highway and a dozen miles from Tannersville, she reaches over to her glove compartment and pulls out her mobile phone. She hasn't checked her phone the entire weekend. The screen shows she has one message.

"Helen…it's your mother. …Call me as soon as you get this. And whatever you do, don't go to Angela's house! Something bad happened; she's in the hospital. So don't go to her house! Call me as soon as you get this. …Love you!"

Eight

A Serious Crime

Helen reaches over and takes Angela's hand; Angela opens her eyes as much as possible. Her face is bruised and swollen and bandaged. Cuts surround her eyes. She lost two teeth in the back of her mouth, and the ones on her right side are loose. Her body is battered harshly, but all bones are intact.

"What happened?" Helen asks.

Angela speaks slowly and softly. It is painful to move her mouth, and she cannot open it more than an inch or so.

"Two nights ago at home, I looked out my window. I saw the figure of a man standing across the street looking at the house. When he saw me at the window, he walked on. I didn't think anything of it at the time. But the following night, I looked out and there he was again, just staring at the house. It was dark; I couldn't make him out. I felt tempted to call the police. . . . I should have. . . . It was foolish not to, but I didn't. When I looked out the window again, he was gone. Just then, the phone rang. It was the hospital telling me about an emergency. I told them I'd be there as soon as I could.

"I remember going into the garage and opening the garage door. Just when I placed my hand on the car door, a man rushed in and started beating me. I fought back, but it was useless. . . . He was too strong. I tried to scream; he started hitting me in the face. Eventually, I lost consciousness.

"When I didn't show at the hospital and they couldn't get me on the phone, they called the police. They found me lying on the floor of the garage.

"I told the hospital to contact you. I didn't want you to go to the house alone. They have your address listed with your parents. So they called your mother. . . . I'm sorry."

"Did you get a good look at him?" Helen asks.

A look of disturbance mingles with the look of pain on Angela's face.

"Not really. . . . he wore black gloves and a black ski mask."

Helen releases her hand from Angela. Her face goes pale, and she begins to tremble.

"It was him. . . wasn't it?" she says.

Angela tries to sit up. When she can't, Helen places a pillow behind her to prop up her head.

"I'm going to tell you something I didn't even tell the police," Angela says. "I don't believe it was the same man who attacked you. I think it was someone who wanted me to think it was. The ski mask was all wrong; it didn't have the yellow markings you told me about. While he was hitting me, he was grunting. His voice sounded familiar; everything about him was familiar. At one point, I got a clear look into his eyes. . . . They were wild, like an animal's eyes. . . but I knew who he was."

"So who do you think it was?"

"I believe it was Richard. I looked into his eyes. It was Richard – I know it!"

"Richard? Why would he do anything like this?"

"He came to my office. . . . He said things. . . horrible things. . . . He threatened me, so I kicked him out."

"Angela, why didn't you tell the police?"

"Because there's no proof; it's just a feeling. But in my heart, I know it was him. Helen, you must stay away from him. . . . He's dangerous. I'm so sorry! I'd feel so frightened for you if you stayed at my house alone."

"Don't worry. I can move back in with my folks."

"Just promise me you'll stay away from Richard," Angela orders.

"I promise. . ."

****

In her car, Helen still has the overnight bag from the Tannersville trip, though most of the garments need cleaning. She has some belongings at her house, but she is just not up to a private one-on-one with Richard – if he is home at all. Besides, she promised Angela she'd stay away from Richard. Only possible solution is to get her possessions from Angela's house.

At such a late hour, Helen's father insists he drives her. She agrees; the company is welcomed.

During the drive to Angela's, her father questions her about Richard.

"It's your home as much as it is his," he demands. "Why doesn't he go stay with his folks and you stay at the house?"

"Dad. . . Richard's parents live three states away."

"Well, that would solve everything then!" Her father begins to laugh, and Helen joins in.

"Dad, it's all right. I know you and mom worry, but I'm a big girl now. I can take care of myself."

"What about the gun I gave you?" her father asks.

Helen goes speechless for a minute. Her mind races for an answer. She has not told her parents about the Sandy Beach incident – or anything else for that matter.

"The gun I gave you, does Richard still have it?" he insists.

"I suppose he does." Helen says, trying hard not to sound like she is lying.

"I know he's your husband, but it was wrong of him," roars her father. "Especially since some of the goings-on around here lately…your safety is in question."

He is never able to call what happened to her by its true name. It embarrasses him somehow.

He points to the glove compartment.

"Will you open that for me, sweetheart?"

Helen clicks the latch open. First thing she sees is a gun similar to the one he gave her.

"The gun I gave you…originally, I bought for your mother, but she hated the thing. That one's mine; I want you to have it."

"Daddy, I'm not sure." She takes the gun in her hand.

"Nonsense!" he bellows. "You need protection. I want you to take it. Keep it with you always…until this craziness stops."

He feels uncomfortable using true, clear terminology.

"Just promise me one thing," he continues, "Don't tell anyone you have it…not Richard…not Angela…not the police…and definitely don't tell your mother!"

Before putting the gun in her purse, she checks the bullets in the cylinder of the gun – these are not blanks.

They park in back of Angela's house and go in the backdoor. Helen is just about to flick on the light when her father stops her.

"Don't turn on the light," he says, pointing toward the large picture window in the living room. "Who the hell is that?"

There on the front lawn is the silhouette of a man – moving about as if he is casing the house.

Then Helen remembers Angela telling her about a strange man staring at the house for two nights in a row. Angela suspects her attacker and the strange man are one and the same – Richard. But even though it is too dark to make out his features, this without a doubt is not Richard.

The stranger creeps alongside of the house, working his way to the back.

"We'll just see what this is all about," says Helen's father, flicking on the outside lights.

"No…Dad…don't!" Helen calls after him, but it is too late. He is outside confronting the stranger. Helen runs out and stands near her father. She keeps her hand in her purse, gripping the gun. She is ready to take it out and use it if necessary.

"Can I help you?" he says to the stranger.

The man is young – early to mid-twenties, perhaps. He is tall and lanky with an innocent face and dark wavy hair.

"Ah…I'm sorry," the young man fumbles over his words. "I was looking for somebody. I guess I've got the wrong house. …I'm sorry." He starts to back away.

"Who are you looking for?" Helen asks, walking toward him, no longer afraid.

"I told you," he says, "I've made a mistake. The person I'm looking for obviously doesn't live here."

"You're lying," Helen says. "You've been staring at this house for the last few nights. Now tell us what this is all about or I'm calling the police."

The young man becomes nervous; he shifts his weight onto one leg and then the other. He looks as if he is ready to bolt any second. Then he slips his hands into his pockets and seemingly calms down, as if he comes to some resolve in his mind.

"I'm looking for Angela Mitchell. …She…she…she's my mother."

"Poppycock!" says Helen's father. "I'm calling the police."

"No, wait a minute, Dad. He's telling the truth," Helen says, carefully eyeing the face of the young man.

Helen sees it all now – he has Angela's nose and chin, and her eyes. He clearly has his mother's eyes.

"What's your name?" Helen asks.

"Thomas…Thomas Nyman."

Helen releases her grip on the gun and lets it fall to the bottom of her purse.

"My name is Helen Haywood, and this is my father. I'm friends with your mother. Why don't we go inside and talk about this? Are you hungry? Would you like something to eat?"

"No, thank you. I've got food."

For some reason, Helen feels immediately protective of Thomas. But his tone of voice implies she should not take his young and innocent appearance as a sign of incompetence.

Sitting at the kitchen table, the atmosphere becomes more somber as Thomas tells his story. He'd been raised by a couple who adopted him at birth. They were always loving and caring toward him, and he could not have asked for a happier childhood. When he grew older, he learned of his adoption. But on the same account, no other information was offered. There was talk about a "natural mother" who gave him up for adoption, but the identity, circumstances, and reasons never revealed to him.

"I never understood the term 'natural mother'," says Thomas. "That implies my mother was unnatural, but she was the most loving woman I ever knew.

"My father died while I was in college. He never got to see me graduate. My mother just recently died. While going through her effects, I came on some legal documents – adoption papers, hospital records – all the stuff my mother never wanted to talk about.

"I drove over a thousand miles to speak with…Angela. I'm on a two-week holiday. I've got to be back to work in four days. I can't explain why I've come. I just know now that mother is dead, I need to do this."

Helen listens intensely and then takes her time relaying what she knows – choosing her words cautiously.

"Angela…isn't here. …She's had an accident, nothing serious, and she's in the hospital. I don't know if it would be a good idea to spring you on her now. She should be home in two days. Why don't we wait till then? Where are you staying?"

Thomas lowers his eyes. "I've been sleeping in my car."

"Well, that won't do. Why don't you go get your stuff? You can stay here," Helen says.

A smile grows across Thomas' face. He jumps from his chair. "I won't be long. …My car's right down the block. I don't have much stuff. I won't be any trouble."

The boy heads out the backdoor to his car.

"You sure you're doing the right thing?" Helen's father asks her.

"I think I am," Helen says. "He's her son. …Did you see his eyes? Angela couldn't deny him if she tried. I'm sure she would agree with my actions. Anyway, he's not looking to do harm to anyone; he just wants some answers. I definitely know what that feels like."

****

Helen does not take Angela's warning about Richard lightly. She moves in once more with her parents. But she knows sooner or later she and Richard will have to talk about their problems and work out their differences.

It has been weeks since she stepped into her own home and almost as long since she last saw Richard. She chalks up his behavior to his feelings of shame at having his affair out in the open. Up till now, she left the ball in his court – and he has done nothing with it. She decides to take the initiative.

It is clear Richard is avoiding her. She tries to phone him at home – the answering machine, which the police confiscated, he hasn't replaced. He never answers his mobile phone – perhaps because he sees her number on caller ID. She feels tempted to call him from an unfamiliar number but decides not to, feeling it would have been as childish as not answering.

She tries him at work, but they tell her he is away from his phone, in a meeting, unavailable, or out of town on a business trip. None of her messages receives a reply.

She has a notion to go down to his office and confront him, but she knows how that will turn out. And she wants answers, not a confrontation.

Finally, when all her efforts to contact Richard turn up futile, she decides to try an unexpected approach – she phones Francis Crawley.

"Francis Crawley here. May I help you?"

The voice sounds sophisticated, self-assured, and businesslike.

"Hello…this is Helen Haywood and…"

Before she can say another word, Francis hangs up on her. The hum of the line is all Helen hears.

The ball is in Helen's court now.

****

It has been a long and tedious   s day at work for Francis. All she can think of during the drive home is sipping a martini while soaking in a hot tub.

She parks in front of her townhome and starts up the stairs. At the top stands a woman looking forlorn with piercing eyes following her every move.

Francis stops midway. "May I help you?"

"Francis…? My name is Helen Haywood. …I'm Richard's wife. We need to talk and you can't hang up on me this time."

There is an awkward smile on Francis' face.

"Sorry about that, but you can't blame me. I suppose I have been avoiding this. Care to come in?"

Inside, the townhouse is large and luxurious. On the mantle over the fireplace sits a framed picture of Richard. Francis heads toward the kitchen.

"Would you like something to drink?" she calls into the living room. "I'm having a martini."

"This isn't a social call, Francis," Helen says, standing in the center of the living room.

"No, I suppose it isn't. Please, sit down."

The two women take seats opposite each other – Helen on the couch, Francis in the armchair.

"So, what is it you want to know?" Francis asks.

"That's not how we're going to start," Helen says. "I want you to tell me everything."

"Everything…?" Francis says, wearing a bitter smile, "Very well…everything."

She gets up from her seat, walks over to the bar and makes herself a drink as she speaks. "Are you sure you don't want a drink?"

Helen nods that she doesn't.

"Everything…" continues Francis. "A year ago, Richard and I started going to lunch together once or twice a week to discuss business. …It was all very innocent. It was clear we held an attraction for each other. There was the usual flirting…all in good fun, but I made it clear from the beginning I wasn't interested. After all, he was married. I've always considered nothing good can come from being with a married man…and I mean that." Francis says to Helen who is wearing a look of disbelief.

Francis sits back down with her drink and continues.

"Well, one night we were working late together at the office; we were alone. I always keep a bottle of scotch in my office. I don't know why. …I guess I shouldn't have, but I poured us both a drink. Well, one drink led to two and three, and one thing led to another. Next thing we knew…well, you know."

"Right there in the office?" Helen asks with an unyielding look in her eyes.

"Yeah…" chuckles Francis, sipping her drink. "Sounds kind of cheap and sordid now that I think about it. Well, that's how I was feeling the next day. I guess we both were feeling guilty. We tried to stay out of each other's way for the next few days, but it was useless. …Our offices are right next to each other, and we had to conduct business. I knew it was wrong, as well as he, but the urge was all consuming. We started to meet here every chance we could. Richard even trumped-up an occasional false business trip now and then, so we could spend a weekend together."

Francis finishes her drink and walks to the bar to make another.

"You sure you don't want a drink?" she asks. Helen doesn't reply.

"Well, anyway, weeks turned into months, and here I am…against my own better judgment, having an affair with a married man. I never pressed him about what his feelings or his intentions were. We never spoke of love till recently. But, once the subject came up…I'm afraid I hounded the man. I wanted him so badly. …I love him so much. I asked him if he would consider divorcing you. For a while, that's all we talked about, until you had your incident."

"You mean when I was raped," Helen says coldly.

"Yes...when you were...raped," Francis downs her drink, as if that word put a harsh taste in her mouth. She makes herself another drink and continues.

"Anyway, at that point, all talk of him divorcing you stopped."

Francis' speech becomes slurred as the alcohol begins to take effect.

"I think I will have that drink now," Helen says.

"Good idea," says Francis, staggering to the bar, and then returning with two drinks. She hands one to Helen who places it down. Francis sits, and immediately sips at her new drink, she continues. The drinks loosen her tongue.

"Anyway, all of a sudden, Richard says it's best we forget about him divorcing you. He said if whoever is after you succeeded in killing you, we obviously wouldn't have to split anything with you...you know, community property and all. And if whoever it was...that guy...didn't kill you, you'd probably go crazy and he could have you committed. He said he was going to do everything in his power to make that happen. ...I don't know how, though."

Francis finishes her drink with one quick swallow. She looks at her empty glass in dismay.

"Here, have mine," Helen says, handing her drink to Francis. She wants to loosen her tongue even more and keep her talking. Francis takes the drink.

"So, Richard never told you how he was going to make this all happen...how he was going to help the one who is after me?"

"Nope," Francis shakes her head, sipping her new drink.

"A gun...did Richard have a gun?" Helen asks.

"Oh, that thing...yeah, I saw it."

"Did Richard substitute blanks for real bullets in the gun?" Helen asks.

"What a great idea," laughs Francis. "You'd be trying to gun down your assailant and all you would be doing is making noise. ...What a great idea! No...Richard didn't do that...I don't think...I mean...he's not that smart, I don't think."

Helen realizes she is slowly losing Francis.

"Francis, I've been trying to get in touch with Richard lately, but he's been avoiding me. ...Do you know where he is?"

"Welcome to the club," laughs Francis. "I haven't seen him in weeks. I don't know where he is. I miss him, you know?"

"I'm sure you do," Helen says. She gets up and makes her way to the front door.

"You know something?" says Francis in a drunken stupor. "Life for Richard and I would be so much better if you would just somehow die."

"I'm sure it would be," Helen says, gently closing the door behind her.

As Helen descends the townhouse stairs, her mind reels. How much of her misfortune is not from her attacker but from Richard? And what will he do next?

****

It is the end of a long day, at the end of an equally long week for Goebel and Benson. They retraced their steps in the Haywood case, starting back to square one.

Goebel looks at his watch "Six thirty! Hell…I need a drink. What do you say we head over to Max's for a beer?"

Benson nods in agreement.

Maxwell Sullivan had been on the force nearly thirty years before he retired. It took less than one year of retirement to make him realize being away from the job he loved was too much to bear. He was too old to rejoin the force, so he did the next best thing and opened a bar one block down from the station. His regular customers are all his old friends who he worked with for years. It is like he never left; only now, he can drink on the job – legally, that is.

"Hey, Maxie, how you been?" Goebel asks as he and Benson take their places at the bar.

"Doing just fine," Max says. "You boys been okay? What are you having?"

"Two beers, Maxie, and keep them coming," Benson says, grabbing a handful of salted peanuts.

"So, are they going to let you finish the investigation on the Haywood deal or are you going onto something new?" Max asks, placing two beers down in front of them.

"What the hell are you talking about?" Goebel says. "Why wouldn't we continue the investigation?"

"Didn't you guys hear?" smiles Max. "They got the guy. …He walked into the Tannersville Police Station and confessed to everything."

"Where the hell did you hear this?"

"Your boss, he came in about an hour ago. He's in a booth in the back." Max picks up the bowl of salted peanuts and moves them away from Benson.

"Damn…well, let's go see," Goebel says.

They find Captain Vega sitting in a booth in the backroom with two of his buddies. Two pitchers of beer, one already empty, sit in the center of the table, glasses all around.

"Hey, look what the cat dragged in! If it ain't the Rover Boys! Pull up a chair and join us," Vega says in an uncommonly friendly tone.

"What's this we hear – someone confessed to the Haywood case?" Goebel asks.

"Yeah, a guy walks into the Police Station in…what was the name of that hick town?" Vega snaps his fingers as he asks his pals.

"Tannersville…"

"Oh, yeah…Tannersville. …A guy walks in today, gives himself up, and confesses to everything."

"That's our case, Vega. How come we had to find this out from a bartender?" Benson demands.

"Relax…don't go jumping on my case. I just found out about it a little over an hour ago myself. Besides, Max is okay. …He probably knows more about what's going on at the station than we do." Vega bursts into laughter, so do his companions. Goebel and Benson are not laughing.

"So when do we get our hands on this guy?" Goebel asks.

"Tomorrow…they bring him to us tomorrow. I want you two to grill him. Get it all down on paper, signed nice and neat. The guy also gave up lots of physical evidence. Have Dodson run tests on everything. You sure you guys don't want to sit down?"

"Thanks, but no thanks," Benson says. The two detectives back away and return to their places at the bar.

"Say, Maxie, what happened to my peanuts?"

****

The Police Station at Tannersville was quiet for weeks, not that any real serious crime ever happens in Tannersville. They have their share of family spats, loud parties, drunk and disorderly cases, but nothing of any genuine, newspaper-headline crimes. And even such petty crimes have been few and far between lately. It has been quiet.

It is nearing the end of the workday at the station. Making their daily reports and preparing for the night crew are all three daytime officers – Sheriff Gibson, and Officers Wilson and Pearce.

Front door of the station opens and in walks a man carrying a shopping bag in one hand. He is wearing khaki pants, heavy work boots, and a thick flannel lumberjack shirt. But the one striking feature he's wearing is a black ski mask with yellow make-believe eyebrows and lips.

The three Police officers look up and catch sight of him all at the same time.

"Put your hands up and don't move," Sheriff Gibson shouts, taking his gun from his holster and pointing it at the man. The other two officers do the same.

"I've come to confess. I did it all," says the man.

"That's good. ....Now just listen to me. ....I want you to raise your hands slowly and place them on top of your head," says Sheriff Gibson.

The man follows their orders. In an instant, all three officers rush him, forcing him down to the floor and into handcuffs. They turn him over and pull the ski mask off his head – it is Victor Russell.

"Victor, what the hell are you doing, scaring us like this? Are you drunk?" the Sheriff asks.

"I've come to confess."

"And what do you have to confess…jaywalking?"

"I've come to confess to the rape and beating of two women…and murder. ...I committed murder…one woman and some guy in a gay bar."

"You taking to hanging out in gay bars, now, Victor?" Sheriff Gibson laughs sarcastically. "How about we toss you in the drunk tank overnight and let you sleep it off?"

"Don't be so hasty," says Officer Wilson. "Get a load of this!"

He empties the contents of the shopping bag onto the floor. There is a knife, pins, nails, a gun, a woman's dress soaked with blood, and a human ear.

"I told you…I want to confess." Victor has a solemn look on his face.

"You're sober, aren't you, Victor?" the Sheriff decides.

"Yes, sir, I am…though I wish I weren't, but I figure it best under the circumstances."

"Okay, boys," says Sheriff Gibson as he stands up. "Put him in the back cell. Let's get down to business; we've got a serious crime on our hands."

Nine

Is Everybody Happy?

Walter Lieberman drives into the parking lot. His excessively large luxury sedan takes up nearly two spaces, which is fine with Walter. That way, nobody parks near him – no door dings. He pulls up the front of his car mere inches from the wall of the building so no one can walk in front of his car.

Walter is in his late sixties with thinning white hair combed over his bald spot. His camel-hair coat covers his large gut. He bends low and looks in the mirror on the side of his car. Finding a hair out of place, he licks the small finger on his right hand, the one with the pinky ring, and pushes the strand flat to his head.

He walks to the front entrance of the restaurant and looks at the overhead sign – "Great Wall of China Buffet."

"God, how I hate Chinese Food…" Walter murmurs.

There is a sign in the window – "All you can eat $9.95." Walter just shakes his head in dismay.

Inside, he walks past the maître d' before the man can say a word. He finds Goebel and Benson sitting at their usual booth in the back.

"Why the hell do we always have to meet here? I hate Chinese food! Don't you know they make this crap with cat meat?"

"Meow!" purrs Goebel. Both officers laugh and continue eating. Walter has one of the waiters bring him a menu.

"I'll have that," he says, pointing his order out for the waiter.

"But, sir, that is children's platter," says the waiter, his Asian accent making every syllable count.

"I don't give a damn. That's what I want…a hot dog, macaroni and cheese, and French fries…good American food!"

The waiter walks off, shaking his head.

"So, do you two want to do this or do you want to stuff you faces with that dog food?"

"We're listening," Benson says, between bites.

"Well, first, I want it understood this meeting is off the record, and if anyone ever asks, this meeting never happened," Walter announces.

Goebel puts down a sparerib he is working on. "For Pete's sake, Walt, we've been doing this for how many years…twenty? We know the ground rules. Just tell us what you know."

"Well, I met with my client this morning. As you know, he refused to talk until given counsel from his appointed lawyer…yours truly. I believe he's ready to talk, but before I disclose anything he says in confidence, I'd like to know how much the police know."

"Not much more than you do," Benson says, putting his fork down. "Victor Russell walked into the Tannersville Police Station four days ago carrying a shopping bag filled with several incriminating items from the crime which the man confessed to. Mrs. Haywood, the woman he claims he raped, identified one of the items. …She recognized the ski mask as the one worn by her assailant. The bloody dress they identified as the one worn by Carol Hastings the night of her abduction. We checked the numbers on the gun found in the shopping bag. …It's registered to Tom Russell, the father of Mrs. Haywood…"

"That part puzzles me," Walter interrupts. "The gun was loaded with blanks…why were there blanks in the gun?"

"The gun was a gift to Mrs. Haywood by her father, but her husband took it from her and was in possession of it for nearly two weeks. He and his wife have been separated for some time now, and we suspect he substituted blanks for the bullets in hopes of leaving his wife defenseless to her assailant. But like I said, we suspect him of doing this. We have no proof…so we haven't called him on it, but we're keeping him under tight surveillance."

"What about lab tests?" Walter asks.

"We're still conducting tests. There are no fingerprints on any of the items. The blood on the dress is still undergoing tests, but we're reasonably sure it's Carol Hastings' blood. We're running tests on the ear, but again, we're thinking it is Carol Hastings'. And by the way, there are semen stains on Carol Hastings' undergarments…they're still being tested. But if I were a betting man, I'd bet the stains were made by your client. We'd like a blood sample to compare DNA to the stillborn caused by the rape of Mrs. Haywood. We're still waiting on a court order. When we get it, we're hoping all evidence points to Victor Russell."

"That's what we know," Goebel says, putting his fork down at the center of his now empty plate and pushing it toward the center of the table. "Now tell us what you know."

Just then, the waiter brings Walter's order. Walter waits until he is out of hearing range.

"Like I said, I met with Victor this morning; he's eager to talk. But I'll tell you one thing…after talking to him, the man's not right in the head. Get this, when I asked him why he cut off Carol Hastings' ear, he said she wouldn't listen, so he cut her ear off. When I asked him what he did with her body, he said he forgot. And here's the best part. He hears voices; he talks with his deceased father. …The man is nuts, I tell you."

"So, what are you telling us? You're going for an insanity plea?" Benson asks.

Walter takes a bite of his hot dog, spits it back out, and pushes his plate away.

"They probably use real dogs to make their franks," he says, wiping his mouth on his napkin.

"Forget the food," Goebel says. "Tell us what you know"

"I'll make a deal with you," Walter says. "I'll do everything in my power to help you get a conviction, but I want him examined by a physiatrist of my choosing. I want him committed. I'll be doing the world a favor if he gets put away. I tell you, he's a danger to himself and others. I just want the chance to prove it."

"Fair enough," Goebel says, "as long as we get a conviction."

"Don't worry…you will," Walter says.

"Fair enough," Benson says. "Let justice ring," he says handing the bill to Walter and walking away.

"He wants me there in the room when you interrogate him," Walter calls out.

Goebel stops and looks back. "I don't care if Santa Clause is in the room! I want his butt, and I want you to give it to us."

****

While at work, Helen receives an unexpected call – it is Richard.

"We need to talk," he says.

"Go ahead; I'm listening."

"Not this way, not on the phone. Meet me at the house."

With all her suspicions, Helen feels it unwise to be alone with him.

"No, I don't feel comfortable meeting you at the house…alone…not anymore. Why don't you come here to my office?"

"Gee, I suppose I should feel insulted."

"Don't play the martyr, Richard. Sackcloth and ashes doesn't become you. I'll block off three to four on my schedule. If you're serious, you'll be here."

She hangs up.

She assumes the office is a good choice. He will have to go through security to enter and exit the building. There will be no way he can cause any trouble.

One minute before three, Richard knocks on her door. He looks worn and haggard, as if he slept in his clothes. Only his eyes tell a different story. It's clear he hasn't been getting any sleep.

"Close the door behind you," she says coldly.

Richard sits down facing her.

"Well, you're the one who wanted to talk. So...talk."

There is no expression on Helen's face, or emotion in her voice.

Richard fumbles in his chair for a moment and looks down at the floor. Then, he sits up straight, lifts his head, and looks directly at Helen. He speaks as if he has found new conviction.

"I suppose the only thing to do now is to come right out and say it. I've fallen in love with Francis. I'm sorry, but I want a divorce."

"A divorce? I thought you wanted me dead..."

"I don't know where you get such nonsense."

"Oh...lots of different places...your girlfriend for one!"

"I heard about that; Francis told me all about it. She said the two of you were drunk and..."

"She was drunk! I wasn't drinking."

Richard pauses; a look of irritation comes over him. The moment passes; he shakes it off and continues.

"Whatever...Francis said some things that were easy to misinterpret...and you did."

"Misinterpreted...?" Helen laughs.

Resisting the urge to argue, Richard pushes down his anger and continues, "I realize you're upset; I don't blame you. I didn't plan to fall in love with Francis; it just happened. I would have told you sooner, but I wanted to spare you the pain of a divorce at this time."

"Richard, you're not only a martyr, but you're a saint, as well." Her words hang heavy with sarcasm.

She sits forward and directs her gaze at Richard's eyes. Her face once more goes cold as a marble slab.

"I'll tell you how I see it: you fall in love, so you say, with this...woman. You'd like to ask me for a divorce, but you don't want to part with half of everything we own together. The car, the house, the investments – you want it all...but how?

"Then one night, I'm raped and nearly killed. I don't think you had anything to do with that or what happened to Carol, but I'm sure now you did your best to leave me defenseless...hoping that madman would do the dirty work for you."

"Helen, what are you talking about? I gave you the gun back! If I wanted you harmed, would I have given you the gun back?"

"You gave it back to me, all right...after you exchanged the bullets for blanks!"

"You're out of your mind," he insists. "All this has made you paranoid."

"Paranoid...am I? Out of my mind...am I?" Helen stammers nervously, "I presume what happened to Angela was just a hallucination!"

"Some old dyke gets beat up in her garage, and because I had a few words with her, right away I get the blame!"

Helen stops and freezes for a moment. Her eyes become wide and hateful.

"I never told you what happened! There's no way you could know that! It was...it was you!" she says, horrified.

Richard says nothing; a look of sheer animal anger comes over his face. His lips grow thin as he grinds his teeth together. His chin goes up, and he looks down his nose with contempt at her.

"I used to think I loved you, Richard," she says, "but then again, I used to think I knew you. Well, I realize now I never truthfully knew you, so it's clear I no longer love you. Get out of here and get out of my life. You'll get your divorce and everything of value...you can have it all. ...I don't want it. You can have the car, the house, and the money. I don't want you to have any reason to hurt me or anyone I love. Get out of here!"

Richard says not a word; he just holds a cold, icy stare at her. He has the look of a wild beast as he gets up and walks to the door. Helen chose wisely; if they had not met at her office – if they had been alone – he would have attacked her. She knows it just by looking into his eyes.

"Fine..." he says, standing in the doorway. "I'll take your terms, and I'll leave you alone. But that's not going to stop him. Whoever he is, I hope he never stops until he kills you!"

Richard slams the door. Helen doesn't even flinch.

****

Angela sits up in bed, smiling when Helen enters her hospital room.

"Well, look at you," Helen says, smiling back. "You look so much better."

"I feel lots better, too. They say I can go home tomorrow. I can hardly wait to get back to work; this lying around is driving me crazy. You know it's true what they say about hospital food. I don't think I've had one meal that..." Angela stops midsentence. She can tell just by looking at Helen that something is not right. "Helen, what's wrong?"

Helen sits down near Angela.

"Angela, I've never forgotten all the help you've given me as my doctor, but I've also come to think of you as a good friend, and I hope you feel the same."

Angela nods.

"Because…" continues Helen, "I've done something I believe only a friend would do…at least, I thought it was the right thing to do at the time. But now I'm not sure. And if you're offended by what I've done, then it's going to take a good friend to forgive me."

"Forgive you? Helen, what are you talking about?" Angela is still smiling.

"The other night when I went to your house to get my things, something happened. I don't know how to say this…"

"Then just say it." Angela's face turns somber.

Helen moves her chair closer.

"You remember you told me someone was watching your house at nights. Well, it wasn't the man who beat you."

A questioning look comes over Angela's face.

"And you remember once you told me how you gave the baby up and how you had…"

Angela starts shaking her head back and forth. "No…no…I don't believe this. …This can't be happening!"

Helen tries to take hold of Angela's hand, but she snaps it away.

"After all these years…my God!"

"It was a boy," Helen says, joyfully. "Actually, he's no longer a boy. …He's a young man now. And Angela, he's so handsome! He has so many of your features! He was the one you saw from your window those nights. He's been hanging around like a lost puppy for days. I couldn't send him away, so I've let him stay at your place for the past two days. Please, don't be angry with me."

There are tears in her eyes. She looks at Helen. "I'm not mad at you. I'm just scared…no, I'm terrified. What can I say to him?"

"You're a physiatrist; you won't have any trouble."

"That's like saying, 'If you're a bartender you can never have a drinking problem.' I bleed just like everyone else! I don't have any magic phrases to get me through this. What can I tell him?"

"Tell him the truth; that's all you can do."

Angela raises one hand to her head and then the other to her face.

"My God, I look a fright! I'll scare the poor boy away!"

"Don't worry," Helen says, "We'll do your hair up real nice. Some makeup will cover up those burses."

"I haven't worn makeup since…since…" Angela begins to cry.

Since you were raped, Helen finishes the sentence gently in her own mind. "It's all right," smiles Helen, taking Angela's hand once more. "It'll all work out fine…you'll see."

****

Not surprisingly, Victor adjusts well to life behind bars. For the first time in a long time, he feels safe. Not having a drink is difficult for him. But at least he doesn't have to sleep with one eye open.

Early morning in his cell, Victor sits on the edge of his bunk, eating his breakfast of cold coffee, powdered eggs, and toast. He looks up to see a guard standing in front of the cell.

"Russell, your lawyer's here to see you," the guard speaks in an official monotone voice.

"But I haven't finished my breakfast."

"It's your breakfast and it's your lawyer, buddy; you decide which is more important. But if I were you, I would lean more toward the lawyer."

Victor scrapes up the powdered eggs and carefully places them on top of his slice of toast. He stands up, toast in hand, and grabs his paper cup of coffee. "I'll see my lawyer, please."

It is a stark room with two chairs and a plain wooden table in the middle. The guard sets Victor in the chair that's bolted to the floor and handcuffs him to the chair's arm. An overhead lamp with a protective wire grid hangs over the table, giving no more light than a full moon. It's just barely enough to light up the tabletop; there are no windows.

"I'll be just outside that door," the guard tells Walter Lieberman, pointing to the door. He then leaves, closing and locking the door behind him.

Seated at the table, facing Victor, Walter is busy going over papers with pen in hand. Victor is still busy with his breakfast, cup of cold coffee in one hand and egg on toast in the other.

"So, Victor, I've asked for court approval to have you analyzed by a physiatrist. …How do you feel about that?" Walter asks, putting down his paper and pen and finally paying some attention to his client.

"Why? I'm not crazy," Victor mumbles calmly, with a mouthful of toast and powdered eggs.

"Of course you're not, Victor. It's just a formality. Now, when you're talking to the doctor, I want you to make sure you tell him what you did and how your dead father told you what to do…how he talks to you in your head."

"He doesn't talk to me in my head!"

"How's that…?" Walter looks at his client, confused.

"He doesn't talk to me in my head. He comes and visits me, and then he tells me what he wants me to do."

"Whatever…" Walter whispers under his breath, taking his pen and making a note of the information.

"In fact, he came and visited me just yesterday." Victor finishes his egg and toast, takes a gulp of coffee and swallows. "He told me I was a good boy and he was proud of me."

"You mean, your father came into your cell and spoke to you?" Walter asks, putting his pen down.

"No, not in my cell, sir; you're not allowed visitors in your cell. He came by and we visited in this here room."

"Of course, what was I thinking?" Walter says. *This is going to be easier than I thought,* Walter thinks, smiling.

Victor puts down his coffee cup; Walter puts down his pen.

"You should be set up with an analysis in two days."

"Yeah, sure," Victor says. "Listen, I don't want to appear rude or anything, but I'm allowed an hour of TV every day, and I wouldn't want to miss it. You don't mind if I go back now?"

"Of course not. We wouldn't want you to miss your shows, now…would we?" Walter smiles, gets up from the table, and signals for the guard. "We're through here, thank you."

As they guide Victor back to his cell, Walter gives him one last word of advice, "You just hang in there, Victor, and I promise you everything is going to turn out just fine."

Victor nods, more concerned with missing his TV time.

This is going to be so easy, Walter thinks.

He stops at the guard desk and smiles.

"Say…did Victor Russell have any visitors, yesterday?"

"I'm not sure, sir, but I could look it up," the guard says, pointing to the computer.

"Nah, that's all right…thanks though." Walter walks away, smiling. "I must be getting soft in the head…believing what some loony tells me. Next thing you know, he'll have me talking to his dead father, too."

Ten

Too Many Chefs in the Kitchen

Dodson walks down the block toward Max's tavern. He is regretting his promise to meet Goebel and Benson after hours. There are sure to be people in the bar – maybe too many people – and people only make him uncomfortable.

"Hey, Dodson, I didn't know they allowed you out of the basement before dark," Max jokes from behind the bar when he sees Dodson standing in the doorway. "If you're looking for Goebel and Benson, they're over there in the booth by the window."

"Thanks, Maxie," Dodson says, making his way across the barroom. He is thankful and relieved to see there are only a small handful of patrons in Max's.

A waitress is putting two beers down on the table when Dodson takes a seat across from his two associates.

"What will it be?" asks the waitress, between snapping her chewing gum – which irritates Dodson to no end.

"A Pink Squirrel, please."

Benson looks at him through squinted eyes and a pouting mouth.

"What?" Dodson says, shrugs his shoulders, "I like cream drinks."

Benson shakes his head in disbelief. Goebel pulls his beer in close and waits until the waitress leaves.

"So what do you have for us?" Goebel asks.

"Some new pieces to the puzzle, only I don't think these pieces are going to fit anywhere in the big picture," Dodson says, opening a manila folder in front of him. "First off, the gun is the same gun registered to Mrs. Haywood's father...the one he lent her...the one her husband withheld from her. There are no fingerprints on it except for those of Mrs. Haywood, and they're a bit smudged. Whoever had it last wiped it clean...real clean. The blanks that were in the gun cylinder were clean also. Blanks are not like live ammo; you don't have to register to buy them, which make them hard to trace. They're usually used as starting guns at sporting events. The company that makes them won't ship out an order unless the request comes on a legitimate letterhead...you know, high schools, colleges, sports arenas. There might be a lead in there somewhere.

"The ski mask was a match to the gloves we found around the neck of the dead cat, made by the same Swiss/Italian company, the one that went out of business in the '60s.

"The human ear is from Carol Hastings; we're sure of it. It matches the blood on the dress, as well. Also, tests show that the knife in Victor Russell's possession when arrested is the same knife used to cut off her ear. There are no prints on the blade except his, and I found traces of her blood on all the sharp items in the shopping bag."

The waitress places Dodson's drink down. Benson looks on it with loathing and distain. The waitress walks away.

"And finally, the last piece of the puzzle. I did some tests on the bloody dress against medical records. . . . It was Carol Hastings'. Next, I did a blood test on Victor Russell and compared it to the semen stains on Carol Hastings' undergarments. . . . It was a match. Then, I compared Victor's blood with the sample taken from Mrs. Haywood's stillborn, and the match was close. . . it looked like he could be the father."

"Looks like? Very close? He could be the father? What the hell are you talking about?" Goebel demands.

"This isn't an exact science! Nothing's a hundred percent. You do a DNA test and you get ten positives out of a million. . . . That's pretty good odds. His DNA showed there was a fair chance Victor might be the father. . . . That's the best I can offer you."

"Well, maybe you made a mistake. Maybe you need to do the test again?" Benson says.

"That's exactly what I thought," Dodson replies. "And that's what I did. I ran another test on the semen stains on the undergarments, only this time I took a sample from another part of the garment, and what I found confused the hell out me."

Dodson stops to sip on his drink.

"For Pete's sake, put down that pink slosh and tell us what the hell you found," Goebel hollers.

"Well, when I ran the new test, the DNA matched the dead baby's samples but it didn't match Victor's blood sample."

"I don't get it," Goebel says, "What the hell are you telling us?"

"I'm telling you there are two different semen samples on Carol Hastings' underwear! One is Victor Russell's; the other is somebody else. And whoever he is, he's the father of the dead baby and the man who raped Mrs. Haywood."

"You mean, two guys came on Carol Hastings' panties. . .at the same time?" Benson says, sounding nauseated to his stomach.

"It would seem so," Dodson says.

"That's sick..." Goebel says.

Dodson takes another sip from his glass, places it back down, and then continues.

"I ran the entire test again...just to make sure, but I was right. Reason I wasn't sure at first was because the DNA was so similar. I would say the two men...Victor and your mystery man are blood relatives...most likely brothers."

"But the report on Victor shows his brother died years ago in a car accident," Benson says.

"Maybe we should get in touch with the authorities in...what's the name of that hick town?" Goebel asks.

"Tannersville," Benson answers.

"Maybe we should get in touch with Tannersville and recheck the records?"

"Oh, and another thing," Dodson adds, "The voice test on Richard Haywood doesn't match the voice on the answering machine. And before you two ask me, I took the liberty of getting a court order to test Victor's voice against the voice on the answering machine."

"And...?" Benson asks.

"It's not his voice either."

****

Goebel and Benson dread a return visit to the Velvet Hammer, but the cruel and senseless shooting of Donald Johnson is a key part of their investigation. And now with a confessed prime suspect, it is time to go back.

They phone ahead to be sure Tink will be bartending. He bursts into greeting when they approach the bar.

"I knew you two would be back. Decided to try the gay life?"

"No! I'll have you know, my partner and I are both happily married," Goebel says.

"What...to each other?" Tink explodes into laughter.

"No, wise guy...to our wives!"

"Well, you know, you won't be the first guys to hang out here with that same affliction. So how can I help you, detective?"

"Just a few questions," Benson says, "if you don't mind?"

"I don't have enough mind left to mind!" laughs Tink. "Say, how's your investigation going?"

"About as well as expected," Goebel says, taking his place on a barstool. "We talked with Donald Johnson's neighbors, friends and coworkers. ...They all say the same: 'He didn't have an enemy in the world.' Everything points to a stranger he must have picked up here."

"That's the trouble with one-night stands," Tink says, "If they don't break your heart, they shoot you in the head!" He goes into another fit of laughter. Not finding any humor in murder, both detectives remain aloof.

From his topcoat pocket, Benson produces a mugshot of Victor Russell. He hands it to Tink.

"Take a look at this. Tell us if he looks familiar to you."

Tink looks at it for no more than a second.

"Hell, yeah, I remember this dude. I never forget a weirdo. . . . They haunt my dreams.

"He came in one night…never seen him before. …He plants himself up against the jukebox, and he stares at everybody. He doesn't dance…just nursed one drink all night…hardly talked. …He just stared. Did that every night for about a week, and then he disappeared. …Never seen him again. The guy gave me the creeps!"

"This wouldn't have all happened the week of the Donald Johnson killing?" Benson asks.

Tink thinks for a minute.

"Now that you mention it, I think it was the same week. I guess I never connected the two, but I believe you're right."

"Do you think Donald might have been involved with this guy?" Goebel asks.

"I told you I don't think the guy said more than two words the entire week he was here. And as for Donald, I told you I saw him here that night, but I never saw who he was with or when he left."

Tink hands the photo back to Benson.

"So who's the guy in the picture?" Tink asks.

"Just a guy…" Benson says.

"That must be an old Army picture or something like that, huh?" Tink asks.

"What do you mean?"

"I mean, that must be an old picture of the dude."

"Why do you say that?"

"Well, because that picture must be at least twenty years old. That's the same guy, all right, but he's not so young anymore. I mean…his hair is gray now, and he's got himself a good-sized gut. Nothing's so big a turn off as a big old gut on a man, don't you think?"

Goebel and Benson look at each other, confused.

"Well, thank you again. You've been a big help," Benson says.

The two detectives start toward the door.

"So long, you two," Tink calls out. "Come back anytime you like. Don't forget…every Friday and Saturday night is all you can eat."

"You have a buffet?" asks Goebel.

"A buffet? Who said anything about food?"

Outside, they hear Tink's laughter.

Eleven

Getting Reacquainted

"Tannersville Police Department, Officer Wilson speaking. How may I help you?"

Sheriff Gibson is on his way back to his office when he hears the call come in. He hovers over Officer Wilson's desk, listening.

"Yes, sir…I understand," says Officer Wilson, "I think it would be best if you spoke with Sheriff Gibson. …One moment. I'll see if he's in." Officer Wilson covers the phone receiver with his hand. "It's a Detective Benson. …He wants to get some info on Victor Russell. …You want to talk to him?"

"I'll take it in my office."

Officer Wilson removes his hand from the receiver. "The Sheriff will be right with you, sir. Please hold." He presses the transfer button and hangs up.

Sheriff Gibson places his hat on the hat rack by the door, sits down behind his desk, takes up the phone to his ear, leans back in his chair, and places his feet up on the desk.

"Sheriff Gibson here. Can I help you?"

"Sheriff, this is Detective Benson, one of the officers working on the Victor Russell case. I was hoping to get some more information."

"Didn't we send you a full report when we sent Victor to you?"

"Yes, sir, you did…thank you. …It was very helpful, but we were wondering if we could get some information on the suspect's family sent over, please?"

"Well, heck, ain't any reason for somebody to mail something and waste a stamp. I've lived in this town all my life, and I've been Sheriff here since Victor was a little boy. I could probably answer your questions. …Ask away."

Well, sir," Benson says, "we've been having some concerns about his father and his brother."

"Concerns…what's all the concern about? They're both dead…been dead for years," says Sheriff Gibson. "Jerry…Victor's father died about the time his two boys were going into high school. Nicholas, his brother, died in a car crash. …Real nasty business."

"Can you tell me something about the father…about Jerry Russell?"

"Jerry? Jerry was a good ole boy. He and I knew each other since grade school. Everybody liked Jerry. He always willingly gave of his time for civic duties, especially when it came to boys' sports at the high school. He died of a heart attack on vacation with his wife in Europe. By the way, I wouldn't go calling his widow about any of this. Poor woman had a stroke a few years back, and she ain't been much good to anybody since. …Knocked her porch light out, if you know what I mean?"

"We have it on report that when her husband died, she had him cremated in Europe?" Benson asks.

"That's right. …Seems it was a heck cheaper than shipping the body back to the states."

"So you never saw the body?"

"I saw an urn full of ashes, if that's what you mean."

"And Nicholas…Victor's brother?"

"When their father died, the two of them boys got pretty wild. Nicholas, I'd say, was the worst. He'd always be racing around town in his car, half the time high on something. Well, one night, he pushed his luck too far. He slammed into a light post, and the car exploded into flames."

"And, you got to see the body?"

"Sure did! It was black as a piece of burned toast and just about as crispy."

"Then, how did you know it was Nicholas Russell?"

"Well, for one, it was Nicholas' car … and anyway, the body was identified."

"By whom?"

"Why, the brother, of course."

"Why the brother? Why not the mother?"

"You can't expect a mother to look on her child looking the way he was…like…like a used matchstick."

"What were the results of the autopsy?"

"Autopsy? For what? The boy looked like a burned marshmallow that fell off the stick and landed in the campfire. Weren't no reason for no autopsy."

Benson goes silent for a moment, thinking.

"Are you still there?" Sheriff Gibson asks.

"Yes, Sheriff, I'm still here. One last question, please. This is going to sound a bit crazy. But do you think it's possible, since both bodies were in a condition difficult to identify…do you think it's possible either Victor's father or brother might still be alive?"

Sheriff Gibson lets out a long, hard belly laugh. "You're right, boy. It does sound crazy. But, I'll tell you, if either one of them are still living, they sure as hell haven't been doing that living here in Tannersville!"

"This is ridiculous! There's no need for all this fuss. I can walk myself out, thank you." Angela complains, sitting in a wheelchair.

"Spoken like a true patient," laughs the nurse. "You know hospital policy as well, if not better, than I do, Angela. So just relax and enjoy the ride."

The automatic front-door opens, and the nurse wheels Angela out to the curb. Helen is waiting in front of her parked car.

"See? That wasn't so bad," says the nurse. She then turns to Helen. "She may be a wonderful doctor, but she is by far a terrible patient."

"I just hope you never have to go through it," Angela remarks, getting out of the wheelchair.

"If I do, I just hope I get a nurse as sweet as me," laughs the nurse.

Angela sits in the front passenger seat of Helen's car. She lowers the window, and smiles at the nurse.

"Despite all my bitching, I do appreciate all you've done for me, and I thank you very much."

"Don't mention it," says the nurse with a smile. "All in a day's work. When will you be coming back to work?"

"Monday…I'll be back Monday."

"See you then." She waves as Angela raises her window and the car pulls away.

They take the main highway toward the Madison District.

"Gee, you're driving so fast. What's the speed limit?" Angela is digging her fingernails into her own knees.

"Will you relax?" laughs Helen. "I've never seen you like this."

"It's just…I'm scared." Angela shakes her head in dismay. "What if he doesn't like me? What if he hates me?"

"Calm down. He's probably just as nervous as you are right now, thinking the same exact things. If you don't calm down, you'll scare each other to death."

"Do I look all right?" Angela is taking stock of herself in the car visor mirror.

"You look just fine; stop worrying."

Angela goes silent. She gazes out her window at the world quickly passing by, each mile bringing her closer to a meeting with her son, the child she never knew.

Helen walks into the house first, and Angela follows coyly close behind. They find Thomas in the living room, sitting on the divan by the window. He jumps up and stands at attention. There is a long and uncomfortable silence as Angela and Thomas just stand staring at each other.

"I suppose introductions are in order," Helen says, standing between the two of them. "Angela, this is Thomas. . . . Thomas, this is Angela."

Thomas takes a step forward.

"I'm not sure what I'm supposed to do," he says. "Do we hug or just shake hands?"

"I guess we can start with a handshake and see where that leads," Angela says, offering him her hand.

"It's a pleasure finally to meet you," he says.

"Yes, it is. . .I mean. . .it's a pleasure to meet you, too." Angela is staring, taking all his features in at once.

"Well, I best be going," Helen says, turning toward the door.

"Oh, must you?" Angela says, nervously. "Can't you stay for just a little while?"

Helen looks at the two of them and smiles. "No, I need to go, really."

Helen places her hand on the doorknob and looks back once more, smiling.

"Thank you, Helen. Thank you for everything," Angela calls out to her.

"Don't mention it. . . . All in a day's work."

"So. . .?" Angela says, timidly turning to Thomas.

"So. . .?" he echoes.

"Sit. . .please." She motions him back onto the divan and takes a chair facing him.

"Helen told me you drove over a thousand miles to get here," Angela says, trying to engage some small talk.

"Yes. . .I have to get back soon. . .for work. I'm afraid I'll be leaving early in the morning."

Angela thinks for a moment.

"That's too bad," she says. "Perhaps, since it's such a long drive. . .if you're tired. . .we could do this at another time?"

"No. . .I've waited a long time for this." His voice has the sound of a pleading urgency.

"So have I," Angela says softly.

"I don't think I could sleep now, even if I tried. Besides, I've got so much to ask you. . .so much I want to know." His eyes speak of sorrow. "It won't be the first night I've spent without sleep."

"Nor mine," Angela says to herself as well as him.

She rises from her chair. "It seems we have a long night ahead of us. This calls for a big pot of coffee. Do you like coffee?"

He smiles at her. "It's my fav!"

Twelve

God's Lips

The interrogation room is wired for sound; every word is recorded. There is a large dark-wood table with chairs in the center of the room and a two-way mirror along one wall with no one on the other side. The room is dim save for a desk lamp on the table.

"Now, Victor, you understand everything you say is being recorded?" Benson warns.

Victor nods an affirmative.

"No, Victor, it's a tape recording. You can't just nod your answer; you have to state your answers loud and clear. Again, Victor, you understand everything you say is being recorded?"

"Yes, I do."

"And we are in the presence of your lawyer, Mr. Lieberman, who also knows that this is being recorded?"

"Yes, I do," says Lieberman.

"Now, Victor, let's start at the beginning. What is your relationship with Mrs. Helen Haywood?"

"Why...she's my cousin," says Victor, sounding a bit put off, as if it is an unnecessary waste of time to state the obvious.

"Your cousin, you say. ...In what way?"

"My father and her father are brothers." Victor sounds more put off.

"Have you ever had sexual relationships with Mrs. Haywood, your cousin?"

Victor looks to his lawyer who gives him a nod to answer.

"Yes...once when we were very young and a few months ago when I raped her."

"You say the first time was when you were both young. How young were you?"

"Oh, I don't know. ...She was maybe nine or ten. So, I guess that would make me thirteen or fourteen."

"And, what were the circumstances of this first time?"

"I don't know. ...It was a long time ago. It was at some lake. The family was having a picnic at some lake. My brother and father were with me and..."

"Was it a common practice for you, your bother, and your father to have sex with young girls?" Goebel interrupts.

"No, that was the first and only time."

"I thought you said it was the first time. How many more times was there?"

"I'm not sure. I don't remember."

"But you did have an ongoing sexual relationship with your brother and your father?" Goebel presses the issue strongly.

Victor goes silent for a moment.

"I don't understand what you mean."

"I repeat...did you have sexual relations with your brother or your father?" Goebel demands.

Victor becomes flustered. "What do you mean by sexual relations?"

"Okay, Victor, let me spell it out for you. Did you...with your brother or father...at any time...take your clothes off...and while naked...touch, fondle, or caress one another?"

Victor looks as if his head is about to explode; he looks to his lawyer for advice who again nods to answer.

"Yeah...I guess so...something like that happened."

"You 'guess so'...'something like that happened'? We need a straight answer, Victor. Were you and your brother molested by your father or not?"

"Yes...damn you...yessss!" Victor slams his fist down on the table.

"Was it all touching, or was there oral contact...was there any penetration?"

"I told you yes! What more do you want to know? What good are details now?" Victor sounds drained of all energy.

"Okay...okay...take it easy, Victor. Tell us about the time at the beach with your cousin, Helen."

"I told you it was too long ago. We were all naked..."

"Who was naked?"

"Me...my brother...my father...Helen. ...My father made Nicholas and I do some stuff to each other and then Helen. I don't know if we were too young or too scared, but we couldn't...my brother and I couldn't penetrate her. My father made us hold her down while he had her."

"Then you're saying you helped your father rape her?"

"Something like that."

"'Something like that'? Yes or no, Victor!"

Victor looks to his lawyer for guidance, but Lieberman is ecstatic by the way things are going. With this interrogation recording, he will have the jury crying for the judge to show mercy. *Ladies and gentlemen of the jury...yes, Victor Russell committed these crimes! But in light of his tortured past, how could any of us not show pity on him? From such a perverted childhood, how could you expect any other outcome? Victor Russell is as much a victim as any of his accusers,* Lieberman rehearses his speech in his mind.

"All right, Victor...just calm down. We're your friends. We don't want to hurt you. We want to help you."

Victor lowers his head, he looks up at them, his eyes tired and exhausted.

"So, that was the only time...with a girl...at the beach?"

Victor nods.

"We need you to answer, Victor."

"Yes...yes...yes!"

Goebel and Benson look at each other; they know they have him on the run.

"Tell us how you raped your cousin, Mrs. Haywood."

"I told you, it was my father...at the beach."

"No...not the time at the beach...years later."

Victor runs his hands over his face, trying to clear his thoughts.

"I waited for her...where she works. I hid behind her car."

"Why then, Victor? You don't see Helen for years, and then suddenly you decided to travel all the way to the big city to rape your cousin. We don't get it, Victor. Why?"

"It a long story...you won't understand."

"Try us," Goebel says.

Victor goes silent.

"Why did you wear a ski mask and gloves?"

"I didn't want her to recognize me. ....That's why I put dark makeup around my eyes, so she would think I was black."

"She hadn't seen you in how many years? And you were afraid she'd recognize you?"

"Not recognize me. ...I meant...have a description of me."

"Did you know she became pregnant that night?"

Victor looks at the two detectives, wide-eyed. "No...I didn't." He sounds sincerely moved by this information.

"Don't worry; she lost the baby before birth."

"That's a shame," says Victor.

"So after you raped and beat your cousin, you ran off. Why didn't you kill her?"

"I'm not a murderer!" There is anger in Victor's eyes.

"No...you're not a murderer? Then tell us about Donald Johnson."

"Oh…the black guy in the gay club. I didn't mean for it to happen that way. I figured, with all the investigation, if I could get some stuff from a black guy on the panties, it would confirm that whoever did it was black."

"So why did you kill him?"

"We were in his car…after he…I started to wipe him up with the panties. He started to freak out, so I shot him."

"Which bring us to the twenty-four thousand dollar question: how did you come in possession of the gun?"

"I can't tell you that…not yet."

Goebel and Benson exchange glances again.

"Okay, Victor, forget that for now. What about Carol Hastings, Mrs. Haywood's assistant?"

Victor grows silent again.

"Why did you take Carol Hastings, and where did you bring her?"

Victor begins to shake his head back and forth.

"You know your blood type doesn't match the blood of Mrs. Haywood's stillborn. …That means you can't be the rapist!"

"We found your semen stain on Carol Hastings' underwear, but there was someone else's semen next to yours. Who's your accomplice? Who are you covering for?"

"Stop it…stop it…! I told him this wouldn't work! It's too much information for one person to keep track of. I told him this wouldn't work!" cries Victor.

"That's it. …This investigation is over right this minute." Lieberman jumps from his chair. "Stop the recording! I want to talk to one of you two outside," Lieberman says to Goebel and Benson, and then storms out of the interrogation room.

Goebel follows him out into the hallway. "Walt, what the hell are you doing?"

"I was just about to ask you the same thing!" Lieberman points his finger at Goebel's face. "I thought we worked this all-out. I was going to help you get a confession and a conviction in exchange for an insanity plea!"

"What the hell do you think we were just doing?" Goebel tries to keep his voice and his anger down.

"I don't know, you tell me! I thought this was all going to be cut-and-dried, but suddenly we've got other things in the mix. Why wasn't I told about the blood and semen tests and the possibility of an accomplice?"

"We only just found out about this. . . . There wasn't time. We're on your side, Walt. Nobody wants to go around your back," Goebel pleads. "Just tell us what you want and we'll make it happen."

Lieberman takes a deep breath and calms down.

"Well, for one, I don't want to continue without Victor being examined by a psychiatrist. We both know the guy is buggy, but I want it on paper that he is. Once I got that, I don't care what you ask him or what direction you want to take this."

"It's a deal," Goebel says.

"I'll call you and let you know who and when," says Lieberman.

"Now, I've got one demand to make, as well," Goebel adds. "I want the doctor's examination done here in this same room, and I want the tape recorder going. I want it all to go on record as just another part of the investigation, and I want to make sure it's admissible in court."

"You took the words right out of my mouth. I'll call you early tomorrow." Lieberman starts down the hall.

Goebel walks back inside the interrogation room. "Well, that about winds everything up for today. It's back to the cell for you, Victor."

Benson rises from his chair, walks over to the far corner of the room, and motions for Goebel to approach him.

"Lieberman wants Victor looked at by a doctor," Goebel whispers low enough so Victor can't hear. "I told him it was okay, as long as we get to tape it."

"Well, whatever we do, we better do it soon," Benson says. "This guy isn't going to standup to much more of this."

Goebel looks over at Victor. "Yeah, he does look pretty spooked."

"I think he's about to crack up," Benson says. "Which, as you know, can be a good thing or a bad thing...depending on the timing. If we get him when he's just about to crack, he'll spill his guts, but if he goes over the edge, he's useless."

"Yeah, I think you're right. We've got to make sure the doctor gets to the point we want him to and no further. There's ways to get that done. . . .We've done it before." Goebel turns from Benson toward Victor, "Back to the cell, Victor. It's TV time."

****

Early morning sunlight pours golden into the kitchen; the coffee turned cold hours ago. If only Angela can hold back the dawn, if only she can have her son stay for just a few minutes longer, but the earth turns without giving apologizes.

"It's morning," Angela says, stating the obvious. "Would you like more coffee? How about breakfast? I could…"

"No, thank you. I need to get going. I've got such a long drive home," Thomas says. "I'll just go get my stuff."

"I'll make some sandwiches to take with you," Angela calls out to him.

"That would be nice," he replies, disappearing into the bedroom.

Angela's hands are shaking as she makes up the sandwiches. *Now's not the time to break down*, she says to herself. *I won't make a scene!*

But in her heart, she is crying. She wants so badly to run to him, throw her arms around him, and beg his forgiveness. To hold him close and cherish him, to never let him hurt or want again, to make up for so many lost years. Has he forgiven her? She tried so hard to explain the past, but is it enough to make up for a lifetime of never being there. Has he learned enough to hate her, or worse, enough to never want to see her again? She can never bear that, not after seeing him, not after hearing his voice. It is better to be hated than forgotten.

She puts the sandwiches in a paper bag, and then takes a deep breath, trying to calm herself. She puts a smile on her face. If this is the last time they see each other, he will not have to carry the memory of a pitiful woman with him for the rest of his life.

"I'm ready." Thomas is standing at the doorway with his overnight bag.

"Here, nothing special, just ham and cheese," she says. "Come on, I'll walk you out."

Outside, his car looks out of place in such a well-off neighborhood. It is old, the paint is fading, and a collection of dirty clothes cover the backseat. He opens the car door and tosses his overnight bag in the back and turns to Angela.

"I wish I didn't have to go. It's been…" He stops in mid-sentence. "Oh, heck, I don't know what to say. I had a speech all planned out, but now I don't even remember the first word."

"Maybe it's one of those moments in life where nothing needs to be said. Maybe words are not what are needed?" Angela says, surprised at her own wisdom.

"Could I have that hug now?" It was clear he is holding back so much.

"I thought you'd never ask." Angela extends her arms, and he falls into them like a trapeze artist landing into a net with his eyes closed.

She holds him so tightly; she wants her arms and hands to always remember what he feels like. She inhales long and deep, wanting the smell of him to go deep into her lungs and rest there – to be able to recall his scent whenever she misses him. And she will miss him.

He straightens up and slowly backs away. "I really do have to go," he says as he makes his way into the front seat. He turns the key and the rusty old motor turns over one more time. His window is down. Angela reaches out and takes his hand.

"I've got your phone number," he says, "and you have mine. . . .I don't want this to be the end of it."

"Neither do I."

"I'll call you. . . .Maybe you'll come visit me next time?" He puts the car into drive.

Angela feels as if her heart is leaving her body.

"I'll call you when I get home," he says as he pulls away. "Thanks for everything, Mom!"

She stands there, watching the car go off into the distance. She stands there after there is nothing left to see or say. He called her *Mom*, and the word feels as if the lips of God rest on her forehead in a gentle kiss.

Thirteen

Top of the City

Tannersville is just a small backwoods town, but a person has to have a lot on the ball to be elected sheriff year after year, as Sheriff Gibson has. He is dedicated, smart, personable, and he makes the townspeople feel safe. But to most city folk, Sheriff Gibson comes across as just another country bumpkin, and he knows it. Often, he will use this to his advantage. Many times, a criminal looks back to see if old Sheriff Gibson is on his trail only to see nothing, because Sheriff Gibson is usually a couple of steps ahead of them.

The phone call from Detective Benson disturbs him. For days he thinks of little else. He keeps going over and over in his mind the night they found Nicholas Russell dead, if that's what really happened? The phone call floods his mind with doubt. Had he missed something?

And then there is his memory of Jerry Russell's funeral. There had been no body, just an urn full of ashes. He accepted and believed, as everyone else in Tannersville, that Jerry had been cremated in Europe – there was no reason to suspect otherwise.

Late that night, while lying in bed next to his wife, he questions her on the subject. He shares nearly everything with his wife. Over years, Rita developed a keen sense of the criminal mind, as well as powerful intuition and just plain good sense. He respects and relies on her opinions.

"What a weird thing to ask, 'Do you think Jerry or Nicholas Russell are still alive?' What did you answer him?"

"What do you think I said? I just laughed it off, but now he's got me thinking. I mean...no one ever did see Jerry's body, and Nicholas was nothing more than a cinder."

"As I see it," says his wife, "the question isn't *how* someone could do such a thing and get away with. ...The question is *why*. If Jerry Russell faked his death, what would be the reason to do so?"

"Well, for one, insurance. His wife, Eleanor, did well for herself when he died. Maybe they split the money? Who knows, maybe Jerry stayed in Europe?"

"And what about Nicholas?" Rita asks.

"I can't think of a reason." He shakes his head.

"You need to check insurance records on him also," she says. "But first, you know who you need to talk to? Old Doc Miller – he oversaw both cases for the state. You should talk to him."

"Not a bad idea," he admits.

"Besides, it's been months since you drove out to see him. Since his retirement, he looks forward to seeing all his old friends. It would do you both good to chew the fat together."

"You're right. I think I'll head out to Doc's place after lunch tomorrow."

****

The drive out to the Millers' place takes a little more than fifteen minutes from downtown Tannersville.

Doc Miller bought the property and the old house years ago for a song, with the intent he and his wife, Grace, could spend their golden years there together. The house was what most folks call a fixer-upper; it was in great need of repair. For years, Doc spent all his holidays, vacations, and free time working on the old place. Now three years into his retirement, it is still a work in progress.

Sheriff Gibson parks and looks around. Doc has done wonders with the place – it is a fine spread, indeed.

"Land sakes, Sheriff Gibson!" exclaims Grace as she pushes the screen door open. "Haven't seen you in a coon's age! What…you come here to arrest old Doc?" she says, jokingly.

"No, not this time…" He smiles up the porch stairs at her.

"Too bad. …The old goat could probably use a little excitement…get his blood stirring! Lord knows a pretty face don't do it for him anymore." She strikes a pose like a fashion model. "He's around back puttering in the garden. Why don't you go surprise him? I'll bring both of you some lemonade."

"Good to see you, Doc," says Sheriff Gibson as he turns the corner of the house.

Doc is leaning most of his weight on a tall shovel, surveying his backyard.

"Damn rabbits…damn those rabbits! I put poison out, and I swear it just gives them an appetite…kind of like a hors d'oeuvre!" He turns to see Sheriff Gibson and his face lights up with surprise. "Well, if it ain't Sheriff Dave Gibson! Good to see you. Hell, I thought you was dead."

"No, at least, not yet," laughs the Sheriff. "You're looking fit, though."

"Fit? Hell, I'm on my last leg! Of course, I'll still outlive you. …You look terrible! Here, sit down and give me an update on all the local gossip."

The two sit at a round patio table. Grace brings out a tray holding three tall glasses of ice and a pitcher of cold lemonade. After serving, she sits down also.

Sheriff Gibson enlightens them both on all the local talk going around town, which leads to the subject of Victor Russell.

"I know," Grace says. "We read about it in all the papers. Poor boy...must have gone mad to do all those horrible things."

"That's really what I came here for, Doc: to ask you what you remember about the deaths of Jerry and Nicholas Russell. Seems some city detective suspects one or both of them may still be alive."

"I can't see how that could be," Doc says. "I checked Nicholas' dental records myself. That charred body was definitely Nicholas Russell."

"What about Jerry?"

"What about him? His ashes were sent back home with all the right paperwork. I signed the receiving papers myself."

"Do you think it's possible," the Sheriff asks, "the documents could have been tampered with?"

Old Doc makes a fist and gently taps the Sheriff on the forehead. "Hello...is there anyone at home? What...were you born yesterday? You've been in law enforcement for how long, and you're asking me if it's possible to pay off a government official to falsify documents?"

Sheriff Gibson can't help laughing when he realizes the foolishness of the question.

"But why would Jerry Russell fake his own death? That is...providing this fantasy is true."

"Insurance money," answers the Sheriff.

"Maybe so," says Doc, "but that was a long time ago. If he were still alive, someone would have seen him eventually, unless he's been living under a rock."

"That pretty much sums up my feelings on the matter, too," says Sheriff Gibson, getting up from his seat. "Well, thanks for the drink; but I do need to get back to work."

"Wait one minute, Sheriff," says Doc. He turns to his wife, "Grace, go inside and get my camera."

Sheriff and Grace both look at him, questioningly.

"I just want to take your picture for a keepsake. Seeing how, I'll probably never see you again."

"No...I promise...I'll be back for a visit real soon."

"You're just afraid of getting your butt whipped at chess again," says Old Doc.

"That's not the way I remember it, but I'll take that as a direct challenge! I'll just have to come back and teach you what-for," declares Sheriff Gibson.

"Good!" smiles Grace.

***

Helen looks at the wall clock. At three in the afternoon, the project she is working on is only half complete. It will be another late night at the office for her.

She spins around in her chair from her computer to her phone, when she hears it ring.

"Helen Haywood speaking."

"*Bonjour, chérie…*"

As expected, the slightest mummer of a foreign word sends cold shivers all through Helen. But in the next instant, she knows it isn't him. The voice sounds much too friendly.

"Who is this?"

"It's me…Kyle Adams. You said to give you a call if I were ever in town. Well…I'm here!"

"Kyle, you took me off guard. I wasn't expecting to hear from you so soon."

"Neither did I, but something unexpected came up."

"Where are you staying?" she asks.

"I'm here at the Durham Hotel."

"Oh…the Durham," she says, sounding impressed.

"Yeah, only the best," he says, jokingly. "Say, they've got one of the swankest restaurants in town on the top floor; it's got a great view of the city. Why don't you come over and have dinner with me? I'd really like to see you." He puts a soft whispering emphasis on the last sentence.

Helen is silent, as she looks at the pile of work on her desk.

She shakes her head. *I'll just have to come in early in the morning*, she thinks.

"So, what do you say?" Kyle asks.

"Kyle…there's something you need to understand. My husband and I have separated, and we're sure to divorce soon, but it doesn't mean I'm looking to start up with someone. If anything, I'm a bad candidate for such things right now."

"We're talking just a friendly dinner…no strings attached," Kyle replies.

She thinks for a moment.

"Okay, but I've got some work to finish first. I won't be able to get there till…" She is going to say seven, and then she remembers she has on her business suit, hardly fitting for a romantic rendezvous – "nine o'clock…is that all right?"

"Nine o'clock it is! I'll be counting the minutes."

Helen puts down the phone and looks at her workload once more.

"Heck with it," she says out loud as she shuts down her computer and grabs her purse.

****

It has been a long time since Helen had a reason to get dressed up. Walking across the hotel lobby and passing the front desk, she feels all eyes on her. It is a good feeling to know she can still turn heads.

"Good evening, Ms. Haywood," says the concierge.

Helen giggles, clearly taken by surprise. "How do you know my name?"

"Monsieur Adams described you to a tee…although I believe his description, though complimentary, does not do you justice."

Helen feels a hot blush coming on.

"Monsieur Adams asked me to tell you he waits for you at our Top of the City restaurant, which is atop the hotel. The express elevator is down this hall to your left."

"Thank you," she says, making her way in the direction he points.

In the express elevator, Helen finds only two buttons – one marked "Lobby," the other "Top of the City" – she presses the later.

Her breath is taken away as she soars up along the outside the building to the top floor. The doors open; she is greeted by the maître d' who escorts her to a table where Kyle sits waiting.

He smiles and rushes to his feet the instant he sees her. He has on a dark suit and tie, looking debonair. He offers her a single long-stemmed rose as she sits down.

"Why, thank you," she says, holding the flower to her, and taking in its fragrance.

From that moment on, the evening is a fairytale. Kyle orders for the two of them – a chance to make use of his fluent French. They drink nothing but champagne. They dance to soft romantic music and hold hands as they look out at the view of the world far below. The city lights are like stars sprawled at their feet and the lights of the moving cars bustling up and down dark streets are like white and red corpuscles flowing through the veins and the arteries of the city.

"If you don't mind me asking, what's this unexpected something that brings you into town?" Helen asks.

"You may not believe me if I tell you."

"Go ahead…try me," she says, smiling into his eyes.

"You…you're the reason I'm here…the only reason. I was so desperate to see you."

"I'm glad you did," she whispers as he pulls her in closer to him and kisses her – soft, gentle, and quick.

****

They are alone in the express elevator. Kyle presses the Lobby button.

"It makes me feel so dizzy to look down," she laughs nervously.

"Then don't look," Kyle says, holding her tightly and kissing her.

Downstairs in the lobby, Kyle begins to guide Helen toward a row of elevators.

"Kyle, it's not that I don't want to," Helen says, pulling on his arm, trying to steer him in the opposite direction. "I really do want to be with you. …It's just it's all too fast."

"Just for one drink, if I promise to be a perfect gentleman? Besides, I have something very important to show you."

She reflects a moment and decides she believes him. "Well, just one drink. …That's all."

Up in his room, there are glasses and a bottle of champagne on ice.

"Just one drink…" he says as they click glasses.

They hold hands, sipping their drinks.

"So what is it you need to show me?"

"I have something I want to give to you." His face grows serious. "But first, I want you to understand…I'm only giving it to you because I care so much for you. As for me, I would sooner destroy it, but I think it's something you can use."

"What are you talking about?"

He breaks free of her hold and walks over to the bed. He bends down, pulls something out from under it, and places it on top. Helen moves in slowly to get a better look – it is a small, gray metal box.

"My God, it's the box from the basement!" Helen says in horror. She looks at Kyle, questioning. "Was it you that night in the basement?"

He shakes his head. "No, it wasn't me. …It was my mother."

"Your mother…? I don't understand."

"Joyce McDonald, your aunt's caretaker…she's my mother."

"But I could have sworn it was a man who pushed me aside in the basement!"

"My mother has been a caretaker since I was little. Years of lifting deadweight from beds onto wheelchairs, into tubs, and out of tubs…she's surprisingly strong."

"But I don't understand!"

Kyle sits down on the edge of the bed and buries his head in his hands.

"It was a long time ago," he speaks softly as if others might be listening and he doesn't want them to hear – only Helen. "I was only eleven at the time. Victor and Nicholas were friends from school. I used to go to their house to play. One day we were playing in the basement, and their father came down. He asked me if I wanted to be a member of their secret boy's club. Victor and Nicholas were members, and it would be fun.

"Next thing you know, we're all drinking whiskey, smoking cigarettes, and reading girly magazines. I thought I was in juvenile delinquent heaven. I became drunk. . . . The rest was all a blur, but I wasn't so drunk I didn't remember what happened."

"Why didn't you tell somebody?" Helen asks as she sits down next to Kyle, running her hand gently over his back in sympathy.

"I couldn't. . . . I was too scared. . . too ashamed. This went on for months; it was like I was trapped and couldn't get out. Finally, I did, and I never went back to the Russell house again. But I never spoke about it to anyone.

"After school, I joined the military and then college. When my father became ill, I returned home to help my mother. Years after his death, my mother remarried. . . . That's why the different name. I took care of my stepfather who died sometime later. My mother gave me the house after his death, and she moved out – she wanted to be alone. I've lived there since then.

"By that time, Jerry Russell had been long dead and so was Nicholas. There was only Victor to contend with. . . only he knew my secret. One night, I confided in my mother. She wanted to go to the authorities, but I pleaded with her not to. I couldn't bear the shame. I just wanted to forget it ever happened. This box of photos is my only reminder."

"If you knew about the photos, why didn't you take them long ago?" Helen asks.

"I was afraid of Victor; he's mad, you know. He always swore if I or my mother ever so much as touched them, he'd kill us both, and I believed him. It was only by sheer coincidence my mother became employed by your aunt. For years, she kept an eye on this box, as did Victor.

"I knew about you from the photos of you and by what Victor told me. . . about that day at the lake. When you came to town, we knew, my mother and I, you had remembered and come for answers. My mother saw you looking at the basement door that night. She was afraid you might go down and find the box, so she waited outside till you turned off the lights. She figured you had gone to bed. She was planning on taking the box and hiding it until your stay was over and then returning it before Victor realized it was missing. But when she saw you in the basement with the box, she panicked.

"When Victor was arrested, there was no need to return the box, no reason to be afraid anymore. All that was needed now was to destroy its contents."

"Why didn't you?"

"Because of you," he raises his eyes to her. "I know what you're going through…the torture of the memory. If these pictures can help you…to help set you free…I want you to have them."

Helen leans over and kisses Kyle. He slowly and gently removes his lips from hers and stands up. He takes the box and puts it under his arm.

"Come on, I'll carry it down to your car for you. I said I'd be a perfect gentleman. So let's go before I try to break my promise."

Kyle places the box in the backseat of Helen's car.

"What will you do with them?" he asks.

"Probably give them to the police." Then she looks deep into Kyle's eyes. "But not until I've removed every picture of the young Kyle Adams from it."

"You don't have to, you know."

"I know, but I want to. I think you've been brave in doing this, and I don't see why you need to suffer any more."

"If that's what you want. They're yours now to do with what you want."

Helen falls into his arms, and they kiss long and hard.

"Call me?" she asks, looking up at him.

"I will, first thing in the morning!"

Fourteen

Spilling Your Guts

Victor is showing signs of cracking up, quickly going over the deep end. He has the faint smell of urine on him. His hair is falling out in handfuls, and his breath reeks sour from stomach problems. His knees bob up and down nervously when he sits. There are dark circles under his eyes from little sleep. When he does sleep, nightmares plague him, and he wakes in a cold sweat.

He's never given permission to socialize with the other prisoners. All conversation is kept down to a minimum of two or three words. He's not released from his cell for exercise and is denied reading material, radio, and TV.

His meals consist of nearly no protein. They allow him as much white bread and pasta as he wants. Vegetables are few and prepared with a high content of sugar. In fact, sugar and white flour are the main ingredients of all his meals. If he is thirsty, only coffee and sugary drinks – never water.

Such treatment is illegal, but who will stop them? Drastic circumstances call for drastic measures. And who can Victor complain to, the guards, his lawyer? Walter Lieberman knows Goebel and Benson's methods and approves of them. The forces-that-be are pressing down hard on Victor Russell. If he knew how far they are willing to go, he would tell them everything and spare himself.

****

Goebel and Benson stand behind the two-way mirror looking into the interrogation room. Benson reaches over and turns on the tape recorder.

Two microphones rest on the table in the room. One faces Victor Russell; the other, Dr. Robert Carver.

"Now, just relax, Victor," says Dr. Carver. "I'm going to ask you a few questions, and I want you to answer them any way you'd like. Don't think about it too long. Just say what comes into your head. Do you understand?"

Victor nods. Dr. Carver gets a good look into Victor's bloodshot eyes.

"Tell me, Victor, do you have trouble sleeping?"

"Yeah, it's real noisy here, especially the guards. They're always banging stuff around."

"I see," says Dr. Carver, writing notes on his pad. "Now, tell me, Victor, when you sleep, do you often dream?"

Victor lies. "No more or less than the next guy, I guess."

"And what do you dream about?"

"I don't know…just stuff."

"Well, give me a 'for instance'. Do you dream of flying? Are they happy dreams? What sort people do you meet in your dreams?"

"There's never anybody in my dreams; I'm always alone."

"I see." Dr. Carver jots down another note. "Now, Victor, when you're awake do you ever hear voices?"

Victor lets out a long sigh and shakes his head. After a long moment of silence, he speaks.

"I realize what's going on here, and I understand my predicament. True…I may be crazy, but I'm not stupid! Do I dream? Do I hear voices?" he says, mockingly. "You said I could answer any way I wanted to. So, why don't I just tell my story and just get it all off my chest. Then you figure out if I'm crazy or not. I couldn't care less, and the police will have what they want…all on tape. That sound good to you, Doc?"

"If that's what you want to do, then please continue."

"That's what I want! You guys getting all this?" He addresses his statement to the two-way mirror – there is no response. He turns his gaze back toward the doctor and begins speaking slowly into the microphone.

"I hate my father! I've always hated him and I always will hate him. He has made my life one long living hell. I used to pray every night for him to die. Finally, one day I got an answer to my prayers. And you know what happened? Nothing happened! Even death doesn't stop him! He rules my life even from the grave!

"As far back as I remember…no…even before that, I'm sure…before any memory I have, my father molested me and my brother. He took advantage of his own two young boys, year after year. He kept us in his web of shame and fear with no way out.

"He even used us to lure other young boys, getting them drunk, and leaving them helpless."

"Your mother," Dr. Carver asks "did she know about any of this?"

"I can't see how she couldn't. It went on under her nose in the same house for years!"

"And these episodes only occurred with your brother and other young boys, never with any girls?"

"My father used to call it the Secret Boy's Club. He wouldn't allow us to mention girls; they were taboo."

"What about the time at the lake with your cousin, Helen?"

"That was an accident...a comedy of errors. She came on us unexpectedly in the woods. ...It was a total nightmare. That poor little girl...I remember...she ran off crying...leaving her doll behind.

"That damn doll! My father kept that doll like a war souvenir, a holy relic, a precious keepsake. He kept that doll! Often, he incorporated it into our sessions locked up in the basement.

"He called it our token female. It was a weird little doll...made up of flags from all over the world. When you pulled its string, it said phrases in different languages. He used to pull that string for hours and answer back to it in whatever language it was speaking. He became obsessed with the damn thing. He took it on himself to learn all the languages the doll spoke...even curse words and swearwords...no...especially curses and swearwords! He even forced my brother and me to learn the different languages...especially the dirty words. Oh, how he loved dirty words!"

Victor falls silent.

"When did your father die?"

"When we were in our teens...my brother and I, we couldn't believe it ... we were finally free...or so we thought.

"A couple of years after his death, he began appearing to us...mostly in our bedroom at night. He also forced us to return to the basement for his sessions. It was like he never died."

"Was this the ghost of your father that you were seeing?"

"'Ghost...you tell me! His fists felt real. It drove Nicholas insane."

"Victor...your brother's accident...did Nicholas kill himself?"

"I don't know... maybe. I wouldn't blame him if he did. I wish I had that courage."

Victor leans forward toward the microphone and continues.

"A few years after Nicholas died, I met my wife. We dated. ...Daddy didn't show for years. I thought things could be normal. We married; we had kids, a house, and a car. I was working; life seemed normal. Then I started to see my father again. He began to appear whenever I was alone. He started telling me to do things."

"What kind of things, Victor? What did your father tell you to do?"

Victor's face grew pale. He hangs his head down and catches it in his hands. He looks as if he is about to cry. There is a crack in his voice.

"He told me to…" Victor can hardly speak. "He told me to…touch my boys…my sons. He wanted to start a new secret boy's club. I knew it was wrong, but he has this power over me!"

Victor is nearly screaming at this point. Then he pauses, calms himself, and continues.

"My wife found out and kicked me out of the house. I don't blame her. I would have done the same. I moved into a small apartment on the other side of town. I started drinking heavy again. Occasionally, at night, my father visited me.

"Then one night, he was angrier than I've ever seen him before. He had the doll with him…that damn doll. After years of pulling on its string, it finally broke. It was useless…but to him, it was dead."

"The death of the 'token female'?" interjects Dr. Carver.

"Exactly, and now he wanted the original, my cousin, Helen…to have his way with, like he did with the doll.

"I told the police I wasn't a murderer, and I'm not! Everything…the rape of my cousin…the killings of Donald Johnson and Carol Hastings…the phone calls…even the dead cat…I had nothing to do with any of it!

"He told me every detail of each incident, because he wanted me to confess to all of it. As usual, I had no power to fight against him. I did what he asked."

"How is it we found some of your semen on Carol Hastings' clothes?" Dr. Carver asks.

"He brought them over one night. It was during one of his sessions…he…"

Victor's voice trails off to a whisper. He can say no more about it. Dr. Carver immediately changes the subject.

"Victor, why are you telling us all this now? Why not before?"

Victor looks into the eyes of the doctor and smiles – a madman's smile.

"You see, doctor, as much as I hate my father, there are two things stronger than my hatred: the hold he has on me and the fear I have of him.

"That's why I did all those horrible things he told me to do for so long…and I never told a soul. But these past few weeks have taught me something. If I'm locked behind brick walls and iron bars, he can't touch me.

"I tell you, Doc, either you claim me insane and put me away for good or I swear I'll kill someone, so they lock me away for life or they hang me. Either way is fine with me. Never release me, please. I never want him to touch me again."

Victor sits back in his chair. There is a look of calm resolve on his face.

"Victor…" Dr. Carver starts to speak.

"No more questions," Victor interrupts. "There's nothing left to say." He stands and shouts at the two-way mirror, "Did you get it all? Is that what you wanted, you filthy sons of bitches?"

****

Helen waits with the phone receiver to her ear. A guard escorts Victor to a chair facing her. He sits down and just stares at the phone.

"Pick up the phone, Victor," Helen shouts, but all is silent on the other side of the two-inch-thick Plexiglas. She makes a fist and starts to pound on the glass. The faint thumping catches Victor's attention. She motions for him to pick up the receiver.

"Yes?" he says into the phone.

"Victor, it's me, you cousin, Helen."

"I know who you are. You're International Nancy!" As if a song from a long-forgotten children's TV commercial he sings, "Wherever I go…I always know…just how to say hello."

"I'm not Nancy…I'm your cousin, Helen!"

"Helen…yeah, right, Helen…our token female!"

"I need your help, Victor," she pleads into the phone, looking at him through the Plexiglas.

"You need my help?" He starts to laugh. "All I can offer you is advice. You need to get yourself locked up…like me, immediately. You need to get yourself into a prison or an insane asylum…or something…anything!

"You see, the world has it all backwards. Prison means freedom! He can't get at you in here. Outside is prison!"

"Who's outside? Tell me, Victor, is it your father? Is your father still alive?"

"No…Daddy's dead, but don't let that fool you cause that don't stop him!"

"Victor, I found the box of photos in the basement. I gave them to the police, but I kept a few of them. Can you tell me about these?"

Helen holds the photos taken that day at the lake up against the glass pane.

"Oh, look," he says, smiling, "you've brought the family album with you!" He starts to laugh again. "There's Victor…and Nicholas…and Daddy…and – oh, look – a picture of you! What a pretty little girl you were."

"Victor, tell me what happened that day?"

"Don't you know?"

"Not all of it. It's all a big blur. I need to know, Victor!"

"You were initiated into the Secret Boy's Club...an honorary member...our 'token female'."

Helen realizes she isn't getting anywhere fast. She decides to ask as many pointblank questions as she can.

"Victor, tell me, is Nicholas really dead?"

"If he isn't, he sure knows how to play dead real good. Sit, Nicholas, sit. ...Roll over, Nicholas. ...Now, play dead...good boy!" Victor speaks as if he were in pain, "He was ashes...just like Daddy. Even his sneakers melted."

"Is he really dead, Victor, or is he playing dead?"

He doesn't answer. She is losing him, and she knows it.

"Victor, tell me, is your father dead or is he playing dead?"

He smiles. "Only one person I know who's dead for sure...really dead...and that's International Nancy. He pulled her string too hard and *boing*...she was dead. Now he needs you...the token female."

"He needs me for what, Victor?"

"You know," he sneers, "to do dirty things with...to curse in German and French, to...to pull your string."

"But if he pulls my string...he'll kill me?"

"Eventually, but not for years. Anyway, he won't hurt you much. He needs you. It's the people around you that he'll hurt."

"What are you telling me, Victor?"

"Exactly what I just said. Oh, he may slap you around a little, but it's the people you love...they're the ones he'll kill. That's how he gets to you."

Victor begins to cry. "Like wives...he'll go after wives...and sons...especially sons...he'll kill them if you don't do what he says."

Victor looks into Helen's eyes, "My wife...my children...make sure they're safe...for me...please?"

"I will."

"No...swear...swear you'll make sure they're safe!"

"I swear!"

"You've got to get them someplace safe," he continues. "Get them locked up, if you can. You, too, get yourself and your loved ones locked up, so he can't get at you.

"Do something crazy...molest a child. ...That's always good for one free admission to the nuthouse. Don't worry; you don't have to mean it. God will understand."

Just then the guard reappears to take Victor back to his cell. Before Helen can say another word – before she can say goodbye – Victor hangs up the phone, gets up, and walks away.

Helen watches as they guide him out of the room; he is still mumbling. Her focus changes, and she sees her own reflection in the Plexiglas. She is crying.

****

It is clear Helen has taken Victor's warning seriously, but was it merely a warning? Perhaps, more like a prediction. Was Victor in the know? Had he been told what would be the next course of action?

That evening, Helen returns to the home of her parents. She finds them sitting in the living room and watching TV.

"Hello, dear, I didn't know you'd be home so early," her mother says, smiling. "I would have kept something out for you." She rises from the couch.

"That's all right, Mom. I had something while I was out."

Helen looks across the room at her father, sitting in his recliner.

"Dad…what's with the sunglasses?"

"I don't want to talk about it," he says bluntly, never taking his gaze from the TV.

Helen steps in closer for a better look.

"Your father got into a fight earlier this evening outside the mall."

"Did someone beat you up?"

"No one beat me up! Didn't you hear your mother? It was a fight…and not even a fair fight. …There must have been at least two or three of them."

"You were jumped?"

"No…it was a fight! I told you I don't want to talk about it. I'm going to lie down and read." He storms into the bedroom and slams the door behind him.

"I don't understand? Is he all right? Did you tell the police?"

"Come, dear," says her mother. "Let's go sit in the kitchen. I'll make us some decaf, and I'll tell you all about it."

"Mom, tell me what happened?"

Her mother takes her time stirring her usual two teaspoons of sugar and cream into her coffee.

It doesn't surprise Helen the flippant manner in which her mother relays the story of her husband's misfortune. She shows little sympathy in her speech, and delivers the facts as if reading a grocery list.

"You need to understand, Helen, your father is a proud man. When we first met in college, he was captain of the boxing team. You should have seen him then…quite a figure of a man.

"All his life he was always able to take care of himself. I've never seen him back down from a bully who wanted to scrap, not once. But now he's gotten old and that's the one part of aging that bothers your father…not being able to defend himself. He feels helpless. …He feels less of a man."

"Mom, what happened?"

"Oh, your father was at the mall. When he was locking the car, someone came up behind, put a beating on him, and stole his wallet."

"Was it really three men?"

"No…just one. That's your father's pride talking; it sounds better if it was more than one."

"Did he get a look at the man?"

"No, it all happened too fast."

Her mother takes another sip of coffee and continues.

"He hobbled to the mall, and they called an ambulance. They took him to emergency…just a few small cuts and a big black eye. I'm sure it doesn't hurt half as much as his wounded pride."

She takes another sip of coffee, places the cup down, and looks into her daughter's face.

"Strangest thing, though…the man who did this…while he was hitting your father, he was yelling in foreign languages. Not just one language, mind you; he was yelling in all sorts of languages…German, French, Spanish…all very strange.

"Then, just before he ran off, while your father was lying helplessly on the ground, he kicked your father hard one last time and said, 'That's for Nancy!'"

"What does that mean? Who is Nancy? He must have mistaken your father for somebody else."

She goes back to her coffee.

Helen rises from her chair. "Excuse me, Mom, I've got to pack my overnight bag. I'll be gone early in the morning."

"Oh, no…not another business trip? You poor dear, they're trying to work you to death. Where are you going this time?"

"Back to Tannersville. I've some unfinished business there…something I should have done the last time I was there."

Fifteen

A Better Epitaph

Helen calls ahead to tell her Aunt Eleanor she'll be in the area on business and to ask if she can stop in for a visit. Helen also phones Kyle. He is ecstatic when he hears she is coming. Against her better judgment, Helen consents to stay at Kyle's home during her visit to Tannersville. He vows she'll be and feel safe from any approach from him. He'll sleep on the couch and offers the bedroom to her. He swears to be a perfect gentleman. But it isn't Kyle's intents putting her ill at ease. It is her attraction to him she questions. Could she trust herself being alone with him?

On her arrival at Tannersville, Helen's first impulse is to go to Kyle, but she tries to focus on what motivated her to revisit Tannersville in the first place – her Aunt Eleanor. Still, she cannot forget her solemn vow to Victor, to see to the safety of his family.

It takes a few minutes of wrong turns through town – relying on her memory, but she finally finds the home of Teresa Russell and her children. She parks the car a few houses down and is just about to get out when she sees Kyle leaving the Russell home. Teresa is with him, the two hug, they speak for a moment, and he leaves. Teresa watches from the porch as he drives off and then goes back inside.

Helen feels a twinge of jealousy coursing through her veins and mistrust for Kyle. Then, she stops herself. She has no ties with Kyle; he is free to come and go as he pleases, as is she. Besides, she is being too quickly judgmental, and perhaps the visit is all very innocent. As she was told many times before, this is a small town and everybody knows everybody else. She is being childish – reading more into what might be nothing more than a friendly visit.

The screen door swings wide. Teresa emerges, baby in tow and one clinging to her side.

"Helen?" she says, surprised.

"Teresa, I was wondering if we could talk. May I come in?"

"Yes, of course, come in."

The living room is small, clean, and sparse – what little furniture she owns looks old and worn.

"Please, sit; can I get you anything?"

"No, thank you, I only have a minute." Helen sits down. "I saw Victor the other day, and I promised him I would look in on you."

"Victor…is he all right?"

"He's worried about you and the children's safety. He talks as if he knows of some impending doom. He believes there might be someone out there who wants to do you and the children harm."

"I can't think of anyone who would."

"Nonetheless, there's a ring of truth in what he's saying. Please, be careful for the sake of the children."

Teresa sits down in a chair opposite Helen, the baby still in her arms.

"Tell me, what is going to happen to him?"

"I have no idea. I wish I had something more to report to you."

Helen finds it impossible to tell Teresa the truth. How ill Victor seemed during their last meeting. That even if he isn't convicted of any crime, he is sure to be put away for mental instability.

"I couldn't help but notice as I was pulling up to the house…was that Kyle Adams leaving?"

Teresa goes pale white and silent for a moment.

"Oh…yes…that was Kyle. We've been friends since we were kids and lived in the same neighborhood. He drops by every once in a while and does little odds and ends for me around the house. There are just some things a woman needs a man to do."

"I see," Helen says.

"Jeez…that didn't come out sounding right," Teresa says. "I mean he's been nice enough to help out. Plus the boys need a father figure around. He takes them down to the gym where he works every once in a while. It's good for them to be around a grown man. I'm on a tight budget, as you can imagine. He fixes stuff for me…you know…leaky faucets…backed up toilets…"

Teresa stops in mid-sentence, gently places the baby down on a blanket on the floor between the two of them.

"Who am I kidding?" she says. "Kyle and I have been seeing each other nearly as long as Victor has been gone. At first, it was just friendly concern on his part. He'd come by and check on us once in a while. If money was low, he always offered some to me. If it weren't for the children, I never would have taken it.

"Everything was very platonic for a long time, but you understand how things are. You talk, you listen, you laugh, you cry, you care, and the next thing you know…

"Hey, it's a small town, and nobody's going to knock down the door of a woman with three kids. Oh, I'm not living under any illusions. Kyle's a nice guy, and God knows he's lonely, but I know he doesn't love me. And…I suppose I don't love him, either."

Helen listens. She remains silent, which is like torture to Teresa.

"There is one thing I think you best know," Teresa says, "something important…"

"And what is that?"

"Kyle told me about you when he came back from that weekend trip he took to see you."

"Did he tell you about the photos?" Helen asks.

"Photos…what photos? I don't know anything about any photos," Teresa says. There is a look of sincerity on her face. It is obvious Teresa knows nothing of what Helen is asking.

"Never mind," Helen says. "It's not important. Finish what you were saying."

"I'm saying, Kyle doesn't love me. He's never loved me and he never will. He told me about you from the start. He has strong feelings for you.

"You need to know why he was here just now. He came by to call it off between us. He's so excited he's going to see you today, he can hardly contain himself. He doesn't want to live a lie with me anymore. He's hoping for a new start with you.

"Please, don't judge him or me; we did what we needed to do to survive, and now it's over. Don't ruin what might be between the two of you over what could never be between the two of us."

Helen looks at the baby on the floor and then into Teresa's face. "Thank you for telling me this. I wish…" Helen isn't sure what to say.

"He's a good man," Teresa says. "I envy you."

Helen stands up. "I do need to go. Is there anything you'd like me to tell Victor if I see him again?"

"Yes, tell him I love him."

****

Helen pulls her car behind Joyce's car in the driveway. On the porch, she puts her hand over her eyebrows and looks through the screen door into the dark house. She pounds gently on the side of the door, and the next moment Joyce's smiling face appears.

"Helen, we didn't know when to expect you! Come in! Your aunt has been waiting."

Inside, it takes a minute for Helen's eyes to adjust to the darkness of the house. The air is stale and warm; there is a silence over everything.

"So how have you been?" Joyce asks.

"Good…I've been good… and you?"

"Not so bad. It's not that I don't have complaints, but who'd listen?"

"I know what you mean," Helen agrees in a sympathetic tone.

"Listen, there's something we need to talk about. I want to apologize for what happened that night. I mean, I didn't mean to scare you, and I definitely didn't want to hurt you."

"I understand," Helen says. "Kyle told me everything. Under the circumstances…"

"Kyle has been talking about nothing but you for the past few weeks. I think you've made quite an impression on him."

"The feeling is mutual."

"I need to tell you something about your aunt," says Joyce. "She hasn't been well lately, and her strength has been failing. She has been spending most of her time in bed, and when she's not, she's in her wheelchair. She hardly comes out of her bedroom. That's where she is now. Go to her, she's been so excited about your visit."

Helen walks to the bedroom door. She takes a long breath and knocks.

"Who is it?" the feeble voice of her sickly aunt seeps through the door.

"It's me, Aunt Eleanor…Helen. …May I come in?"

"Come in, darling…come in!"

Helen enters. If the rest of the house is too dark to make out colors, Aunt Eleanor's bedroom is too dark to make out shapes clearly.

"Helen, it's so good to see you again." Aunt Eleanor sits in her wheelchair close to the window, though the shades are down. Helen kisses her on the cheek and sits on the edge of the bed.

"I don't see you for years and now I see you twice in the same year," smiles Aunt Eleanor. "You are going to be staying with us? I've had Joyce make ready your room."

"Oh, no, Aunt Eleanor, I'm just in for the day on business. I just have time for a short visit."

"Well then, we'll just have to make do, so let's visit," says the old woman.

The next few minutes they fill with idle chitchat. Then a silence comes over the women. Helen's mind races, she thinks of what she'll ask and how to ask it. Finally, Helen starts slowly but straightforward with her questioning.

"There's something I've wanted to ask you, Aunt Eleanor, something I should have asked you the last time I was here."

"What is it you'd like to know?" her aunt asks, smiling.

"I was very young when Uncle Jerry died; I hardly remember him. Tell me about him, please."

"Well, let's see…he was a loving husband, a good provider, a good father, and a credit to his community. I doubt there's a better epitaph I could write for him than that."

"And how did he die?"

"Heart attack. …We were on vacation in Europe and the poor man fell over on the steps of a church in Barcelona. It happened oh so suddenly. As I remember it, he grabbed hold of his left arm as if in pain. He went sheet white, fell to the ground, and the next moment he was gone."

"You say he was a good father?"

"Of course, he was! You just ask either one of my boys; they'll tell you."

"Your boys…I thought Nicholas died years ago in a car accident?"

The smile leaves the old woman's face.

"Yes, I didn't mean to suggest otherwise. It's just it's been such a long time ago…I meant just ask Victor."

"I did speak to Victor, and he paints a much different portrait of his father than you do…a very dark portrait."

Her aunt's tone turns cold, "I don't know what you're trying to suggest."

"Aunt Eleanor, do you know where Victor is right now? Do you know how he's been living and where?"

"Of course, I do! He's married and he lives with his lovely wife, Teresa, and their three children. He works at the cement plant as a supervisor. They're all very happy!"

"Aunt Eleanor, Victor and his wife have been separated for months. He's in jail right now!"

"Jail…" whispers the old woman, as if not surprised, as if she knew it was a question of when and not if. Yet, outwardly, she does not accept what she knows in her heart. "That's impossible," she snaps. "What would Victor be in jail for?"

"He's been accused of murder!"

"There must be some mistake; Victor never hurt anyone!"

"That's what he says, and I agree," Helen says. "He says someone else did the murders, and that someone told him…no…forced him to confess."

"Who…who would do such a thing?"

"Victor says it was his father."

"His father!" exclaims Aunt Eleanor. "But Victor's father has been dead for years. I don't know where you're getting all of this, young lady, but…"

"From Victor…Victor swears his father is still alive. …He visits him and tells him to do things."

"Well, I don't believe a word of it. Poor boy must have lost his mind!"

"Perhaps he has. But I think it a strange and callous conclusion for a mother to arrive at so quickly. Unless, Aunt Eleanor, I think you know more than you're telling me. I think you're hiding something."

"I don't know what you mean!" The old woman's voice grows cold as do her staring eyes. Helen realizes she hit a nerve.

Helen presses on. "All those years, living under the same roof, you must have known what was going on. You at least had your suspicions. Or did you turn your eyes from what was happening and bury your head in the sand?"

"Young lady, what are you implying?"

"I'm talking about your two boys…your two sons…and their father locked for hours together down in the basement. I'm talking about the endless line of young boys coming and going."

"I still don't know what you're talking about!"

"I think you do! The more I think about it, the surer I am you knew."

"Knew what?" she demands.

"That your husband molested your sons and other young boys."

"That's a lie! You're lying! Who told you this…Victor? He's a liar! No one will believe him, and no one will believe you! There's no proof. …You have no proof!"

"You did know…didn't you?"

"He wasn't like ordinary men," argues her aunt. "His taste for life was deeper than other people. He was a genius, and a genius needs to drink from many wells!"

"Who told you that? Did he tell you that? And you believed him? Those were your sons, your own flesh and blood!"

"Go ahead, say whatever you want, tell whoever you want, it doesn't matter. You have no proof!" Her voice goes hoarse.

"No proof…I'll show you proof!"

Helen reaches in her pocket and pulls out a handful of photos – pictures taken from the basement.

"Where did you get those?" The old woman leaps from her wheelchair at Helen. "Give me those, you little slut!"

The old woman grabs the photos from Helen. She holds herself up for no more than a few seconds and then goes crashing to the floor. Joyce comes rushing in and falls to her knees alongside Aunt Eleanor, taking the pictures from her grasp.

"This wasn't why we gave them to you!" says Joyce, handing the pictures back to Helen.

"I hope he kills you!" Aunt Eleanor hollers, gasping for breath and choking on her words. "I hope he kills you!"

Aunt Eleanor's eyes roll back in her head. In one quick motion, Joyce picks up the old woman and drops her down on the bed.

"There's a phone in the kitchen; call for an ambulance!" Joyce commands Helen.

Ten minutes later, the paramedics are storming into the house.

"She's in there," Helen says, pointing at the bedroom door.

They run in, slamming the door behind them.

Helen waits nervously, pacing the floor. She played her hand and laid down all her high cards. She questions herself over and over if she did the right thing.

A few minutes later, Joyce steps out of the bedroom.

"Well, she's going to be all right for now, no thanks to you," says Joyce. "Whatever possessed you to do such a thing?"

"I'm just trying to get at the truth. That woman knows more than she lets on."

"You think I don't know that?" says Joyce. "Of course she knew! But what good is it to rub her nose in it now?"

"I just thought…"

"Well, you thought wrong! I think it would be best if you just leave."

Helen opens her mouth, but before she says a word, Joyce insists once more.

"I said…I think it would be best if you just leave."

Helen starts for the front door. She hears Joyce's last remarks.

"And I wouldn't come back, if I were you!"

Sixteen

Music Lover

Kyle spends most of the day cleaning his house and stocking the fridge with treats. He buys two bottles of the best champagne his budget can handle. He has a roast slowly cooking in the oven – all in preparation for Helen's visit.

He starts setting the table, when the phone rings.

"Kyle, it's me," Helen sounds nearly close to tears.

"Helen, what's the matter?"

"Oh, Kyle, I think I've done something horribly wrong. I know you weren't expecting me till later, but would you mind if I came over now?"

"Mind…? Of course not! Helen, are you all right? Do you want me to come and get you?"

"No, that's all right. I'll be fine. See you in a few minutes."

When Helen pulls up in front of Kyle's house, she finds him standing on the front porch, waiting for her. She flies up the stairs and into his arms.

"Helen, what's the matter?" He holds her close.

"I…I…" Helen is unable to speak.

"Come inside." He guides her through the front door and sets her down on the couch. "Wait here, I'll be right back."

He returns a minute later with a small box of tissues and a snifter of warm brandy.

"Here, take a sip of this; it'll calm you down." He hands her the glass and rests the tissue box down on the coffee table.

Helen alternates – first the glass, then the tissues, then back again. A minute later, she begins to calm down.

"So, tell me," Kyle says, "why are you so upset?"

Helen takes her time and slowly tells him what happened between her aunt and her – omitting nothing.

"When I left, your mother said she was all right. But I'm not sure now if I've done the right thing."

For a moment Kyle seems lost for words.

"Wow, that's pretty heavy! What made you do it?"

"I thought I could get my aunt to talk. I think she's hiding something."

"Hiding something? What can an old woman hide?"

Helen places the brandy snifter down on the coffee table and looks into Kyle's eyes.

"Kyle, I know this is going to sound crazy, but I believe it's possible either my cousin Nicholas or my Uncle Jerry…or both…may still be alive."

"Gee, Helen, I don't know. Are you sure? I mean, what makes you think so?"

"It's a long, strange story."

"And I want to hear every word of it, but I've got a roast that needs taking out of the oven. Help me finish setting the table, and you can tell me everything over dinner."

Throughout the three-course meal, Helen relays her story to Kyle. He listens to every word intently, without making a comment. When she finishes, he speaks.

"What did your aunt mean…'I hope he kills you'? He who?"

"That's just the point; that leads me to believe there's still a possibility my cousin and or my uncle is still alive…and my aunt knows it!"

Kyle shakes his head in disbelieve, "I just don't see how it could be true or why anyone would try to pull off such a…a hoax?"

They sit silently for a moment. The sun has long since set. Moving shadows fill the room, cast by the light from candles on the table. Kyle notes the smoothness of Helen's skin under the glow of the candlelight. The reflections of the flames dance in her eyes.

"It would be best if I start for home now," Helen says, not sounding too thrilled at the proposition.

"I thought you were going to stay the night."

"That was before my confrontation with my aunt. There's nothing left for me to do now."

"Nothing…?" Kyle pours the last of the wine evenly into their glasses. "You know, I have a confession to make," he says.

Helen remains silent and listens.

"There's a woman here in town…I was having a relationship with. …I should have called it off a long time ago. We didn't love each other. …We were just lonely together.

"I called it off today because you were coming. I wanted a clean slate. I don't want anything to come in the way of any possibilities there may be for you and me."

He goes silent, waiting for her response.

"I'm glad you told me," Helen says. "Is there a you and me?"

"There can be." He takes her hand. "Oh, Helen, there can be!"

He stands up, lifts her from her chair, takes her in his arms, and kisses her.

"I need to get back to my job," she whispers, silently wanting deep inside for him to say something that will stop her from leaving.

"You can leave with the morning light; you'll be home in time for lunch."

That is all she needs to hear. She rests her head against his chest. Still holding her, he leans across the table and blows out the candles – the room goes dark.

****

"Knock, knock," Goebel says as he and Benson stand in the doorway of Captain Vega's office.

"Come in boys; take a seat," says Captain Vega. His tone of voice sounds excessively syrupy and sweet – something is up.

Goebel and Benson sit down. It is impossible not to notice the large reel-to-reel tape recorder on the Captain's desk.

"You know, fellas," says Vega, "I like going to the movies. You guys like to go to the movies?"

Goebel and Benson look at each other, confused.

"What's that got to do with the price of tea in China?" Benson asks.

"Just let me finish," says Vega. "My wife likes girly romance pictures, and so that's mostly what we see. Now, me…I like a good action flick, and not just any kind of action flick, I like police action movies. …Man, I love 'em."

The strange smile that adorns Vega's face disappears.

"But there is one thing I hate about police shows. Whenever the hero or heroes get into trouble they wind up being called to the Captain's office. He's usually some old fart…balding head…drinks and smokes too much, and has high blood pressure. He's always screaming at the top of his lungs about how if the hero doesn't fly straight he's going to put them on suspension.

"Now me…I'm not an old fat or bald, am I? I don't smoke…except for a good cigar now and then. I keep my drinking down to a minimum and only on weekends…and my blood pressure couldn't be better.

"That's why I'm not going to scream and threaten you with suspension. I'm calmly going to tell you if you pull another stunt like this one, I'm going to have your badges. You can kiss my butt goodbye and go home and dream about retirement."

"What stunt?" Goebel asks. "What the hell are you talking about?"

"This is what the hell I'm talking about," Vega says, turning on the tape recorder. It is a conversation between Victor Russell and Dr. Carver – the psychiatrist assigned by Victor's lawyer to examine him.

Goebel and Benson listen carefully to the electrical voices. Dr. Carver is asking Victor a series of typical questions used in psychoanalysis – when suddenly Victor interrupts him.

"Say, Doc, you've been asking all the questions. Mind if I ask you one or two?"

"Well, it's highly irregular, but I suppose it would be all right. What would you like to know?"

"Tell me, Doc, do you play piano?"

"No, I don't."

"Do you play guitar?"

"No, I don't play guitar."

"And, what about trumpet, do you play a trumpet?"

"No, Victor, I don't play trumpet. In fact, I'm sorry to say, I don't play any musical instrument."

"Oh, that's too bad! And are you planning to take up a musical instrument sometime in your life?"

"No, Victor, I'm not. Why do you ask?"

"I see…" Victor says.

The next sound coming from the small speaker of the tape recorder is loud and over modulated. There is the smashing sound of chairs hitting the floor, followed by a piercing scream from Dr. Carver.

The next sound is of two police officers rushing into the room and subduing Victor to the floor – all the while, horrific screams continue from Dr. Carver.

At that point, Captain Vega reaches over and shuts the machine off, and looks at Goebel and Benson for an explanation.

"Son of a bitch jumped over the table at Dr. Carver, grabbed hold of his hand and chewed his little finger clear off!"

"Damn, that's got to hurt!" Goebel exclaims.

"This isn't funny!" Vega shouts, slamming his fist down on the desk.

"Nowadays…can't they stitch a finger back on?" Benson asks.

"They can if you have the finger to stitch back on! Crazy bastard swallowed the damn thing. Later, when we were questioning Victor, he said he bit the small finger off so the doctor could still hold a pen and write. He said he wouldn't bite off a finger if the doctor played a musical instrument, because he likes music. When we asked him what he would have done if the doctor did play a musical instrument, he said he would have chewed off his nose!"

"So how's any of this our fault?" Goebel asks.

"Because you authorized the doctor's second interview and you knew what state of mind Victor was in. He even admitted he would go so far as to kill someone to insure he would not be released. I'm holding you two responsible. I want this case solved and closed soon or you're off it…you understand?"

Goebel and Benson walk sheepishly out of the Captain's office.

"Looks like Victor Russell got his wish," Benson says to Goebel as they stand in the hall outside the Captain's office.

"Yeah," Goebel replies. "He may never see the outside world again. If he plays his cards right, they'll lock him up forever."

"Safe from Daddy," Benson adds.

Seventeen

Bingo

Rita looks at the clock on the nightstand – it is ten thirty at night.

"This better be important," Rita says as she walks into the kitchen to answer the phone.

"Sheriff Gibson's residence. May I help you?" she says, sounding almost mechanical.

"Rita, this is Eleanor Russell. May I speak with the Sheriff, please?"

"The Sheriff is getting ready for bed right now. He'll be in the office at seven in the morning. I'll have him call first thing."

"I'm sorry to be calling so late," says Eleanor, "but it is important…so may I please speak with the sheriff?"

"Like I said, he's getting ready for bed. …He's in the bathroom just now. I'll have him call you as soon as he gets out."

"Oh, that's all right. I don't mind holding," Eleanor insists.

"Okay, just hold on." Rita puts the phone down on its side and walks off in search of her husband. She knocks on the bathroom door.

"Yeah?" her husband responds from within.

"Eleanor Russell's on the phone. …She wants to talk to you."

"Tell her to call the office in the morning."

"I told her that, but she says it's important."

"Tell her I'll call her back in a minute!"

"She says she can't wait. …It's too important!"

After thirty-five years of marriage, Rita knows her husband's moods and ways. She backs away from the closed bathroom door. She knows all too well he'll come storming out any second, angry as a wet hen and wild as a bull in a China closet – cussing everything and everyone that gets in his way.

The door swings open; he is tying the sash of his robe as he stomps toward the kitchen. He grumbles obscenities under his breath so his wife can't hear. But after thirty-five years, she has heard it all before and is not easily shocked.

In the kitchen, the Sheriff takes a moment to calm down before putting the receiver to his ear. People are always calling him at home for the most minuscule of reasons – a neighbor's barking dog, a loud party across the street. They all think calling the sheriff direct yields more immediate results. This is the curse of being a paid city official. He knows this, accepts this, but doesn't like it.

"Sheriff Gibson here…"

"Sheriff, this is Eleanor Russell. I'm sorry to be calling you so late, but I couldn't sleep if I didn't speak with you."

Sheriff Gibson has heard it all, but he tries to remain polite.

"How can I help you, Eleanor?"

"I have some important information I need to share with you…something that's been bothering my conscience all day since my niece came to visit me today. She was right. …I did know about it all. …I never wanted to admit it. I need to clear my conscience. …I need to confess."

"Eleanor, what are you talking about? Confess what? What important information?"

"About Victor…about his brother…and about my Jerry. …Could you come to my home tomorrow morning?"

Eleanor's plea befuddles the sheriff but leaves him with questions.

"Why wait till morning? Tell me now."

"I couldn't…not over the phone. Besides, it would take too long."

"Okay, I'll come over in morning on my way to the office. Seven o'clock all right?"

"No, that's when Joyce serves me my breakfast. Could you perhaps come later? Could you make it eight?"

"Eight o'clock will be just fine." Sheriff Gibson rolls his eyes. "Now, is there anything else, Mrs. Russell?"

"No, not at the moment."

"Well, then, I'll see you in the morning. Goodnight, Mrs. Russell." He hangs up before she can respond.

"What was that all about?" Rita asks, standing at the kitchen doorway, listening in.

"Crazy old goat!" he says, making his way back to their bedroom – Rita close behind. "She wants me to go to her house early tomorrow morning…something important to confess to me about her boys and Jerry…something she wants to get off her chest."

"A confession…?" Rita asks as she gets into bed next to her husband. "Maybe she killed Jerry, and years of guilt have been torturing her, and now she wants to confess it all?"

"You need to stop reading those silly crime novels," he says. "She probably wants to tell how innocent her son Victor is and if there's anything I can do on his behalf. Only she didn't have to call me in the middle of the night!"

He turns out the light. He feels around in the dark till he finds his wife's lips and kisses her goodnight. He turns on his side grumbling, "Crazy old goat!"

****

Sheriff Gibson pulls up in the driveway of the Russell house. He shoots a glance at the dashboard clock; the digital numbers reads seven thirty-five.

"Dang, if she thinks I'm going to wait out here in the car for another twenty-five minutes while she eats her breakfast, she's got another thing coming."

Standing on the porch, he raps his knuckles hard three times on the screen door. There is no response from inside. He hammers his fist a few more times, a little bit harder – still no response.

He presses his face against the screen door, but the house is dark and he is unable to see anything.

"Joyce!" he cries into the house. "It's Sheriff Gibson!"

There is no sound coming from inside the house. He tries the door – it is open. He slowly walks in. Everything seems as it should be. He walks passed the living room, the dining room, and toward the kitchen. He sees Joyce standing at the kitchen sink.

"Joyce…it's me…Sheriff Gibson," he says gently enough not to frighten her, but loud enough to be heard over the sound of water running in the sink. She shows no response. Then, he notices she isn't bending over the sink, but in fact bending down into the sink.

"Joyce?" he says once more as he enters the kitchen.

It does not take the eye of a criminal expert to see what is wrong. As he approaches Joyce, he sees the top portion of her back. It is bloody from multiple stab wounds.

Her eyes are wide open and lifeless. Her face presses against pots and pans – the same ones she used to prepare breakfast only a few minutes ago. There is blood all over the utensils, save for the ones under the stream of running water.

There is no question in Sheriff Gibson's mind she is dead, but he wants to be fully sure. He reaches out and places the first two fingers of his right hand on the side of her throat – there is no pulse. The body still holds warmth to it, meaning the murder has taken place recently – perhaps only moments ago. That means it is likely the killer is still on the premises. The Sheriff takes his gun from his holster and carefully and slowly searches the house. There is no sight or sound of anyone.

When he approaches the bedroom behind the stairs, the door is slightly ajar. He looks in and then pushes the door open and steps inside.

There on the bed is the dead body of Eleanor Russell. She is sitting up with two large pillows propped behind her. None of the food is touched on the breakfast tray on her lap. He reaches over and places the back of his hands against the scrambled eggs in the plate – they are still warm.

Her head tilts way back as if someone pulled her by the hair, forcing her head far back. Her unblinking eyes stare at the ceiling. In all his years as sheriff, he's seen few dead bodies and even fewer that were murdered. But he knows that whatever killed Eleanor Russell was a complete surprise to her, had taken her off guard.

Her throat is cut from ear to ear. There is no need to check her pulse – the front of her nightgown, the sheets, and the top portion of the covers blood-soaked.

The room is in shambles as if someone was desperately looking for something.

Satisfied that all danger is passed, Sheriff Gibson puts his gun back in his holster and slowly backs out of the room. He makes his way out of the house and back to the squad car. Reaching in through the open car window he pulls out the microphone of the police radio.

"This is Sheriff Gibson. . . . Is anyone reading me? Come in, please."

The police radio crackles with empty electronic static, then a click.

"Wilson here, Sheriff. What'cha need?"

"Wilson, listen carefully. I'm out here at the Widow Russell's place. There's been a double homicide. The widow and Joyce the housekeeper have both been murdered. I want you to rustle up all our people. I want them to go over the entire crime scene from the basement to the attic. . . . I want no stone left unturned."

"Sure, Sheriff. . . right away!"

"Oh, and Wilson, I want you and everyone else concerned not to say a word to anybody about this. . . especially to the papers. . . at least not yet. I don't want this to turn into a circus."

"Not a word," vows Wilson.

"Wait, Wilson, there is one person I want you to tell. Go into my office. . . . On my desk, you'll find a number for a Detective Benson. Call him and tell him what happened. Tell him if he wants to come to Tannersville, he's welcomed to."

****

Five hours later, Sheriff Gibson and his crew are still busy collecting evidence at the Russell home. The paramedics bag Joyce and Eleanor, and ever so gently carry them out to the ambulance. There is a small crowd of interested citizens gathering outside. It won't be long before the newspapers arrive – maybe even TV coverage. It can't be helped. In only a few more hours, that circus Sheriff Gibson tried to avoid will come to town. Everyone feels uneasy, but still there is a small amount of civic pride. To be mentioned on the news, even for murder, is a reason for the citizens of Tannersville to feel pride. Whatever it takes to get on the map is a good thing.

****

He stands at the front door watching the ambulance drive away when a dark unmarked car pulls up. Three men get out. They are not reporters; their suits are too old and too cheap. Sheriff Gibson can smell a city cop from a mile away. Perhaps this is that Benson he spoken to on the phone.

"Sheriff Gibson, I'm Detective Benson. I'd like to thank you for the heads-up on these killings. We got here as soon as we could. This is my partner, Detective Goebel, and our head of forensics, Lieutenant Dodson."

"Forensics?" Sheriff Gibson questions. "I've already got our people on it."

Sheriff Gibson sounds insulted, but Dodson is used to small towns taking offence, so he trudges on.

"I'd just like to take a few pictures," Dodson says, holding his camera.

"Yeah, well, we've already taken pictures!" Sheriff Gibson sounds put out. "I know, you get a hell of a lot more killings where you boys come from, but this ain't our first rodeo, and I'm ashamed to say it probably won't be our last. We know what we're doing. I'd be glad to share any pictures we have as soon as my people develop them."

There is an awkward moment of silence that Detective Goebel breaks.

"Well, you mind if we come in and look around?"

"Not at all," Sheriff Gibson says, backing from the door.

Inside, the trio stand looking around, then at the Sheriff, waiting for what information he is willing to share – there is none.

"So, where are the bodies?" Goebel asks.

"Gone. . . . That ambulance that just left while you were coming in, the bodies were in it."

"Why did you give permission to take the bodies away before we arrived?" Goebel asks.

"Listen, gentlemen, let's get one thing straight from the get-go," says Sheriff Gibson. "You're here on an invite. I thought maybe we could help one another, but this is our investigation. You three are just guests in our home, so please act like gracious guests.

Now, take a look around all you want, but don't touch anything and please don't get in the way."

The Sheriff walks toward the kitchen.

"Do you mind if we at least sit in on the autopsy?" Dodson calls to the Sheriff.

Sheriff Gibson turns around to face Dodson.

"You can view the bodies later…after the autopsy. I'll be going to the morgue myself, later; I'd be glad to drive you three with me."

Sheriff Gibson turns and disappears into the kitchen.

"Idiot," Dodson says softly, but loud enough for Goebel and Benson to hear.

"Now, now…let's not be an ungracious guest," Goebel says.

****

Sheriff Gibson pulls the squad car into the parking lot of Kathleen's Copper Kettle. Benson sits in the front seat with the Sheriff; Goebel and Dodson are in the back. All three men look at the Sheriff, unaware of his plans.

"I figure you boys must be starving. You probably ain't had anything to eat since you left for Tannersville early this morning. And once we get busy at the morgue, it'll be hours before any of us get a chance to eat.

"Now, I hope none of you has a weak stomach? I mean, eating a meal before looking at bodies after an autopsy?" Sheriff Gibson turns to direct his statement to Dodson.

"I can eat raw eggs while performing an autopsy," Dodson boasts, putting emphasis on the word performing.

"Raw eggs, eh? Well, I think we can do a little better than that. Kathleen makes a mighty fine hamburger; ask anybody in town. Come on, it's on me. I'm buying," he says.

They all huddle around one small table near the window overlooking the parking lot. It is late afternoon, too late for lunch and too early for dinner. The restaurant is empty with only one waitress on duty. Of course, she and the Sheriff know each other.

"Hamburgers, fries, and cokes all the way around. Thank you, Sara."

"Coming right up, Sheriff."

He then focuses his attention to the other men sitting at the table.

"You know, fellas, I didn't come here just to feed our faces. I didn't want you to think I'm that heartless. I'm sure you have several questions and I'll do my best to answer them."

The pride of all three officers is slightly dented, but they are willing to play Sheriff Gibson's game.

"What time do you estimate the killings?" Dodson asks.

"Well, let's see…I got to the Russell place a little after seven thirty, and everything was still warm and fresh, so I'd estimate it at just after seven in the morning."

"Why were you there in the first place?" Benson asks.

"Eleanor Russell called me the night before. She insisted I come over first thing in morning. She said she had something she wanted to tell me…something to get off her chest."

"And what was that?"

"I never got the chance to find out."

"Didn't she give you an inkling of what it was about?" Benson asks.

"It wasn't clear – something about her sons and her husband…a confession, she said. Whatever it was, someone thought it important enough to kill her."

"Then why would they kill the housekeeper?" Dodson asks.

"Just because she was there. …Wrong place, wrong time, as they say. It would have been near impossible to get to the Widow Russell without going through Miss Joyce."

"Do you have any suspicions who might have done this?"

A smile comes over Sheriff Gibson's face; he shakes his head and lets out a soft laugh. "No, not really, but I'll tell you who we've spoken to. Of course, you have Victor locked up, but I wouldn't put it past him to have his own suspicions. I'd question that boy if I were you.

"We spoke with Teresa Russell, and she doesn't know or care about any of this. She's more concerned with her three kids. Also, I don't think she benefits from the Widow Russell's death. I don't think Eleanor liked her much. You know the type, "no one is good enough for my boy."…And she avoided her grandchildren like the plague.

"Miss Joyce…well, she lived alone here in town most of her life. Just an old spinster; she never married. She does have a son though…Kyle Adams. He works as a gym teacher over at the High School. No one knows who his father was…at least, Joyce never told anybody. She raised him till he went off to the army. When he came back home, he started working for the school and bought himself a good-size house here in town. He and his mother never lived together from that point on, but still they were close."

Later, after the investigations, the detectives found it strange how off base Sheriff Gibson was on the information on Kyle Adams. For such a small town, one would think such information would be well known. It was as if the sheriff was purposely lying, or no one in town had the true knowledge on Kyle.

Sheriff Gibson continued, "Earlier, I went over to tell Kyle the bad new; I didn't want him hearing it from gossiping neighbors. He took it pretty bad; got all shook up about it…crying like a baby."

"Did he say where he was this morning? Does he have an alibi?" Goebel asks.

"Strangely enough, he does." There is a knowing smile on Sheriff Gibson face. "And I used the word strange on purpose. Seems Kyle Adams' alibi is he spent the night with a lady friend, if you get my drift. And now here's the strange part…the woman Kyle spent the night with was Helen Haywood …Eleanor Russell's niece…Victor Russell's cousin!"

Goebel and Benson look at each other in bewilderment. As well, Dodson knows enough about the case to find this information interesting.

"Damn, the plot thickens," Goebel says to his partners.

"Did you get to speak with Ms. Haywood?" Benson asks.

"No, she was long gone when I got to Kyle's place. We haven't been able to reach her. She might still be in route to her home.

"Kyle says she spent the night and left early in the morning."

"I don't own an almanac, but if I remember correctly, the sun rises at six in the morning this time of year. Maybe we make a point to talk to Mr. Adams before we leave town," Goebel says.

"Here's the burgers. . . .Eat up, boys. Soon as we're done, we'll head for the morgue."

****

The morgue is small, but well equipped. Dodson finds it easy to work in. He studies the two bodies carefully. Whoever performed the autopsy has not botched it; they have done well. Dodson reads the autopsy notes as he goes over every inch of the corpses. He looks over photographs of the bodies at the murder scene over and over, trying to place pieces of the puzzle into their respective places.

Goebel and Benson examine photos taken at the Russell home. Sheriff Gibson looks on quietly.

There is the sound of footsteps coming down the stairs. Each of them stop what they are doing and look to see an elderly gentleman approaching. Sheriff Gibson does the introductions.

"I hope you don't mind, gentlemen, but I've asked Dr. Miller here today to see if he could be of some help. Doc was the only medical help in town for years until they built the medical center. He's also a good old friend, and I respect his opinion."

To the annoyance of Dodson, old Doc Miller circles a few feet around him like some old vulture looking for scraps – looking over Dodson's shoulder.

Twenty minutes later, Dodson announces he has finished his analysis. All the men huddle about, eager to hear his findings.

"Well, first off, looking at the notes of the autopsy, I must agree with most of their suspicions. From the angle and the force of the stab wounds on Joyce, the housekeeper, I would say without a doubt it was a man…a right-handed man. The cut across Mrs. Russell's throat reflects these findings, also. The knife, based on the looks of the cuts must have been a large hunting knife, held in the right hand, and cut from her left ear to the right. The cut was also deep, all the way to the neck bone, which also reflects the strength of a man.

"Looking at the photos of the room, it appears the killer ransacked the bedroom, perhaps to rob something or to at least make it look like a robbery. Was there anything missing?" Dodson is addressing Sheriff Gibson.

"A few things, we believe. We never found Joyce's purse. In the bedroom, there was nothing left of value. All her jewelry taken. Not a single earring found."

"I see," Dodson says. "Then I'd like to propose another scenario. As much as we might think these killings have something to do with the Helen Haywood case or with Victor Russell, possibly, they might be completely unrelated.

"I don't know if anyone else noticed there is a railroad crossing less than a mile from the Russell home. It is possible, and it wouldn't be the first time, a transient hopped off a train and went into the first house he came to. Noticing the only inhabitants were older women, he killed them and ransacked the house. Then he made it back to the railroad crossing and hopped on the next train out of town.

"From the bodies' positions, he took them by surprise. They found Joyce facedown in the kitchen sink, three stab wounds in her back, and the water was still running. I doubt if she knew what happened.

"As for Eleanor Russell, it appears he rushed into the bedroom, and before the old woman could make a peep, he cut her throat."

"What about fingerprints?" Benson asks.

"He never touched anything. He stabbed Joyce, took her purse. Killed the old woman, rummaged through some clothes to get to a jewelry box. It's not surprising there were no fingerprints."

"And what about the murder weapon? Where is it?"

"Like I said, it looks like it was a hunting knife...probably his own knife. ...He took it with him. I'd say the killer is long gone."

A moment of silence goes over the room as each man tries to absorb what he just heard.

"Well, what do you think, Doc?" Sheriff Gibson asks.

Old Doc Miller moves in closer and looks carefully at the bodies and photos.

"Well, I'd say that was some darn good work of deduction on this here young man's part. And I agree with a good amount of what he said; only I don't believe a stranger done this. I'd say it was somebody they knew and felt safe with."

"Oh...and how did you come up with that?" Dodson asks.

"Well, like you, I remembered the Russell place was close to the railroad crossing. So when the Sheriff here called me and asked me to come take a look-see, I thought I'd do some investigating of my own. I called the rail company and found out only trains coming through these parts today were coal cars. And no self-respecting hobo, or transient as you call them, hops a coal car; they'd get filthy. And there was no sign of coal dust or shoe marks at the murder scene. So that eliminates any hobos...I mean, transients.

"Now, I do agree it was a man...a right-handed man, but he was no stranger. Look at the three stab wounds in Joyce's back."

They all gather around and look at the now clean wounds. Doc Miller continues.

"Notice anything strange? Now, all three wounds...the same knife made them, only this wound is slightly larger than the other two. That means it was the first; she was relaxed...not expecting it. The other two are smaller because she tightened her muscles."

"Then why did he stab her in the back? He must have snuck up on her!" Dodson says.

"You were inside the house," old Doc says. "These old houses around here – some of them are over a hundred years old – the old wooden floors creak with the slightest touch. You couldn't sneak up on anyone in the old Russell place if you wrapped pillows around your feet. The killer just didn't want the hassle of having to fight with her, if he didn't take her by surprise.

"Same goes for Mrs. Russell in the bedroom. She knew the killer, she was at ease. Look at this photo of her lying in bed with her throat cut. ...Look at the breakfast tray. I realize she was an old woman, but no matter how weak and slow she was, if someone rushed her, she would have at least been strong enough and fast enough to spill her glass of orange juice."

Everyone looks at the photo. Sure enough, there on the breakfast tray is a full glass of un-spilled orange juice.

"No, she didn't see this coming any more than Joyce did," concludes Dr. Miller.

"Then who do you think did it?" Goebel asks.

Old Doc looks down and scratches his head.

"Well, there's your mystery. I haven't the foggiest. Only people who would have anything on these two women are Victor…and there's no way he could have done this. Teresa, Victor's wife…but she would have no reason for killing Joyce, and I'm sure Eleanor wouldn't leave anything to her in her will, anyways. Then there's Kyle Adams. …Of course, he might have wanted his mother dead, but I doubt that. I've never heard an unkind word between them, and Joyce didn't have any real money to speak of. And again, what reason would he have for killing Eleanor Russell? He surely had many other opportunities to kill his mother if he wanted to without involving Eleanor Russell.

"No, this is a mystery to me, because it would have to be someone associated with both victims, and I can't think of whom that would be. I haven't the foggiest."

****

Goebel, Benson, and Dodson, go through the formality of interviewing both Teresa Russell and Kyle Adams. They have to agree with Old Doc that singularly each as a suspect makes little sense. But still they do the interviews in hopes some light might shine on the mystery.

Teresa Russell shows little remorse for the loss of her mother-in-law, even a slight amount of hostility toward the old woman.

"She was always babying Victor," Teresa says. "He had the chance of being a good man, but she made sure he would never grow up. She accepted me only on terms I stay out-of-the-way of her relationship with her son. Because he wanted me, she was willing to tolerate me. I hardly ever saw the woman, except for holidays.

"When the children came, she accepted them because they were her son's, but she did little else. Her own grandchildren! She never visited them or had them over to her home. On their birthdays she sent a card with ten dollars in it…same for Christmas.

"So she's dead…big deal…who cares? She meant nothing to me. You might have told me a stranger got killed, because that's what we were to each other…strangers.

"When Victor and I separated, she knew how hard it was for me…alone with three children…her grandchildren. She never once offered me a nickel. She never offered, and I never asked. We just stayed out of each other's lives. Strangers…that's what we were. And, good riddance to her, the old bitch…that's what I say."

"Mrs. Russell, you mentioned you and your husband, Victor, were separated. May I ask why the two of you separated?" Benson asks.

Teresa's face goes blank. She seems taken off guard by the question. After a moment of long thoughtfulness she speaks.

"It was because...because of someone else," she says shyly.

"When you say someone else, what do you mean? Did he have someone else, or did you?"

Again, she goes into a moment of thoughtfulness.

"Both," she finally answers in a whisper.

"I see," Benson says.

****

If Teresa Russell shows little remorse for her mother-in-law's passing, or for Joyce, for that matter, Kyle Adams is the exact opposite. He trembles and cries as he speaks of his beloved mother.

"Why would anybody do something so horrible to two old women?" Kyle asks, with tears in his eyes.

"That's what we're trying to find out," Goebel says. "Is there anything you can think of that might help us?"

"I can't think of anything. My mother didn't have an enemy in the world! And to die so horribly...I don't understand!"

Kyle covers his face from the officers as more tears roll down his cheeks.

"Kyle, we realize this is a difficult time for you, so we'll make it as short as we can...just a few more questions," Benson says.

"Tell us about your father, Kyle. Do you know where he is?" Goebel asks.

"I don't know who he is. My mother never told me. And honestly, I seriously think my mother didn't know either. She always spoke about being married, but I've never seen any documents to prove it. She was single, young, and foolish when she had me, as she used to say to me. Who knows, maybe it was a one-night fling with a traveling salesman. I couldn't say, and if my mother were still alive, I doubt if she could either."

"You live in this big house alone? Why didn't your mother live with you?" Goebel asks.

"I begged her time and again to move in. I told her there was plenty of room. But she wouldn't hear of it. She said no woman wants a man who lives with his mother. But I think she liked her privacy, besides doing what she thought was best for me. She was always thinking of me, putting me first."

"What I don't understand," Goebel says, "is when we spoke to some of the townspeople about your mother; they all gave us a different story. Some spoke of her as being a widow and others tell us she never married, as well as you saying you never knew your father."

"That was just my mother trying to do the best for me as she knew how. I guess she felt sorry for me…having to live with the stigma of not even knowing my father. Sometimes she told people she was a widow and that her husband died and left me this big house because he loved me.

"Other times she gave people a different last name than Adams, so no one would make the connection, or she said she was widowed twice over, which explained the name difference."

"Don't you think that was strange for your mother to do?" Benson says.

"I guess so," Kyle says, "but my mother had her quirks, especially when it came to the subject of my father."

"Now, you told the police you were with someone last night. With Helen Haywood…how did that ever come about?"

"Helen and I met last time she came to town to visit her aunt. We hit it off right from the start. I went and visited her a few weeks ago. When she told me she was coming to visit her aunt again, I invited her to stay with me."

"Do you know she's married?"

"Not for long," Kyle says sharply in his own defense. "She and her husband separated and are planning to get a divorce."

"And how did you two meet?"

"Through my mother…I mean…I should say, because of my mother. I went to visit my mother one day when she was working for Mrs. Russell. Helen was there, and I asked her out to dinner that same night."

Strange that Kyle would lie, but he did.

"Did she tell you why she came to visit her aunt?"

"She said she had come to town on business…something to do with her job. She just happened to be in town, so she spent a day or two at her aunt's."

"Did she tell you what happened or what transpired between her and her aunt during her visit?"

"No, we never spoke about her aunt." He tells another lie.

"Well, thank you for your time and for being so understanding, Kyle. We'll be in touch. Call us if you think of anything else."

"Glad to be of help, if I can," Kyle says.

"So, now what?" Dodson asks, sitting in the backseat as they drive back to the city.

"That's simple," Benson says. "We talk to Victor."

"Definitely…Victor," Goebel adds.

****

"Isn't my lawyer supposed to be here?" Victor asks as they usher him into the now familiar interrogation room where Goebel and Benson are waiting. A dull light from the one table lamp is all that lights the room.

"Your lawyer sends his apologies. He had some important business to attend to, but he gave us permission to talk with you," Goebel says. "Sit down, Victor."

"You guys are so full of it," Victor says, then laughs and takes a seat across the table from the two detectives. "I told you a long time ago, I may be crazy, but I ain't stupid. But, hey, what do I care…? You guys are going to do whatever you want, no matter what the law says. Besides, as long as I'm behind bars, I'm safe. I couldn't give a rat's turd."

"First, let me say, we're sorry for what happened to your mother, Victor," Benson says.

"Sorry? I'm glad to hear somebody's sorry about the old girl's demise, but I'm not." Victor began to laugh as he speaks. "She got off easy, only having her throat cut. She deserved worse and would have got it if time wasn't an important factor."

"What do you mean 'time was a factor'?"

"The Sheriff…she called the Sheriff. She was going to spill her guts to him, so she needed to be taken out."

"How do you know about the meeting with the Sheriff?"

"I know lots a things; I've got the inside track…I get my dope straight from the horse's mouth. She was lucky! If she didn't need to be taken out so quickly, she would have been looking at a month of pain or more. She was always pulling stunts like that…having a conscience and all. I'm surprised he let her live as long as she did."

"Who let her live, Victor? Was it your father?"

"Bingo…give the man a cigar," laughs Victor. "You're finally catching on!"

"But your father is dead. How could he kill your mother?"

"Now, did I say he killed her? No, I said he let her live, even though she was always in the way. No, Daddy didn't kill Mommy…Daddy had Mommy killed!"

"So, who did it? Who killed Mommy?"

"Bubba did!" Victor nearly topples over laughing. "It was my brother. He got the order from Daddy."

"But you said Nicholas was dead!"

"And he is," Victor says, "It's all done with mirrors, I guess."

"Is there another brother…other than Nicholas?"

Victor holds his sides as he laughs.

"Is there another brother?" Victor says mockingly, "Is there another Mommy? Is there another Daddy? I am he, and he is we, and I am she, and she is he, and we are altogether!" Victor said in a singsong manner.

"This is useless," Benson says.

"I agree," Goebel says.

Eighteen

You Could Do It

Helen gets up from her desk, hearing noise in the hallway. "What's all the commotion?" she asks Todd Yeager as he rushes past her.

Todd turns to face Helen. He walks backwards as he speaks, not missing a step. "There's a celebration in John Pierce's office. He just got word he's this year's Employee of the Year. ...Big bonus, you know?" Todd turns again, facing forward and runs off.

"Well, good for John," Helen says, smiling as she goes to join the celebration.

There is a line of cheering coworkers that starts at the water cooler down the hall and flows into Pierce's office, right up to the foot of his desk. Helen pushes her way forward, just close enough to see Pierce standing on top of his desk.

"Speech! Speech!" The cry starts at the back of the hall and ends in the office. Pierce holds out both palms of his hands, signaling for them to be quiet. The crowd goes silent.

"First, I'd like to thank all the little people I stepped on to get to where I am today. And I want all of you to know I won't forget any of you...at least not for the first three months after my promotion," Pierce says, with ice-cold seriousness. Then, unable to hold it any longer, his face bursts into a smile, and then into laughter – as do all the others present.

Again, he holds his palms out, gesturing for silence.

"No, seriously, there are some people I would like to thank from the bottom of my heart. First, I'd like to thank God. Second, my beautiful and blessed wife, Tina, and our two lovely children. But most of all I'd like to thank you, my good friends."

There is a moment of true electric emotion in the air that leaves each person speechless.

"Sentimental horse apples!" someone yells from the back of the crowd, and the celebration returns to its original ear perching shouting and laughter.

Someone shakes a bottle of soda, twists off the bottle cap, and sprays down Pierce in true champagne fashion.

An hour later, when all the coffee and doughnuts are gone, the entire crowd scatters. John Pierce finds himself alone. He begins picking up ripped pieces of paper that had been used as confetti, and places them in the wastepaper basket. He looks up. There is Helen Haywood standing in the doorway of his office, smiling.

"The title of Employee of the Year comes with a promotion, too?" she asks.

He smiles and nods affirmative.

"Yeah, looks like we'll be moving up to corporate. I'll miss you, Helen; you've been a good friend."

"Not as good a friend as you," Helen says, walking into the office. "I never did thank you for that night you and family showed so much concern for me, when I needed it the most...how you said you would pray for me."

"And we still do. Our daughter, Lateasha, says a prayer every night for the nice blond woman who works with Daddy."

"She's a lovely child," Helen says.

"We think so. ...Which reminds me...with all the celebrating, I haven't called my wife to tell her the good news. So, if you don't mind?"

"Oh, not at all. ...Tell Tina hi for me."

"I sure will," John says as he walks to the phone on his desk. "I know my wife will be happy for me, but I sure hope she doesn't mind moving out of state to corporate. She has so many friends here, especially at church. Church..." He bits his lip, as he softly speaks, "Some of the bigwigs are taking us out for a celebration dinner next week. ...I need to call some people from church and see if we can get a babysitter for the children."

"Would you let me?" Helen asks.

"What's that?" John says.

"Let me babysit! Oh, please, it would mean so much to me to do one last favor for you."

"Are you sure?" John asks. "Well, I can't see why not. If it's all right with Tina, then it's all right with me."

****

Back in her office, Helen receives a call from Goebel and Benson explaining all that has gone down in Tannersville. Immediately, she closes her office door and dials her phone.

"Hello?" says a sleepy-sounding voice.

"Kyle, it's me, Helen."

"Oh, Helen...yeah, hi."

"I just heard from the police about your mother. Oh, Kyle, I'm so sorry."

"Oh, yeah...well, you know...I appreciate it."

There is an odd tone to Kyle's voice – not sleepy – drugged or drunk. Perhaps he has been drinking. Helen does not think this an impossibility or odd. Losing your mother in such a horrendous manner – she can only imagine.

"I just wanted to see if you were all right," she whispers, hoping to draw him out.

"I'm okay…I guess."

"Kyle, have you been sleeping? You sound so tired."

"I haven't been able to sleep more than a few minutes the past two nights, not since this happened. I don't remember the last time I ate something. I just don't feel like eating anything right now."

"Of course not. You're still in shock, but it'll all pass," she says, trying to be of some comfort.

There is a rumbling over the phone line, as if Kyle is occupied with doing something else, maybe something in the kitchen. Then there is a loud thud over the line, as if he dropped the phone, followed by crashing sounds, as if trying to recover the phone from off the floor.

"Kyle, are you all right?"

"Helen…you still there?" he says, once he regains the phone.

"Kyle, are you all right?" she repeats. "Do you need me? Do you want me to come to Tannersville? I could be there in a couple of hours."

"No…No…No!" he hollers at her.

"I just thought…" she says sheepishly.

"No…no…whatever you do…don't. …I don't want you to come!"

She thinks this strange. She understands the strain he must be under, but this is something different. Why are his answers so harsh and cold?

"I just thought you could use a friend right now," she says almost in tears.

Then, there is a rumbling once more over the phone line. For a moment it sounds as if he placed his hand over the receiver so she can't hear whatever it is that is taking place. As he removes his hand from the receiver, Helen swears she hears a voice other than Kyle's – another man's voice.

"Kyle, is there someone there with you?"

"No, there's no one here; I've got the TV on. Just give me a second to turn it off."

Again, she senses the palm of his hand covering the receiver. Only, this time she can still hear Kyle's voice.

"No…no…I won't!" she hears him scream, "I will never!"

"Helen?" he asks, returning to the phone.

"Kyle, there is someone there with you! What is going on? You're frightening me! I'm coming over, Kyle. Don't tell me not to. ...I'm coming to you!"

"No, damn it, Helen! I don't want you to come. I don't want to see you. In fact, maybe it would be best if we don't see each other ever again!"

Helen goes silent for a moment, digesting what she just heard.

"Kyle, what are you saying? I don't understand."

"What don't you understand?" His voice becomes cruel. "It was a big mistake! People back out of relationships every day. ...What's to understand?"

"But I thought..."

"Well, you thought wrong. Listen, you're a nice person, and I don't want to hurt you, but it's just not going to work. I'm sorry, but I have to hang up now. And please don't ever call me again."

There is a loud click in Helen's ear. She places the phone down and stares at it. Her mind cannot grasp what he said to her. There is no clear explanation for it. Her first reaction is to dial him up again and demand some kind of answer she can wrap her mind around.

Perhaps she should ignore his wishes, hop in her car, and drive nonstop to Tannersville and demand an answer. Maybe if he sees her face-to-face, maybe then he will talk.

But, a moment later, all those feelings wash away. Somewhere in her mind, she knows there is nothing she can do. She has chosen wrong once more in her life.

She continues to stare at the phone, unable to move. She swears she won't cry as the tears run down her cheeks.

****

Despite their close and ever-growing friendship, there is a part of Helen and Angela's relationship that remains in an official capacity – Angela is still her doctor. Except for the short period of time Angela spends recuperating from her assault, their weekly office meetings at the hospital continue like clockwork. Which is why Helen is so surprised to receive a note from Angela by email, apologizing for not being available for the following day's visit because of unexpected business.

The patient side of Helen thinks nothing of the message, but the friend part of her knows something is wrong. She decides to phone Angela.

"Angela, I read your email. What's up?"

"Do you remember when you were first staying at the hospital; I tried to get you involved in a rehab group?"

"Do I? How could I forget? It just wasn't for me. Those poor women...I felt so sorry for them. ...They all seemed so...so... traumatized."

"Well, do you remember one of the young women...Maria?"

"Yes, I remember her...small Hispanic girl."

"That was her. It seems she took an overdose of sleeping pills last night."

"Oh, my God, but it couldn't have been intentional!"

"I'm afraid so," says Angela. "There was a suicide note found."

"But she was the most hopeful of the group. She had so much faith; she believed it would all work out."

"I suppose that's why I didn't see it coming," Angela says. "I feel terrible. I feel responsible."

"How could you feel that way?"

"She was my responsibility. I'm trained to see the signs and..."

"And the signs just weren't there," Helen insists.

"Anyway, the funeral is tomorrow, and I have to go."

"May I go with you?" Helen asks.

"Why would you want to go?"

"Because, despite what happened, she was a beautiful and fearless woman, and I want to honor her. Besides, from the way you sound, I think you could use a friendly shoulder to lean on."

"You're probably right. Where should I meet you?"

"I'm driving," Helen says. "I'll pick you up at your home tomorrow. What time is the funeral?"

"It starts at one."

"Then I'll see you at twelve."

****

In a spacious gray room with drab green curtains blocking out the sun and rows of metal folding chairs is a small wooden casket at the front of the room. In it lies the body of Maria Alvarado.

In front of the casket sits the immediate family: her parents, siblings, aunts, uncles, and cousins. The sorrow they suffer is clear to see by the gloom that hangs on each of their faces, and the tears that run from their eyes.

Toward the back of the room are friends and neighbors of the deceased. Far-off in a corner is a small group of women who knew Maria perhaps better than anyone else in the room.

"Well, we need to go and pay our respects," Angela says.

She starts toward the front of the room, the other women following – save for Carmen. Angela stops, turns, and looks at her. Not saying a word, she waits for an explanation.

"I can't…" says Carmen, "I just can't…"

Helen looks surprised. Carmen, who always is the more vocal, the hardest and strongest of the group, now reduced to a tearful and sorrowful individual, unable to move.

"It's all right," Helen says. "I'll stay with her."

The small group resumes walking to the front of the room.

Carmen and Helen stand near each other watching in silence. Then Carmen turns to Helen, "He got out, you know. That's why she killed herself; they let him out."

"Who…?" Helen asks.

"Maria's guy…the one who raped and beat her…they let him out early on good behavior. Maria couldn't live with that. …She was so afraid. They don't understand what those bastards do to you! What they take from you! There's no peace. It stays with you for the rest of your life.

"Remember, I told you…he becomes your guy and he lives with you in here for the rest of your life!" She points to the temple of her head.

"I just wish I could meet with my guy," Carmen continues. "I'd know what to do this time."

"Jab your fingers into his eye sockets?" says Helen.

"Oh, you remember me saying that?" smiles Carmen.

"I don't think I could do something like that."

"Most women can't. And it's not just fear stopping them; it's ignorance. Because women don't think…they just don't think! While he's raping and beating them…they just want to get through it alive. …They don't realize it doesn't stop there. If they knew of all the years it will haunt them. How the torture goes on. Then they could do it. Think of how much you've suffered because of him already, and then look out at the years that lay before you. …It with never change till one of you is dead. When you think of it that way…you could do it."

Nineteen

Mothers and Brothers Everywhere

"Try to get him to talk. Once you do, ask him as many questions as you can." Benson is giving some last minute instructions to Helen as they walk down the hall toward the visiting room.

Victor demands to talk to his cousin "one last time," as he put it. When asked what he means by "one last time," he refuses to comment.

"I don't know exactly what advice I can give you," Benson says. "Lately, he's acquired a short attention span. So I advise you to ask as many questions as you can and as fast as you can. But then again, when you bombard him with questions, sometimes he freaks and refuses to say a word. Let's just hope he's in the mood to talk. He might be. After all, he's the one who called this meeting."

They stop just outside the visitor's room. Benson holds the door open for Helen.

"We'll be listening," he says. "Good luck."

Helen walks in alone. Victor is sitting in his place behind the Plexiglas, holding his phone. Helen sits down and puts the receiver to her ear.

"Hello, Victor, how are you?"

"How am I? What the hell kind of question is that?" Victor laughs. "I'm in prison. ...What do you think?"

"I just meant I'm sorry for what happened to your mother," Helen says.

"Why is everybody sorry about what happened to her?" He is still laughing. "She only got what she deserved. I knew it would happen someday."

"Victor, how did you know it would?"

"He always said the days of the club were numbered...that he would break it up someday. So I guess you could say he's started to make good on his word."

"Who is he?"

"Don't play games," Victor says. "You know who."

"Victor, did your father kill your mother and Joyce?"

"No, both mothers were killed by Bubba."

"Both mothers?" says Helen. "I don't understand."

"They were both mothers...right? And Bubba killed them."

"Bubba...? You mean Nicholas?"

"No, Nicholas is dead! Daddy killed him years ago."

"But I thought it was an accident?"

"That's what Daddy made it look like...an accident. Nicholas was getting a bit too rebellious at the time...saying he was going to tell everyone about the club. So Daddy killed him and made it look like an accident."

"So, if Bubba isn't Nicholas...who is he?"

Victor ignores the question and changes the subject.

"That's why I've asked you to come here," he says, "to warn you. Daddy is calling an end to the club. We're all doomed, even you, Nancy. You're an honorary member, but a member, nonetheless. He's sure to kill you, too!"

Helen ignores Victor referring to her as Nancy and continues to ask questions.

"You still haven't answered me, Victor. Who is Bubba?"

That madman smile comes over Victor's face.

"They're both mothers," he says, "Daddy loved them both. Momma was mine and Nicholas' mother, but Joyce was a mother, too."

"Your father had a child with Joyce?"

"Bingo!" Victor laughs. "Mothers and brothers are everywhere. The club needed members...two would never do! The more the merrier!"

Helen's eyes grow wild with fear.

"Victor, are you saying your father and Joyce gave birth to Kyle? Is Kyle your half-brother? Is Kyle Bubba?"

"Bingo!"

He will not stop laughing. He laughs as they usher him back to his cell.

****

Richard reaches across his desk to answer his phone.

"Richard Haywood speaking..."

"Richard...it's me."

Helen's voice is unmistakable to him.

"Yeah?" he says coldly.

"I'm sorry to bother you, Richard, but I've just received the divorce papers."

"Yeah, so what about it?"

"Well, according to this, I get possession of nearly everything!"

"So?"

"I just don't understand. At first, I thought we were heading straight toward a major disagreement. Now you're not even giving yourself a fair share?"

"Hell, I just want out, and as soon as possible. I've asked for a transfer with the company, and they gave it to me. I'll be leaving the state at the end of the month."

Helen knows it isn't her place to ask; nevertheless, she does.

"Is Francis going along with this?"

"It doesn't matter. It's all over between Francis and me. Seems I was only a wrung on the climb up the corporate ladder for her. She found someone with more clout and lots more money."

"I'm so sorry to hear that, Richard."

"What the hell, life's a bitch. In fact, it's one bitch after another."

There is a moment of silence between them. Helen searches for something meaningful to say, but she can't think of anything.

"Well, I guess that's all there is?" she says.

"Yeah, I guess so," he agrees.

"Richard, are you sure you only want half of the bank account? You're entitled to half of everything we owned."

"For what? I've got my car and enough money to start over. I've moved all my stuff out of the house. You can move back in anytime you like."

"Richard, I'm so sorry."

"Sorry? Sorry about what?"

"I don't know. I'm just sorry."

"Don't sweat it." There is a slight chuckle in his voice.

"Richard, is there anything I can do for you?"

"Yeah, there is something you can do."

"What's that, Richard?"

"Sign those papers!"

****

Based on the conversation between Victor and Helen, it is not difficult to gain a warrant to bring Kyle Adams in for questioning, as well as a warrant to search his home.

Goebel and Benson are en route with Dodson and his assistant, Myers, to Tannersville when they are informed over the police radio by Sheriff Gibson that Kyle Adams is nowhere to be found. The sheriff and Officer Wilson meet them outside Kyle's home.

"You're not going to try to pull rank on us like last time, are you, Sheriff?" Goebel voices his concern.

"No, this is your call, and it's your warrant," says Sheriff Gibson.

"So what's the word on Kyle Adams?" Benson asks.

"Don't know. As soon as we got the call, we came here to pick him up, but he was long gone. Neighbors say they haven't seen him or his car in the driveway for days.

"We called his work; they haven't heard from him in three days. They figured he was still in mourning over loss of his mother, so they didn't press the issue."

They all walk toward the house. Sheriff Gibson holds the door open.

"From the looks of inside the house, he packed some of his belongings and got out of here in a hurry. I've put his description, his car, and license number out on a tristate alert."

They enter the house; nothing looks out of the ordinary. Dodson and his assistant get down to work, collecting fingerprints, fibers, hair and skin samples, and much more, while Goebel and Benson ferret through the house.

"We're going to find something on this guy," Goebel says. "He's dirty as sin; I just know it."

"What makes you so sure Kyle Adams is involved with anything?" asks Sheriff Gibson.

Goebel gets up from the floor after looking under the bed and looks the Sheriff's in his eyes.

"Years of experience, for one. I can feel it in my bones; this guy is a nutcase! I mean...just look around!"

Sheriff Gibson does just that.

"I don't know...it all looks normal to me."

"Normal! You call this normal?" Goebel shouts. "Do you know what I just found under the bed?"

The Sheriff shakes his head no and shrugs his shoulders.

"I'll tell you what I found under the bed – nothing, not even one dust bunny...immaculate! The kitchen looks like it's never been used. All the knives in the silverware drawer are facing in the same direction. The bathroom...you could eat off the floor. This is supposed to be a bachelor's pad, man! My old grandma's house ain't half as clean as this is!"

Goebel goes over to the clothes closet.

"The shirts are with the shirts, the pants are with the pants, the jackets are with the jackets, and everything is facing in the same direction. I tell you, this guy is as neurotic as they come. Look, all his shoes have been spit-shined. Say...what do we have here?"

Goebel bends down and moves a pair of shoes, exposing a loose floorboard.

"Jackpot!" Goebel yells. "Hey, Benson, Dodson, get your butts in here. I think I found something!"

Everyone is looking over Goebel's shoulder as he removes the floorboard. He reaches down and rummages for a moment – he comes up with a handful of old photos.

"Oh, man, will you look at these," Goebel exclaims. "Child pornography!"

"Oh, my God…oh, my God," Sheriff Gibson seems in shook. "Oh, my God…that's not child pornography!"

"Like hell it ain't," Goebel says. "Just look at this!"

He fans the photos out like a deck of cards and holds them in front of Sheriff Gibson's face.

"That's not what I meant," says the Sheriff, sounding embarrassed. "I didn't mean to say it's not child pornography…it surely is! But what I mean is…that…that there…those boys in the pictures…that there's Kyle Adams when he was young…maybe ten or eleven…and that's Victor Russell…and the other boy is Victor's brother, Nicholas!"

"Say, who's the naked old guy?" Dodson asks.

"Oh, my God, I don't believe it! That there is Jerry Reynolds…Victor and Nicholas' father."

"And Kyle Adams' father," Benson says softly.

"What are you saying? Jerry was Kyle's father, too?" The Sheriff's voice is trembling.

"Well, that's if you believe Victor Russell's story. …That's what he says."

"I don't believe it," says Sheriff Gibson, mostly to himself.

"Come on," Dodson insists, "we can talk about this later. I've still got lots of collecting to do."

Goebel hands the photos to Dodson and turns to the Sheriff with a wry smile.

"See, I told you," Goebel says, "years of experience. I feel it in my bones. I can see a nutcase a mile away."

****

"You call this coffee?" Dodson asks, placing his cup down on Benson's desk.

"Never look a gift horse in the butt. Next time bring your own damn coffee!" Goebel says as he recovers the cup from the desk and wipes it before a ring forms on the wood.

"So what were the results from the Kyle Adams' home?" Benson asks.

"Well, we didn't get much from the house. The guy is a clean freak. Fingerprints…just his own, his mother's…and of course Helen Haywood's, who we already know spent the night with Kyle. But I did get enough hair, skin, and blood samples to run a DNA test."

"Where the hell did you find blood?" questions Goebel.

"In the bathroom, on the razorblade of his shaver. Must have nicked himself. Anyway…hold on tight, the results of the tests are going to blow your mind!

"Kyle Adams is definitely Victor Russell's half-brother…just like Victor said."

"So, Old Jerry Reynolds was doing Joyce on the side," Goebel interjects.

"It seems so," Dodson continues, "and the semen sample on Carol Hastings undergarments…the one that we couldn't identify next to the smear of Victor's semen…that was Kyle Adams'."

"Jeez, you think they did their thing on the underwear at the same time?" Goebel shutters.

"It's possible…both samples are the same age," Dodson replies.

He puts his hands up and waves them in excitement.

"Now here's the clincher!" Dodson continues. "When I compared Kyle's DNA to Helen Haywood's stillborn, the results came up positive, which makes him the father…which makes him the rapist…which make him…"

"Which makes him our man!" Benson concludes.

"Damn, that's cold!" Goebel says. "How do we tell Helen Haywood, 'the man who beat and raped you…got you pregnant…and has been terrorizing you for months is the same guy you've been sleeping with'?"

"We don't," says Benson. "We speak to Angela, Haywood's doctor. She can tell her in the manner and time she thinks best."

"I'm all for that!" Goebel agrees.

"Meanwhile," says Benson, "we need to put out an all-points bulletin marked urgent to arrest Kyle Adams. …Approach with caution; he is considered dangerous."

Twenty

The Devil Calls for a Date

The day finally arrives. Helen stands at the front door of John Pierce's home and rings the doorbell. A moment later, the door opens and she is greeted by Trent, John and Tina's son. Behind him shyly stands his little sister, Lateasha.

"Good evening, Mrs. Haywood," says Trent in a true well-mannered fashion. "My mother and father are still getting ready. My mother told me to ask you to wait in the living room. My father says my mother makes them late for everything, and she'll probably be late for her funeral."

"Well, I don't think your parents really wanted me to hear that last part," laughs Helen, "but no harm done. May I come in, please?"

"Yes, you may," says Trent, backing from the doorway. "The living room is right this way," he says, walking ahead, Lateasha still close by his side.

It is a lovely home, modern with hints of their heritage. African designs and artifacts are strategically incorporated into the decor. Helen has been there one time before, a Christmas party many years ago. She came without Richard who had to work late – or so he said. She tries to think if she ever invited John and Tina to her home, but they have never been. For her and Richard, their jobs took place over so many other parts of their lives; socializing was low on their priority list. But then again, maybe it was the way things were between them that made their jobs so important.

John comes rushing into the living room to welcome her. He's wearing a tuxedo and the biggest smile. Holding both his arms out, he takes both her hands and shakes them in greeting.

"Helen, thank you for coming. You don't realize how much we appreciate you doing this for us."

"Oh, it's my pleasure."

"Please, have a seat." He gestures to the couch. "Tina will be out in a minute…I hope," he adds softly, as not to be heard by Tina.

Helen laughs and sits down. John sits on the arm of a chair. He looks desperately down the hall toward their bedroom in hopes his wife will emerge at any moment.

"So, you must be excited," Helen says.

"Oh, yes…very excited."

There is an awkward moment of silence. Both of them want to say something, but not knowing what.

"John?" Helen says, finally. He turns to give her his full attention. "John, I have a confession to make."

He says not a word. A deep look of concern comes over his face.

"The night you and your family followed me to the mall parking lot, I saw your face in my mirror. All I could think about was that I saw the face of a black man and I was afraid."

"Some middle-class white guilt?" He begins to laugh.

"No, really…I mean it," Helen says in earnest.

"So do I," laughs John. "Listen, you're a good person…I know it…God knows it…and you know it. You were under much stress at the time. Don't do that to yourself."

"Yes, I know, but…"

"There she is," John announces as Tina enters the room. He stands up, takes her in his arms, and kisses her. "You look lovely," he says tenderly. "But we don't want to be late."

Tina smiles at Helen. "Oh, Helen, thank you for doing this."

"Your husband already thanked me. You need to get going or you'll be late."

"She's right, sweetheart," John says, slowly guiding his wife toward the front door. Tina begins to coach Helen while her husband directs her on.

"The children are already in their pajamas, so don't worry about that. Bedtime is at nine; make sure they brush their teeth first. I made a fruit and vegetable tray, if they get hungry."

"We need to go, honey!" says John.

"The number of the restaurant is near the phone. If you have any questions, feel free to call."

"We need to go, honey!"

"What about TV?" Helen asks.

"We don't watch TV in this house," Tina says. "There's a library of DVDs they're allowed to watch. Let them pick one only or they'll have you changing discs every ten minutes."

"Honey, Helen is a grown woman, she can figure it out. We need to go, or we'll be late." John nudges her forward.

"John, now you just stop it! I'm not leaving this house till I'm sure Helen knows what she needs to know and I've said goodbye to my babies."

"I'm sure I'll be all right, Tina," says Helen.

"I know you will," Tina replies, bending low and holding out her arms to her children. "Come to momma, children!"

Trent and Lateasha rush into their mother's arms.

"Now you two be good and be sure to mind Mrs. Haywood."

"We will," says Trent.

"Honey...?" A sound of urgency is in John's voice.

Tina kisses both her children and breaks free. The next moment, she and John are out the door.

"So, what should we do first?" Helen asks, smiling at both children.

"Noah...Noah...!" Lateasha sings as she bounces up and down.

Helen looks to Trent for an interpretation.

"*Noah and the Ark*...it's her favorite video."

"Well, then *Noah and the Ark* it will be."

It is a cartoon version of the story of Noah. Helen sits on the couch as both children lie on the floor and watch the screen with unblinking attention.

Halfway through the film, Helen goes into the kitchen to get the fruit and vegetable tray and places it on the coffee table. Both children reach behind them for the treats, not once taking their eyes off the screen for even a moment.

When the film finishes, Helen looks at the wall clock. It is eight thirty – still too early for bed. At that moment, the phone rings.

"I'll get it. You two just wait here," Helen says, making her way to the kitchen. She takes the phone receiver and places it to her ear.

Helen speaks into the receiver, "Pierce residence."

There is a dead silence. She listens carefully. She can hear someone breathing.

"Hello, is there anybody there?"

"*Buenas noches, señorita.*"

She recognizes his voice immediately. His dark, low, gravelly voice washes over her entire body like ice-cold dead fingers.

"What do you want?" she says softly, not wanting the children to hear.

"What do I want? What have I always wanted? What does anybody want? A little love and respect from all the right people. Are you one of the right people, Nancy?"

"I'm not Nancy!"

"Oh, yes, you are. You are now, like it or not! I see you're watching over a pair of petite pickaninnies tonight. I've always thought of mixing with the races as, how should

I put this...immoral. In fact, that whole incident with Donald Johnson, that gay black guy...I found that very distasteful, but it had to be done. You see what I have to go through for you? You can only imagine how much I love you.

"But now, these two tiny chocolate morsels you have under your wing...these might be interesting. Especially the young boy...another time and place and he might have been a budding African warrior. I would just love to make a man of him. And the little girl with those big brown moon-eyes. I'd just love to make her watch."

"Stop it...stop it..." Helen shouts. "Why are you doing this? How did you know I was here? Where are you?"

"Where am I?" he says laughing. "Why...I could be anywhere. No...I could be everywhere. I could be on the other end of town, in a trailer and holding a gun to the heads of those children's parents. I could be in the garage just waiting to kick the door in. I could be just outside looking at you right this moment through the kitchen window...and don't turn around to see!

"I'll huff and puff and blow your house down. ...I eat little piggies like you...you three little piggies!"

Helen is shaking and crying, uncontrollably. She finds it difficult to hold the phone – it feels so heavy. She grows faint, but she knows she has to hold on for the sake of the children.

"Listen to me, Nancy, and listen well. One way or another, all our troubles will be resolved tonight. If you want no one hurt, you'll do whatever I say.

"First, if I so much as smell police, I will bring a world of hurt down on everyone you ever loved...especially those two children you have in there with you."

"What do you want me to do?" Helen sobs.

"I want you to leave that house this instant and meet me for one last rendezvous at our spot. ...Come to the lake."

"I can't, I can't leave the children alone."

"To hell with the little bastards. ...I'll crush their black little skulls before your very eyes, if you don't do what I say."

"If I leave the children alone, how do I know you'll meet me at the lake and not come in for the children?"

"You're so mistrusting, Nancy. You have my word. Besides, why would I turn down a chance to be with my favorite girl?"

Helen thinks for a minute.

"No, I'm not leaving these children alone. Their parents will be home in an hour and a half; you can wait till then. I promise, as soon as they come home, I'll come to the lake."

There is another moment of silence.

"Very well," he says. "I'll leave now. ...I'll meet you at our spot."

"By the way," Helen says. "I've got a gun. If you're lying, and you put one foot in this house...I'll kill you!"

"A gun...? How exciting! I hope this time you remember to bring bullets."

The phone clicks dead.

Helen rushes back into the living room. The children are on the floor playing with crayons and paper.

"Come on, children, take your things. ...We're going to stay in your parents' room for a while."

"Why?" Lateasha asks, looking up at Helen.

"Don't ask why," says Trent, picking up his crayons and paper. "Momma said to do whatever Mrs. Haywood tells us to do."

Helen ushers both children into the back bedroom. They all sit down on the floor behind the door, far from the window. Helen holds her purse in her lap; she keeps her hand in it, gripping tightly onto the gun.

The children keep themselves occupied with their drawing. When it approaches their normal bedtime, Trent puts his head down on the carpet and falls asleep. Lateasha continues with her artwork. Helen looks over at the collage of shapes and colors on the little girl's large piece of paper.

"Can you tell me about your drawing?" Helen asks softly, not wanting to wake Trent.

Lateasha starts pointing to the different shapes and interpreting her work to Helen.

"This is Noah's ark," she says proudly.

"And who are those two people on the ark?"

"That's you, and that one is the devil, and you're both fighting."

A shiver comes over Helen.

"And who is that in the sky?"

"That is an angel of the Lord. He's throwing lightning bolts at the devil to kill him and stop him from hurting you."

"I hope to God you're right, child," Helen whispers.

After a while, Lateasha also can no longer keep her eyes open. She, too, falls asleep on the carpet.

Helen gently takes each child, one by one, and places them on their parents' bed. Neither Trent nor Lateasha does more than murmur softly during the transfer. Then, Helen turns off all the lights and opens the bedroom door. She positions herself on the floor at the end of the hallway. From that location, she has a good view of the sleeping children and the bedroom window. As well, she has a clear view down the hallway to the front door.

The bedroom window and the front door are the only possible ways he can get to the children, if he lied about going up to the lake to meet her.

Helen sits in the dark, never taking her hand off the gun, alternating her gaze from the window to the front door and back. She sits for what seems like hours, determined to stay vigilant.

Finally, she hears the rattle of keys at the front door. Most likely it is John and Tina returning home, but Helen isn't going to take the slightest chance. She stands up, holds the gun in both hands, and sets her aim square center on the front door. When the door opens, she clearly sees two silhouettes in the doorway: it is John and Tina.

"Why are all the lights out?" Tina asks aloud as she flicks the light switch on at the front door.

Helen picks her purse from the floor, places the gun in it, and tucks it under her arm. She walks up the hallway toward them.

"Helen, is everything all right?" Tina asks.

Helen is pale and shivering.

"The children are fine, Tina. Both of them are asleep on your bed. They're both fine. I realize this doesn't look good…not what you expected to come home to, and I'm sorry. Someday I may be able to explain it to you, but right now I can't, and I have to be going."

Tina rushes to the back bedroom, and a moment later returns.

"The babies are all right," Tina says to her husband.

"Helen, I don't understand," says John, gently placing his hand on her shoulder.

"Please, John, don't ask me to explain now."

Tina takes hold of Helen's hand and speaks to her softly.

"Helen, if there's something wrong, you can tell us. We care for you; we're your friends."

"I can't," says Helen. "I have to go!"

"You're in no condition to drive. Let John drive you home. You don't mind, do you, John?"

"No, of course not."

Helen pulls herself away and starts running for the door.

"I'm sorry. ....Forgive me...I have to go!" she cries, slamming the front door behind her.

John and Tina rush after her and open the front door, only in time to see Helen's car screeching off into the distance.

****

Foolishly, Helen drives at breakneck speed down the main highway. Thankfully, there are few cars on the road at that hour – and she is lucky not to encounter any police.

The salt in her tears burns her eyes so badly; she continually wipes her eyes with her handkerchief. She swerves in and out of her lane, never slowing down for an instant until she has to slam on the brakes to slow down for the turn off, which she nearly misses. The tires screech in her ears.

Once on the turn-off road, she hammers her foot down again on the gas pedal – rocketing into the night.

Barreling down the dark country road, Helen has only the white line to guide her. Now and then, she reaches across and places her hand in her purse and takes a firm grip on the gun. Somehow it gives her comfort.

Even she cannot believe what she is doing. But talking to him on the phone – the way he threatened to harm the children – that is the breaking point.

Besides, she is tired of living in fear. To live with a sword dangling over her head, with no relief in sight – nothing has helped. Sessions with Angela have not helped. The police are no help; they are no closer to keeping her safe than when they first started. Now she must take matters into her own hands. One way or another, she'll be free.

Twenty-One

By the Light of the Silvery Moon

Off in the distance, Helen sees a small white speck on the horizon becoming larger as it comes closer. A minute later, it is on her. Going as fast as she is, there's little time to read the signpost that says, "Sandy Beach – one mile ahead."

She slams on the brakes when she sees the entrance to the park. But at such high-speed, her tires are unable to take hold of the gravel road. The car spins out of control, off the road and down into a small gully. The engine dies.

Helen takes stock of herself; she isn't hurt. She turns the car key, only to hear the choking sound of the engine trying to kick over.

She waits a moment and tries again – still nothing. She decides to abandon the car. Reaching under her seat, she produces a flashlight. She tries it; the batteries are still good. In her other hand she takes the gun.

She doesn't bother to close the door of the car. The ding-ding-ding of the car door alarm fades as she makes her way down the dirt road entrance to the park.

The sky is becoming clear. Clouds are drifting slowly off into the distance, leaving the nearly full moon as the sole object in the sky. Its light washes over everything with a dim blue haze.

Helen sees beyond the long row of trees that line both sides of the road and the "Sandy Beach" sign spelled out in horseshoes and past the parking lot.

Helen looks around. The parking lot is deserted. The crunching gravel under her feet is all she hears till she gets closer to the lake. Then sand covers the ground, and her footsteps go silent.

She walks past the picnic area and to the lake and then along the beach. Looking out, the water is still and dark – like a monstrous black mirror with only the near-full moon's reflection in it. The lake's only blemish is the white wooden platform in its center. The still, inky water gives the illusion it is floating midair.

When she comes to the diving board, she turns and shines the flashlight down the trail leading into the woods and starts down it.

Her breathing becomes labored; she hears her heart pounding in her ears. Her nervous hand shakes the gun from side to side. She worries if she will be able to aim properly.

Finally, she comes to the clearing. She is alone, yet she has the distinct feeling of being watched.

Slowly, Helen moves the flashlight beam over the ground, over rocks and stones, sand and grass – nothing out of the ordinary.

Then the light shines on a man's hiking boot. She guides the beam up the pant legs, across his chest, and then stops – spotlighting his face covered with a black ski mask.

Helen is shaking like a leaf in the wind; she feels hot and cold all at once.

"I've come," she whispers.

The dark figure just stands there – motionless and silent.

"Well, say something, damn you!"

Her words echo back at them from off the lake.

"I'm so sorry it has to be this way," he says shyly – his voice no longer dark and gravelly.

He slowly reaches up and pulls off the ski mask.

It is Kyle.

"I'm so sorry it has to end this way," he says.

"Kyle?" is all she can say in her confusion.

"You're a girl, and girls were never meant to be in the club," he speaks as if making a decree. "And now that the club is being dissolved, so are we…all its members."

"What are you talking about, Kyle?" Helen's voice cracks – half from fear, half from crying.

"It's all over," says Kyle. "No one gets out of the club alive. I'm sorry, Nancy."

"I'm not Nancy!" Helen cries, tears roll down her face. "Kyle…it's me…Helen. I'm not Nancy!"

Kyle reaches behind his back and pulls out a large hunting knife.

"I'm so sorry," Kyle repeats as he slowly starts toward her.

"I've got a gun, Kyle!" Helen screams, holding out her arm straight and pointing the gun in his direction. "I'll use it, Kyle…I swear!"

"It doesn't matter," he says, continuing to come at her.

Helen closes her eyes and pulls the trigger. The shot roars like a cannon, echoing off the lake. She opens her eyes; she missed. The tears in her eyes make it difficult for her to see, and her shaking hand is causing her aim to be off.

This time, she keeps her eyes open. The bullet grazes the shoulder of his jacket. It does not deter him.

Helen brings her arm holding the flashlight up to her face and wipes the tears from her eyes. She takes a deep breath and holds it.

She fires. This time she shoots him square in the chest. It stops him for a moment, but he doesn't go down. He continues toward her.

Helen then remembers what her father told her, "Empty the gun into him! Don't stop firing until the son of a bitch is dead!"

There are three more bullets in the gun. Helen fires them off in rapid succession. At such close range, she doesn't miss; all three shots enter his chest. Kyle crashes to the ground with a thud.

After the echoes of gunshots fade away, all is silent.

Helen moves the flashlight beam over Kyle's body. There is blood everywhere. He lies there motionless. Surely, he is dead.

"Good work," says a voice in the darkness.

Helen is so startled she drops the flashlight.

"It didn't matter which one of you killed who, though. I'd have to kill whoever survived. If he succeeded in killing you, he would have been mine to kill. But seeing how you were more resourceful…"

The voice is dark, gruff, and, oh, so familiar. It is him. He steps into the clearing, past the shadows, and into the moonlight. Helen can barely make out his silhouette, but even in such poor light, she sees the shape of his head covered with a black ski mask.

Helen quickly raises her arm and points the gun. She pulls the trigger again and again, only to hear a series of metal clicks.

"That's why it's called a six-shooter, you stupid bitch!" he says as he swings the back of his hand around, knocking the gun from her grip. The pistol goes flying off into the woods.

"I hereby call this meeting to order," he growls. "Our first and last course of action is to disband our club with the death of each of its members…including our one and only honorary female member…Nancy!" He grabs both of her arms and pulls her into himself. "All those in favor, say 'aye'!"

Helen feels his hot breath on her face. His hands are all over her body – not caressing, but grabbing and pulling. She desperately tries to get away, but he is too strong. She can't back away from him enough to use her arms and hands to defend herself. In desperation, she brings her knee up fast and hard into his groin. He lets out a painful grunt and falls to the ground, landing on top of Kyle's body. When his hold on her weakens, Helen pulls free and then starts running back down the path toward the lake.

Darkness is all around. Again and again she falls, tripping over rocks and stones and fallen trees cluttering the path. Branches on both sides of her tear and rip at her flesh. Her foot comes down on a large rock. She twists her ankle and hears the bone crack. Lying there, she hears him in close pursuit behind her. She forces herself to stand and continue; the pain is excruciating.

Her mind is racing. In her confusion, she hears a voice – a familiar voice – it is the voice of Carmen. "What's with women and kicking guys in the balls?" Carmen's voice is in her head. "I think they just like doing it. . . . It don't work. I kicked my guy in the balls, and all it did was make him madder."

Helen remembers Carmen's advice.

"When he's on top of you, act like you're enjoying it. When his guard is down, ram both your thumbs into the outer side of his eye sockets. . . hard. . . till both his eyeballs pop out! It's the only way!"

Slapping branches across her face brings Helen back to the present. She hears him close behind, cursing, getting closer every second. She tries to go faster, hobbling down the path, but every time she brings down her injured foot, the pain runs through her like a bolt of lightning. She dares not fall again for fear she may not get up again. She must run past the pain, no matter how intense it is.

When she comes to the end of the path and again in the open, she hears him only a few feet behind her. She is just about to turn to her left toward her car, but with a broken ankle, there is no way she can outrun him for that distance.

With only one course of action left to take, she hops onto the diving board, works her way to the end, and jumps into the water.

She immediately goes under; the water rushes up her nose and into her mouth. She feels water entering her lungs; it makes her cough, which makes her take in more water.

Finally, she begins waving her arms, desperately trying to make her way to the surface. When she hits the air, she howls as she takes in much-needed air.

She points herself toward the white platform in the middle of the lake. She begins moving her arms and legs in a motion similar to the way she has seen other people do – people who know how to swim.

When she is only a few feet from the raft, she hears a large splash in the water – he's dived in after her. As on land, in the water she is no match for him. Seconds later, he is on her, pulling her down, trying to drown her. She struggles, but his weight pressing down on her is too much. She moves her arms and legs, frantically trying to return to the surface. By sheer luck, her elbow smashes into his neck; he begins choking.

Helen uses the time he takes to recoup to make her way to the raft. When she reaches it, she grabs the short metal ladder and starts up. But just as she scales the last wrung, he is on her. This time, he grabs her leg at the ankle – the broken ankle. He pulls hard, trying to get her back into the water. Helen screams in pain.

Finally, she pulls herself free and lands on top of the raft. She tries to stand, but the pain in her ankle makes it impossible. She falls down, helpless.

An instant later, he comes up the ladder. He is soaking wet. The water-drenched ski mask is heavy and drooping over his head; the cutout in the material for his mouth no longer lines up with his lips; and neither do the holes for the eyes.

"You bitch, I'll make you sorry you were ever born," he says as he comes crashing down on top of her.

With one hand he pulls at her clothes, ripping them away from her; with the other hand he works at his pants' zipper, trying to get himself free. His entire bodyweight on her, Helen can barely move.

To his surprise, she stops her struggle. This takes him off guard. He stops what he's doing, trying to make sense of what is happening.

Helen brings both her hands to his face and begins caressing him through the ski mask. She moves under him in a sensual manner. She coos with delight. He looks down at her.

"You bitch, you like this, don't you?" he says triumphantly.

"Oh baby…you're so gooood," she purrs.

He is just about to resume, when he senses her movement. He quickly grabs her left arm at the wrist and pulls her hand from his face. But, he reacts too late; Helen gouges the thumb of her right hand into the outer side of his eye socket. Her thumbnail acts like a knife, cutting through the moist flesh around his eye. She doesn't stop pressing hard and forward until her entire thumb is deep into the socket. She feels her knuckle pressing against his eyeball. With one last motion forward, the eye pops out and hangs along the side of his face by a thin strand of flesh – blood gushes from the opening. He grabs her wrist and pulls her hand out and away, and then jumps to his feet.

He stands there holding his hands over his eye socket. He tries for a moment to place the eye back in; but in his hysteria, only causes the frail skin attached to the eye to break. The eye falls to his feet – more blood flows.

"You bitch! You bitch!" he howls. "I'm going to kill you with my bare hands!"

Suddenly, there is a flash of light. A loud gunshot echoes like thunder. A burst of blood shoots from his chest. Again, another shot, another echo, another burst of blood.

Three more bullets ring out, two more into his chest and the third square in the middle of his forehead. He hits the wooden surface with a loud thud. He lies motionless and dead. All is silent. Then a voice calls to Helen from the shoreline.

"Everything is all right. . . . Stay there. . . . Don't move. . . . I'll come out to get you!"

She is in no condition to respond and much too afraid to believe a strange voice from faraway saying "everything is all right." She rolls to the edge of the platform, and with one swift effort falls off.

In the water, Helen realizes she is unable to swim. She feels herself sinking deeper and deeper into dark waters. At that moment, nothing matters. She no longer cares if she lives or dies. She is about to give up, open her mouth, and swallow as much water as she can, fast as she can, and end it all, when her will to live grows and she starts to flap her arms. She works her way to the surface. The need for air overcomes her and she fears she won't make it. Suddenly, a hand grabs her by the wrist and pulls her up.

She feels strong hands lifting her out of the water and into a small boat. She fills her needy lungs with sweet, precious air. She strains her eyes to see who her savior is, but her eyes will not focus.

A spinning sensation comes over her, and she feels herself falling into a faint. She fights against it, but something tells her she is out of danger, so she allows the feeling to overtake her. Her eyes close as she slips into unconsciousness.

Twenty-Two

The Face behind the Flash

Helen wakes to find herself in bed – a hospital bed. It takes her a moment to focus. She turns to see Angela sitting in a chair at her bedside. Angela jumps to her feet and takes hold of Helen's hand.

"We've got to stop meeting this way," Angela jokes, smiling at her friend. But lighthearted sentiment is lost on Helen who busts into tears. Angela leans over and takes her in her arms.

"Cry if you need to. …Cry all you want…but it's over. …It's really over this time."

Helen tries to compose herself. She looks around the room – Goebel and Benson are standing at the foot of her bed.

"If this is a bad time, we can come back tomorrow?" Benson says to Angela as well as Helen.

"No, don't go, I need to know what happened!" Helen says.

"She doesn't know?" Goebel directs his question to Angela.

"Of course not. How could she?"

An outward show of awkwardness comes over the two officers.

"You see, Mrs. Haywood, It seems you had a guardian angel watching over you all the while," Benson says. "Don Hastings, Carol Hastings' husband, has been following and watching you from afar for months. After his wife's murder, he swore revenge. When he learned your assailant was still in contact with you, he bided his time, watching from a safe distance. …His hunting rifle always close by in his car.

"He followed you out to the lake last night. He waited onshore, aiming his rifle toward the raft, waiting for the assailant to stand so he could get a clear shot at him. When he did, he let the bastard have it.

"It was he who fished you out of the water and drove you here," concludes Benson.

"But who was…*he*?" Helen asks.

Before anyone can say another word, the door flies open. Helen's mother comes storming in. She waves her arms about, tears running down her checks. She speaks in melodramatic tones, as if addressing her own private audience.

"Sweetheart…Darling… my poor baby…don't worry. Mother's here!" She runs to Helen's bedside, leans over, and kisses both her cheeks. "My poor, Helen, what can Mommy do to make it better?"

Helen's mother is in rare form, perhaps a little too overdone even for her.

"My poor child," she continues, "what can I do? I've tried…God knows how I've tried. All your life, I've done everything in my power to keep you safe…and now this. I knew this was going to happen…I just knew it!"

"Mother, what are you saying?" Helen tries to interrupt, but her mother ignores her and continues to ramble on.

"I just knew something like this would happen someday. If I told him once, I've told him a thousand times…I warned him about those boys. I told him…"

Helen reaches out taking a hard grip on her mother's arm and shakes her until she stops talking and pays attention to her.

"Mother, what are you talking about?"

Her mother looks at her with surprise, as if she does not understand how her daughter doesn't understand what she is saying.

"Why, your father, of course. I warned him years ago…if he didn't stop, there would be trouble. First time I saw him with you, when you were a little girl, I told him if he ever laid his hands on you again, I'd leave him! And he stopped…for a long time. Then when I found out about that time out at the lake, with those terrible boys and that filthy brother of his, I threatened to walk out on him. I was going take the baby, I said, walk out on him and never come back. And as far as I know, he never did it again."

Helen cries as she listens. She sees the look in her mother's eyes, a look of madness, as if this has been the final push needed to send her over the edge.

"Oh, I let him keep those filthy pictures, but I warned him never to touch the little girl…never ever touch her again, and he never did, not until now. I didn't know…I swear I didn't know!"

Her mother's words set her memory on fire. Many horrid things she kept hidden from herself now flood her mind. Images locked away now feel like yesterday.

She remembers being a frail, skinny, little girl. She remembers more clearly that day at the lake. There is a flash in front of her eyes, the flash of a camera. The camera moves away, and she sees the smiling face of her father.

"I swear I didn't know," her mother continues. "I've done all a mother could do! I told him I'd leave him! And now he's dead. …He should have listened to me!"

Her mother sobs uncontrollably. Angela gently guides her to the door.

Goebel and Benson slip out of the room silently.

Angel turns to face Helen. "I'll be back in a few minutes." She ushers the old woman out.

"Don't worry. …Take your time. …I'll be all right…I'll be all right," Helen calls out, and something deep inside her believes it.

Twenty-Three

Whatever I Want to Do

Dodson walks into Max's Tavern and looks around. He feels relieved to see the lunch crowd long since cleared out. He walks over to the bar where Max is the lone bartender on duty.

"Hey, Maxie, how's it hanging?" smiles Dodson.

"How's what hanging?" Max asks, dumbfounded.

"You know…it!"

"What is…it?"

Dodson shakes it off.

"Never mind, Maxie. Tell me, where can I find Holmes and Watson?"

"If you're referring to the Rover Boys, they're in the back working on a second pitcher of beer." Max points his bar rag toward the backroom.

"Thanks, Maxie," Dodson says as he walks off.

"You want anything…a Grasshopper?" Maxie calls to him.

"Nah, I think I'll have a Pink Lady."

Dodson disappears into the backroom.

Max shrugs his shoulders and starts to thumb through his bartender's guide looking for a recipe for a Pink Lady.

Dodson finds Goebel and Benson sitting in one of the booths. They have made good work of the second pitcher of beer. A head of white foam at the bottom is the only evidence left.

"Scoot over," Dodson says as he sits down next to Benson. "I've heard from Vega that the Haywood case is closed. So…what happened?"

"It would take too long to explain," Goebel says.

"Hey, I ain't going anywhere. Besides, I busted my hump helping you two on this case. I deserve to get the lowdown."

Just then, Max walks up with a full pitcher of beer and a tall champagne glass filled with a thick, milky pink liquid.

"I figured you guys could use a refill by now." He places the pitcher center stage. Then he puts the drink in front of Dodson, "And a Pink Lady…for the lady."

"Hey, I like cream drinks! So quit busting my chops," Dodson demands.

Maxi walks off, shaking his head.

"Okay, so you want the full story. Well, here it is," Goebel says, pouring himself and his partner another glass of beer.

"It seems Mrs. Haywood's father, Tom Russell, and his brother Jerry, were a couple of perverts. Say…I just realized something. Their names are Tom and Jerry…ain't that a cartoon or something?"

"Yeah, it is!" laughs Benson, taking a sip of beer. It is obvious the two are getting tipsy.

"Cut the crap, you two, and finish the story," insists Dodson.

"Well, as my partner was trying to tell you," Benson continues the story, "The two brothers were a couple of perverts. They probably had been messed up since they were children themselves…that kind of thing can perpetuate from generation to generation. Anyway, they both had this thing for young boys.

"Both brothers dated or married weak, undemanding women – someone they could control. They didn't like women much, but it was a good way to keep up social appearances. Besides, this gave them a continuing supply of young children, which was their victims of choice."

"A family affair," Goebel slurs his words, "real sick bastards."

"As I was saying," continues Benson, "and their victim of choice was young boys. Tom must have put a cramp in their style when he fathered a daughter. Jerry even went so far as to have an extramarital affair with Joyce Adams, particularly to have another son. That's how Kyle came into the picture…Victor and Nicholas' half-brother."

"Real sick bastards," Goebel adds.

"The Russell brothers, Tom and Jerry, went on for years molesting and terrorizing their own children, without anyone the wiser. They both held a good standing within the community. Their women, wives and mistress, turned a deaf ear and a blind eye to what was happening right under their noses, lest they be turned out in the cold without a red cent.

"When the boys began to approach their teen years, the two brothers upgraded their operation. They moved everything down into Jerry's cellar where they started taking photos. They also made the boys recruit other young boys from school…getting them drunk and having their way with them. Surprisingly, no one ever spoke up…that's the power of shame.

"They actually had the gall to claim it their own private, secret boy's club, with Jerry as the head official and Tom as second-in-command."

"How does Helen Haywood fit in?" Dodson asks.

"I was just about to get to her," Benson says. "It seems when she was little, her father tried being a little touchy-feely with her, but her mother caught him in the act and threatened him. He could do whatever he wanted, but when it came to her daughter, that's where she drew the line – which was fine with Tom since that really wasn't his thing."

"His own daughter," Goebel interrupts with a tone of disgust in his voice. "What a sick bastard! I've got a daughter the same age, and if anyone touched her when she was little, I'd kill the son of a bitch…including myself!"

It is obvious the beer is taking its toll.

"As I was saying," continues Benson, "the incident at the lake was a mistake. Young Helen accidentally came onto the family orgy at the clearing in the woods. They raped her. When it was over, she ran off crying. By some saving grace, the memory of it was pushed somewhere deep into her subconscious, which was a blessing or she may have ended cuckoo like her cousins…but I'll get back to that in a minute.

"Anyway, she ran away crying and left her doll. Jerry Russell kept that doll. He claimed it was the honorary female of the secret club. He was obsessed with it…talking to it…having sex with it. He even incorporated it into some of the basement orgies with the boys.

"Over the years, every so often they would bring poor little Helen into one of their meetings. Thankfully, she doesn't remember much of anything from that time.

"Years later, Jerry Russell died of a heart attack while on vacation in Spain. The man is truly deceased…believe me. Now, this makes Tom, his brother and second-in-command, the new leader of the secret boy's club. He inherits everything: the boys, the club, the basement, and the photos…even the stupid doll.

"By this time, the young boys are all well-conditioned and very crazy. They don't know up from down. When Tom claims the new leadership, he also claims to be their father…the poor bastards believe him.

"Everything continued as if nothing happened, as if nothing had changed. But when the boys hit their late teens, Tom found it increasingly harder to control them. He even had to kill one of them – Nicholas, the most rebellious – and make it look like an accident.

"Years go by; Tom visited the boys rarely. I suppose he lost most of his interest in them as they grew closer to manhood and less like children. But he still kept possession of the doll. He became obsessed with it, just like his brother. Till one day, the string in the back of the doll broke. ...The string wasn't the only thing to snap that day. It pushes Tom over the deep end. He gets back in contact with Victor and Kyle and starts running their lives again. He got it into his mind he was going to dissolve the secret club in one last horrific blood-fest...starting with the death of...now get this...the death of the doll. But the doll is broken, and somehow in his twisted mind, he shifts the identity of the doll to that of his daughter...the original owner of the doll."

"Wow, this is starting to sound more like some sick cult rather than a family," says Dodson. "I suppose this is where Helen Haywood comes into the picture?"

"That's right," Benson says. "Tom Russell ordered Kyle to beat and rape her. ...The ski mask and makeup were used to keep us off track. Mrs. Haywood turning up pregnant was an unexpected bonus for him.

"The plan was to terrorize her to the point of madness and then kill her, and they nearly succeeded.

"Tom, himself, started hanging out at the Velvet Hammer intending to get some love juice from a black man to put on Mrs. Haywood's missing panties, reinforcing the black rapist theory. He got lucky, but for Donald Johnson, his luck ran out...it cost him his life. For a smart guy, Russell wasn't so smart. We compared DNA...nothing matched."

"Why did Russell give his daughter a gun?" Dodson asks.

"When Haywood's doctor started poking around inside Helen's brain, several old memories started coming back to her. He knew he could lure her to the lake; so he gave her a gun...a gun with blanks, that is.

"When Richard Haywood took possession of the gun, Tom Russell couldn't have asked for anything better. ...This shifted the suspicion of who rigged the gun with blanks from him to the husband.

"When Helen shot at him, he went down and played dead. When she ran for help, he substituted the body of Carol Hastings for his."

"Which brings up a question," Dodson says, "Why did he kill Carol Hastings?"

"It was just another form of torture. He planned to make Helen's life as miserable as possible by hurting the people she cared for...that is, before killing her as he planned."

"And Victor Russell," Dodson tries to put some of the puzzle together, "he was told to give himself up and confess to everything when it was thought we were getting a little too close to the truth. But of course, the plan failed because of DNA results. But what about Kyle – how does he enter back into the picture?"

"When Mrs. Haywood went to Tannersville to do some investigating on her own, she met Kyle by sheer chance. They hit it off, and the rest is history. The love affair was custom made for Tom Russell's plan."

"What about Dr. Mitchell's beating? Who did that?"

"As far as we figure," says Benson, "and we can't prove it, mind you, but everything points to Richard Haywood. He had words with the good doctor, and swore revenge. He took advantage of the situation by wearing a ski mask…trying to throw us off the scent. But like I said, legally we can't prove anything, but if I had to bet on it, my money would be on Richard Haywood."

"Now, didn't Tom Russell turn up black and blue from a beating he claimed was from his daughter's assailant? What was that all about?"

"Well, it seems during his short visit to the Velvet Hammer that Tom Russell got a taste for the place. One night he picked up the wrong guy…some young stud that beats up on oversexed old men and takes their wallets. The assailant became the victim. But he turned it to his advantage. He drove to a mall as far away from the club as possible and made it look as if he had been beaten up in the mall parking lot."

"What about the killings of Eleanor Russell and Joyce Adams? Why kill them?"

"Killed his own mother…the sick bastard," Goebel interrupts, clearly drunk now. "Tom Russell tells Kyle to kill two old women and up he jumps and does it…his own mother…the sick bastard!"

Benson, not half as drunk as his partner continues.

"Eleanor Russell phoned the local Sheriff the night before. It was clear she was going to spill her guts. Joyce overheard the call. Afraid for her son's safety, she foolishly told Kyle who instinctively told Tom.

"Tom didn't want to take any chances so he made Kyle kill them both. Which only goes to show you how well trained these boys were. I mean…to kill his own mother…but you have to remember, the hold was on these boys from the day they were born."

"Now…the second gun," Dodson says. "The second gun he gave his daughter that didn't have blanks in it! Those were real bullets! What did he have…a death wish?"

"Not at all," Benson replies. "He knew she would shoot Kyle in self-defense. It didn't matter to him, he wanted them both dead. If Kyle killed her, he would have killed Kyle. If she killed Kyle, which is what happened, he planned to kill her. But he never realized there was a joker in the deck. Don Hastings followed Helen Haywood around for weeks with revenge in his heart for his wife and his hunting rifle at his side.

"When he saw the opportunity, he let Tom – the man who raped, tortured and killed his wife – have it…big time!"

"Sending his soul to be with his brother in hell," concludes Goebel.

Just then, Captain Vega walks over and snatched the pitcher of beer from the table. Goebel looks up at him – confused – through glassy eyes.

"That's enough beer for you two. I need you to get your heads back on straight. I need you to answer a call," says Vega.

"But, we're off duty!" slurs Goebel.

"Well, now you're back on. We just got a call…a women was raped in her home by aliens."

"Aliens…? You mean Mexicans?" Benson asks.

"No, not Mexicans…aliens…space aliens. …At least that's what she claims."

"You've got to be kidding," Benson says as he stands up.

"No, I'm not kidding," Vegas' voice is demanding. "Now get your butts in gear!"

"Slave-driving son of a bitch," Goebel mutters under his breath as he and Benson walk out of the backroom.

"I heard that!" Vega hollers. "Say, what the hell is that you're drinking?" Vega is speaking now to Dodson.

"Don't ask," says Max who takes the half-filled beer pitcher from Vegas and walks away.

****

"Hold your horses, I'm coming," Angela addresses the ringing phone.

"Hello?"

"Angela? It's me…Helen."

"Helen, so good to hear from you. Is everything all right?"

"Oh, yeah…sure…everything is fine. Just working, you know."

Angela doesn't say a word. During all the months they have known each other, she's learned to read between the lines with Helen. She knows sometimes when Helen says "everything is fine" it means just that, and at other times it doesn't. This time it doesn't. Angela waits for the other shoe to drop.

"Actually, there is something," Helen says softly.

"And what's that?" Angela tries not to sound pushy, but concerned.

"I went to see my mother yesterday."

"And…"

"And it seems she's doing well. I mean, they take such good care of them at that place. She looks well; they say she's eating. She likes to sit in the garden…"

"Helen…" Angela gently interrupts, "that's not what you called to tell me, is it?"

"No, it's not," Helen moans. "I've got so many mixed feelings when it comes to my mother. I love her so much, but I have such anger for her inside me. All those years she knew and didn't tell anyone. She could have stopped it at any time, but she didn't. I was her child!"

Helen turns silent. Angela waits for her to continue.

"And now I feel so sorry for her…for what's happened to her. …She just sits there staring into space."

"And you think that's your fault?" Angela asks.

"Yes! No…oh, I don't know what I think. She just sits there, not saying a word, oblivious to the world. Sometimes I envy her."

"I know sometimes life seems like it would be much easier if we didn't feel anything," Angela says, "and that's a choice your mother made. You had nothing to do with her choices. And you shouldn't feel like that. You've come such a long way. You're finally starting to heal."

"Thanks to you," Helen says. "I couldn't have done it without you."

"Well, I appreciate your appreciation," laughs Angela.

The two go silent. The mood switches. They have learned naturally to shift from doctor and patient, to friends.

"So, this is a long weekend coming up," Helen says, lightheartedly. "Feel like doing something?"

"Oh, Helen, I'd love to, but my son invited me out to his place for the weekend."

"Say, that's great! It's finally working out for you two!"

"It seems that way. I can only hope. He lives in a small apartment, so we're going to be staying at a hotel close by and…"

"Whoa…*we're* going to be staying? What's this *we* all about?"

"Well, I guess you could say I've been seeing someone," Angela says shyly.

"You guess?" laughs Helen. "Who is he? What's he like?"

"His name is Peter. He's very sweet…a bit of a loner…sort of marches to the beat of a different drummer."

"Sounds like someone else I know," Helen says jokingly. "So where did you meet him?"

"He came with those two detectives. They came by to ask a few questions, and he was with them. He was shy at first; calling me for the silliest of reasons about the case…till finally he got up the nerve to ask me out."

"I think I remember him. …He was in forensics, wasn't he? Now, what was his name…something Dodson…wasn't it?"

"That's him…Peter Dodson! Helen, I hate to ask, but could you do a favor for me? It's been years. …I need some help buying cosmetics."

"Say no more," Helen says. "I know just the place. …We could have lunch and make a day of it. But I insist it's on me."

"Oh, Helen I couldn't…"

"Oh, yes, you could! I won't take no for an answer. It's the least I can do…my gift to you."

"Thanks so much. But now I feel bad…you alone for the holiday weekend. …What will you do?"

"I don't know," laughs Helen, "go to the movies, bake a cake, go skydiving…whatever I want. I'm free to do whatever I want!"

THE END

To purchase additional copies of these books visit our bookstore website at:
www.advbookstore.com

Longwood, Florida, USA
"we bring dreams to life"™
www.advbookstore.com

www.ingramcontent.com/pod-product-compliance
Lightning Source LLC
Chambersburg PA
CBHW051648260626
47170CB00004B/1392